DELAYED EXPECTATIONS

Abigail Shirley

DEDICATION

For my sister, Lianne.

Our story is different to Rose and Myriam's, but our bond will always be the same.

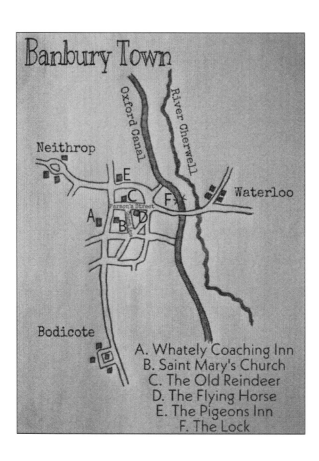

Banbury Town

Oxford Canal

River Cherwell

Neithrop

Waterloo

E

C

Parson's Street

F

A

B D

Bodicote

A. Whately Coaching Inn
B. Saint Mary's Church
C. The Old Reindeer
D. The Flying Horse
E. The Pigeons Inn
F. The Lock

Precious Jewels

We cannot learn
to live
without their love
or
our Grief

But
memories
precious as jewels
whisper through
our thoughts
from
time
to
time

Mabel Drury-Layland

<u>One</u>

August 1837

It was late. It was so late, that it was in fact early, very early. A new day had already started just over twenty minutes ago and it was now no longer today, but tomorrow. As she usually did at about this time most evenings, Myriam climbed her way up the narrow, creaking staircase. She placed each of her steps carefully so as not to awaken those who had long since fallen asleep. The light from her lamp danced with the shadows on the heavy panels that lined the walls of the familiar stairway. She had climbed these stairs so often in this way that her feet now, as if by instinct, naturally fell so as to avoid creaks and groans escaping from the old wooden boards.

But this night was different from usual. As she neared the top of the stairs and her eyes levelled with the landing beyond, she could see a flicker of light coming from under the doorway which was directly opposite. Until that moment she had been feeling somewhat melancholy. It was an emotion she didn't normally associate with herself. At least she hadn't, not for a couple of years now. She viewed herself as a positive, contented person. However, this new, low-spirited feeling was something that she recently sensed surrounding her more and more.

Now though, as the thread of light from

beneath the doorway opposite caught her eyes, Myriam's thoughts were swiftly pulled away from the events which had unfolded earlier. Her thoughts were sent flying towards the day that now lay ahead of her. She placed her hand on the handle, twisted it to release the door and made her way inside the room.

Even though the lantern was still burning, sending out a glow of light from inside the room, it was impossible from outside to know if her sister had managed to stay awake. For this reason, Myriam entered the room in the same way as she usually did on any other night. She crept in softly and carefully. Rose started work early each day, often at around five and so, after Myriam finished her shift downstairs each night, she would quietly come into the room that she shared with her sister. Then, making as little sound as possible, she would climb swiftly and silently into bed without disturbing her. Rose was equally quiet when she awoke each morning. Her clothes were often already laid out on the back of the chair which sat by the door so she could pick them up and leave the room without waking her younger sibling.

Myriam was expecting her sister to have fallen asleep while waiting for her. However, as she tiptoed into the room, Rose let out a little squeal and Myriam relaxed, standing up straight.

"Shush," she whispered, raising her finger to her lips and closing the door as quickly, yet quietly as she could. They weren't the only ones with accommodation on this landing and Myriam was anxious not to wake anyone.

Once the door was safely shut, she turned to face her sister and smiled as she caught sight of her excited, dancing eyes.

"I expected you to have fallen asleep." Myriam took her apron off, stained from food and drink, and placed it in the little basket where they stored their laundry.

"Never!" Rose shook her head. "I'm too excited. Can you even remember the last time we took a day off?"

Myriam slipped off her shoes and sat down on Rose's bed. Pulling her knees up to her chest she let her back rest against the wall.

"I do," she replied. "It was for Grandma Hetty's funeral."

"It seems like such a long time ago now."

"Yes, it does." Myriam thought back to that day, now over a year ago. "It was so hot! Do you remember? It was a relief to be inside that cold church. I remember thinking what a waste of time off on such a beautiful summer's day."

"Poor Grandma Hetty, God rest her soul." Rose closed her eyes and said a brief, silent prayer. When Rose opened her eyes and looked again at her younger sister they flickered with concern.

Myriam had her head back and her eyes closed. Rose had always envied her sister's complexion. It was like ivory, with a soft glaze. Her cheeks always held just the right amount of natural colour, needing no enhancement from a rouge brush. Her perfectly formed lips were soft and plump. But this evening, as Rose studied her face, she could see the tell-tale signs of strain. Her beautiful skin looked ever so slightly duller than usual. Her lips appeared dry and cracked. Rose suspected that Myriam had been chewing them, something she did when she was worried or concerned.

Rose placed her hand on Myriam's. "Are you all right, duckie?" she asked.

Myriam opened her eyes and turned to look at her. In the shadowy light from the lantern, the blue from Myriam's eyes, which usually shone out brightly in the daylight, was lost to the deep grey tones within them. Rose searched her sister's eyes as she responded to her question with a smile.

"I'm fine. Just a little tired," she replied. "The usual Thursday night battle," she explained.

"Ah, I see." Rose knew all about Thursday nights in the bar below.

The two sisters worked at the Whately Coaching Inn. Rose was a kitchen maid and Myriam worked as a waitress in the bar. The coaching inn was situated on the main road though Banbury and so was a busy and popular establishment with travellers passing though. Myriam didn't mind the work although sometimes she thought she would prefer a job that was more behind the scenes. Mr Hamilton had moved her into the bar about a year ago. Tired men, hungry and weary from hours travelling on uneven roads, wanted something pleasant to look at while they ate their meals. Mr Hamilton knew this and therefore had his prettiest girls working in the bar. Being served food by the seventeen-year-old Myriam Evans wasn't going to receive complaints from anyone. She had a pretty face, long dark hair and unguarded eyes. Her figure was slim, womanly and easy on the eye. On the fewer occasions when there were women travelling along with their husbands, Myriam was acceptable to them too. She was innocent and pure. Myriam never made eyes at the men and so their wives had nothing to complain about either. If only all the girls in the bar made Mr Hamilton's life this easy. There were others though who were worldly wise and brazen. Harriet Nicols was one of them. In fact, she was probably the worst. She welcomed the attentions of the lonely travellers. Mr Hamilton found that he had to keep a close eye on her, or the men would spend no money on his well-cooked food and good quality ales, preferring the private company of Miss Nicols. He had considered moving her to work elsewhere, such as the kitchens, but she pulled in the customers. Therefore, since he could keep an eye on her, he kept her where she was.

Twice a month, on a Thursday evening, a certain 'gentleman' broke his journey from London to Kidderminster at the coaching inn. He dressed like a gentleman, spoke like a gentleman and no doubt was occupied secularly with something 'gentlemanly'. Myriam though, failed to view him as a gentleman. She hated the way he looked at her, the way he breathed over her as she placed his food on the table and then, after a few drinks and a bit of time had passed, the way he touched her leg while she cleared his plates away. Mr Hamilton generally looked out for the well-being of the girls who worked for him, but this man tipped well and so Mr Hamilton ignored his behaviour, much to Myriam's dismay. Harriet Nicols sneered each time Myriam rejected the man's advances. Mr Hamilton kept Harriet away from this particular gentleman, but he needn't have worried because this man was only interested in Myriam.

Myriam hated those evenings and each month

they seemed to be getting worse as his eyes lingered longer where they shouldn't. She wouldn't create a scene though. Mr Hamilton was a fair boss, but he wouldn't accept any back-chat or complaining from the staff. Rose had heard about the aggravation this man gave to her sister and it annoyed her, but she didn't know the full extent of it. Myriam made light of it to her, not wanting to cause any concern, and Rose had not seen it with her own eyes. As a result, she couldn't fully empathise with the anxious knots it created in Myriam's stomach each time he walked into the bar on those evenings.

"Bill looks out for you though, doesn't he?" asked Rose.

Myriam pulled her thoughts away from the man with his alcohol filled breath and smiled at Rose.

"Yes, Bill always has an eye on me."

"You know he's sweet on you. You shouldn't take that for granted." Rose's eyes were dancing again.

Myriam rolled her eyes at her sister's implications and shook her head.

Bill was the lad who worked behind the bar. He was eighteen and had arrived at the coaching inn about two years earlier. He was a kind boy. He had a pleasant, happy face and yes, Myriam admitted that it was obvious he had a sweet spot for her. But she didn't feel the same. She enjoyed his company and he was easy to talk to. Nevertheless, something was lacking. His conversations didn't captivate her. When he spoke, he failed to hold her complete attention. She didn't feel that 'thing' she was sure she was supposed to feel if she was to ever fall in love.

Rose opened her mouth to continue but

Myriam had heard it all before. Rose's endless lectures about 'snapping up a good catch when she had one'. She wasn't in the mood for more talk about Bill, lovely as he was.

Myriam spoke first. "I'm really looking forward to tomorrow."

Rose knew that Myriam was deliberately changing the subject. She pursed her lips together and squinted her eyes. Giving in, she replied, "Yes, I am too."

"Now, let's get to sleep or we'll never be able to enjoy it properly." Myriam made her way over to her own bed across the room and then added, "Besides, the *bride to be* needs her beauty sleep."

As Rose turned the lantern down, allowing the light in the room to fade to darkness, Myriam rolled over onto her side and her thoughts drifted to the upcoming wedding. Then she felt it again. That melancholy feeling had returned.

<u>Two</u>

Myriam heard the door close and opened her eyes to see Rose coming into the room. Sunlight was flooding through the small window which was above Rose's bed. Myriam glanced across to the clock they had placed on the small mantelpiece which was fixed above the tiny fireplace. It said it was seven-thirty.

"I'm sorry. I didn't mean to wake you," apologised Rose as she set down the tray that she had been balancing in one hand.

Myriam stretched and then swung her legs to the side of the bed, sitting up. She eyed the plates of freshly cooked eggs and warm bread. There was even a full pot of steaming tea.

"It's not a bad way to be woken up," she replied, smiling warmly. "How long have you been awake?"

Rose raised her eyebrows. "I've been up for about as long as the sun has. I might have a day off but try telling my body it can sleep in, I don't think it agrees."

"Because of habit or excitement?" Myriam asked, pouring out the tea into two small teacups they kept in the room.

"Both!" laughed Rose. She passed a plate of bread and eggs to Myriam. "It's not every day I get to go and buy a wedding dress."

Rose sat down and began to eat. Myriam was

already chewing on the warm eggs and bread. They both looked up and their eyes met. As they had been the night before, Rose's eyes were again sparkling with excitement. Myriam swallowed the mouthful she was eating and returned the smile to her sister, but Rose wasn't fooled. She could see the unease etched in her sister's eyes. Those beautiful, blue eyes that usually shone with contentment had appeared dull and distant for weeks now. Rose didn't need to ask the reason for this. She knew why.

As happy as she was to be getting married, she knew that it would mean their separation. It was hardly a separation that others would think twice about. Rose would still be working at the inn and she would still be living there too. They would see each other every day. For anyone looking on, it was hardly going to be a separation at all. Yet, for Rose and Myriam Evans it would be monumental.

Doctor Evans and his wife, Silvia, had both been killed in a tragic carriage accident three years earlier. Until then the girls had led a happy, peaceful life. The family had lived together in Bodicote, a village just south of Banbury. Doctor Evans was cheerful, kind and well-liked by all his patients. Prior to that fateful day he had taken his wife with him to Oxford while he attended a medical lecture. It was their wedding anniversary and so, once the lecture had finished, they had checked into a small hotel for one night as a treat. The following day Doctor Evans had taken his wife around some of the fancy shops in the city and bought her a new shawl and hat for the coming winter. They had had a happy morning together and were returning home when the coach they were travelling in collided with an oncoming, out of control, cart.

The girls, now orphaned, had just two weeks to sort out their parents' belongings and find a new place to live. Grandma Hetty, who at that time was living with the family, went to live with their mother's sister and her husband in Wiltshire. They didn't offer for the girls to go along with her. Myriam was only fourteen, but by then Rose was already sixteen. There were girls younger than they were, already working from ages as young as eleven or twelve and thus, it was assumed that they would be fine. And they were fine. Rose, always strong, determined and practical, found them both work and accommodation at the Whately Coaching Inn. Since that terrible day back in 1834 it had been the two of them together. Rose had done everything for her sister's well-being and as a result they had become inseparable.

Except now they were being torn apart, or so it felt to Myriam. She failed to see how it could be anything else. She desperately wanted to shower her sister with joy and happiness, but she felt sick at the thought of being alone. Rose had been her constant. Rose had held her tight when she had felt that her life was crumbling as the grief over her parents' death had overcome her. If she was honest, Myriam was scared of what it would be like not having her sister to herself any more.

Rose knew this and, to some extent, she felt it too. Her baby sister had become just that to her; her 'baby'. She had loved and cared for her as she knew their own mother would have, had she been alive. Yet Rose couldn't deny the feelings that had developed in her for Tom Watkins. They didn't replace her love for Myriam, but it was different. Someone else in her life was also now important to her. The separation they both faced would be easier for her and she knew it.

Myriam, anxious as she felt, understood this so she quickly finished the last of her breakfast and stood up, planting a wide, open smile on her face.

"Come on then," she said cheerfully to her sister. "It's time to buy the bride a gown!"

Having dressed and gathered together a small picnic, the two sisters let themselves out of the back entrance of the inn and made their way across the stable yard. Rose's eyes were darting everywhere. It was Myriam who spotted him first. She saw the top of his thick, red hair from behind the horse he was brushing.

"There he is Rose," she said, pointing over to him. "He's grooming that grey mare in the corner."

Rose whistled. It was a short, sharp burst of noise and Myriam tutted at her. Tom Watkins lifted his head up and grinned. He put the brush down, patted the horse gently on the neck and made his way over to them.

Tom wasn't what you would call handsome, not by any means. When Myriam had caught sight of Rose giving him a sneaky goodnight kiss one evening, she had felt a bit nauseous. She knew this was mean, but she just didn't find him attractive. He did have a friendly face though. It was rosy and happy but not the kind of face Myriam imagined herself falling in love with. Rose though, loved him and it showed. She skipped about on air in his company and Myriam had to admit that he had a funny sort of charm about him. His red hair complemented his high-spirited

11

character. It was a character which occasionally got him into trouble, but when he controlled it, it was somewhat endearing.

"So, are you ready?" he asked Rose.

"Yes! I can't wait."

He squeezed her hand and then looked at Myriam.

"Find her something really pretty won't you?"

Myriam nodded at him. As anxious as she was about this upcoming wedding, there was one thing she did want more than anything. She wanted Rose to look beautiful.

<u>Three</u>

The town was busy, as it often was in the mornings. It was noisy too. Rose was accustomed to being in the town because, working as one of the kitchen girls, she often had to run to the butcher or the baker to pick up supplies. Myriam however, rarely came into the town. She wasn't particularly bothered by the crowds, but just felt more comfortable outside of the hustle and bustle of town life. She much preferred the quiet country upbringing they had enjoyed as children. Rose asked if she wanted to stop anywhere along their way but Myriam shook her head.

"Let's just go straight to the dress shop," she replied.

They made their way directly to the ladies' dress shop that Rose had decided was where she wanted to buy her wedding gown. Passing the window display on their way to the door, Myriam admired the dresses that were on show. She had never been into a shop like this before. Her simple barmaid clothes weren't sold in fancy shops like this. The bell above the door tinkled to announce their arrival as Myriam followed Rose inside. The interior of the shop was beautiful. Rails of colourful, divinely pretty dresses lined the two opposite sides of the walls. In the centre of the room was an ornate table displaying small brooches and hair ornaments. A vase of flowers was placed perfectly in the middle of this table and the delicious scent of the delicate pink roses played on

Myriam's nose while she admired the surroundings. From the back of the shop a curtain moved and a woman appeared. She was dressed in a simple but elegant gown with her hair pinned neatly at the back of her head. She wore a wide smile as she came into the room to greet her new customers. Myriam noticed though that as the woman's eyes rested on them both and then looked their appearance up and down, those soft and welcoming features on her face hardened just a fraction. It was a small, minuscule set in the woman's jaw, almost imperceptible, but Myriam noticed it and felt her own face react in response.

"Good day *ladies.*"

Rose hadn't noticed the clipped tone in the woman's voice. "Good morning Ma'am," she replied, in her usual harmless, innocent and happy manner.

"Is there something I can help you with?" The woman's smile was dropping and still Rose had failed to notice. She was so busy stealing glances at all the dresses surrounding her.

"I'm here to buy a wedding dress," Rose announced proudly.

The smile on the woman's face had now gone completely.

"A wedding dress you say? From *this* shop?"

Rose frowned and a confused look came over her face.

"Well, ye... yes." Rose stumbled a little over her words. "I've been told that this is the best place to come."

"And you'd be quite right young lady," the woman replied. "This *is* the best place to come." She paused before adding, "Only our *prices* are also the best."

She looked at them and her eyes darted from one to the other, not lingering though to hold Myriam's burning stare. There was an awkward silence. Rose then opened her mouth to reply but the woman spoke again.

"And our *customers* are the best too."

Rose's face crumpled a little. She was trying to reply while fumbling around with her purse. It was Myriam who found words first.

"I think you've made yourself quite clear."

Myriam's voice was steady and controlled but inside she was shaking. This was Rose's special day. How dare this woman try to humiliate her dear, sweet sister. Myriam took Rose's arm and went to lead her out of the shop but she stopped herself. Rose was looking at her with desperate, pleading eyes. They were eyes that normally shone with happiness but were now sad. Myriam realised that if she caused a scene and forced them both out of the shop then Rose's day would be ruined. Affronted by this woman or not, it was clear by the look on Rose's face that she wanted a dress from this shop no matter what the woman thought of her.

Myriam bit her lip. She took in a long deep breath of air, released her grip on Rose's arm and then looked across at the woman.

"As I said, Ma'am, you've made yourself clear but," Myriam forced a sickly, sweet smile onto her face. "But let me assure you that we can afford your dress prices." She nodded and Rose produced a small bundle of bank notes from her purse.

It was true. Rose could afford to buy a dress in this shop. When Grandma Hetty had died last year, it had been a surprise to all the family to discover that she had amassed a sizeable amount of savings. Shrewdly, she had prepared a will which included her two grand-daughters and Rose was using her share of the inherited money to pay for the wedding.

The woman stepped forward to look at the contents of Rose's purse and it was her turn to take in a deep breath. She looked up and there was a moment of embarrassment as her eyes met Myriam's, due to the realisation that she had nearly lost out on a good sale. She then turned her attention to Rose with a warm, welcoming smile.

"Now dear, if you'll follow me out to the back, I'll show you our selection of wedding gowns."

They disappeared to the area behind the curtain and Myriam sat down in a small armchair which was positioned by the window. She amused herself watching the activities that were going on outside. The shop was positioned in the main street on the corner of Church Lane, a busy little walkway connecting a couple of the town's centre streets. Men pushing carts went by. Women walked past carrying washing and trailing dirty little children behind them. A small girl, most probably around five years old, paused as she followed her mother past the shop and stared up at the gowns. She was carrying a grubby little doll. Her eyes were wandering all over the beautiful patterns and trailing lace until she caught Myriam's glance. She then quickly chased after her mother. Myriam smiled sadly to herself. The child's family were clearly poor.

Her thoughts were interrupted by a rustle from behind the curtain. Myriam looked round to see Rose walking through wearing a beautiful, white wedding gown.

A wide, open smile beamed from Myriam's face. Rose looked delighted. It made Myriam feel warm inside.

"Mrs Woods says she thinks she has others that would suit me better but I just wanted you to see this one," Rose said quietly.

Mrs Woods, which Myriam now realised was the woman's name, nodded in agreement.

"Your sister has quite a pale skin tone, despite her rosy cheeks. I think a dress that is slightly off-white would complement her more."

Myriam nodded with a polite shrug to indicate that she didn't know anything about the subject.

Mrs Woods and Rose disappeared again. Myriam felt relieved. Despite the unpleasant introductions that had taken place earlier, this woman now seemed to be giving Rose her full, highest quality attention and she certainly appeared to know what she was talking about.

Myriam found herself again avidly examining the activities taking place outside. She really did love watching people. That was one thing she enjoyed about her work at the inn, she could quietly observe so much.

About fifteen minutes must have passed before Rose appeared again. Myriam felt her breath catch as she let out a small gasp.

Rose was standing there looking every bit the

beautiful bride that she deserved to be. Myriam felt a small sting as tears threatened behind her eyes. Her sister always had been and always would be beautiful to her, but to most people Rose went unnoticed. She hadn't been blessed with Myriam's height or her slim figure. Rose was shorter than average and a little overweight. Her plump little hands, wrists, feet and ankles weren't slender and delicate and Rose lived in the shadows. No one stopped and admired her. Looking at her now though, dressed in this simple, cream lace gown, Myriam was confident that everyone would be giving Rose the highest admiration on her wedding day. Rose stood, anxiously waiting for Myriam to say something.

"So, what do you think?" she asked nervously.

Myriam shook her head. She couldn't find words. Mrs Woods filled the silence.

"I've pinned the train shorter. At full length it was all train and no bride."

Myriam smiled. She stood up and walked over to Rose. As a single tear slipped out of the corner of her eye she leaned forward and gave her a gentle kiss on her soft, rosy cheek.

"You look so beautiful. I just wish mother could see you."

Rose hugged her sister and sniffed back her own tears.

"Do you think Tom will like it?"

"Like it?" Myriam snorted. "You'll have to pick him up off the floor!"

Four

Rose and Myriam left the dress shop and made their way through the town, their arms linked together happily. Rose had paid for the dress and Mrs Woods was going to make some alterations and then have it sent to the inn later the next week. Rose was clearly very happy with her purchase and Myriam was pleased. She loved her sister and even her own selfish feelings about losing her to Tom Watkins on her upcoming wedding day couldn't spoil her delight at seeing how beautiful she had looked back in the dress shop, wearing her wedding gown.

It was by now mid-morning and the warmth from the sun was prickling the skin on their faces. Myriam pulled her arm away from Rose and unbuttoned the collar of her blouse a little, flicking her hair out behind her as they walked. Rose glanced across at her.

"This is going to be such a special day," she said.

Lifting her head upwards and letting out a long breath of air from her lungs, Myriam replied, "I can't tell you how much I've been looking forward to this next part."

They had arranged to meet up with two of their friends from Bodicote. Eliza and Mary Price were going to meet Rose and Myriam at a prearranged point along the canal, roughly halfway between Banbury and their home just outside the village. The Price sisters were Rose and Myriam's closest friends. As young children they had enjoyed playing together and strong bonds had been forged.

Passing through the shops and some of the work yards, Rose and Myriam soon reached the canal. It was always a busy area. The waterway which ran through the town connected Coventry to Oxford and this made it a busy route for transporting goods from the industrial part of England to London and back again. Making their way towards a bridge where they could cross over and onto the tow path, they passed by the many coal sheds. Huge horses hitched to big carts waited outside each shed, willingly eating the contents of their nose-bags while their owners loaded heavy sacks of coal onto the back of the carts. Coal distribution was a big business for the town and the two sisters were used to seeing men with grimy, soot-stained faces around the area.

Before they reached the bridge, they passed the lock and the last coal shed. It belonged to Mr Dickenson. He was a friendly, soft-hearted man who supplied coal to the coaching inn. Rose caught sight of him. He was standing by the lock gate, chatting with a young man and she called out to him politely.

"Good day Mr Dickenson."

"Ah, if it isn't Rose Evans and her sister Miss Myriam." He turned to face them. "Now then, what are the two of you doing down here at this time of day?"

Myriam smiled. He was such a lovely man she thought, always addressing everyone politely.

"We have the day off and so are going to meet up with our two friends from Bodicote," Rose informed him. She didn't bore him with details about the wedding dress.

"Well, isn't that a fair thing to do, and such a beautiful day for it."

"Yes, we've been looking forward to it. We must go though, I'm afraid. We don't want to be late to meet our friends," Rose explained.

"You both have a lovely time." He waved as they continued on their way and the young man he was with raised his hand to them politely.

While Rose had been speaking with Mr Dickenson, Myriam had noticed how handsome the young man was. He was tall and he looked strong. His shirt sleeves had been rolled up, no doubt due to the warm temperature of the air, and Myriam had caught a glimpse of his strong arms. Her gaze had wandered to his face and his crisp jawline. Then, to her embarrassment, the young man's attention had flicked briefly from the conversation between Rose and Mr Dickenson to her. His dark, mysterious eyes had locked for a second with hers and she had felt a sudden heat in her neck as her face reddened. She had quickly looked away and was relieved that the conversation was now over and they were continuing on their way.

Crossing the bridge, Rose looked at Myriam and frowned.

"Are you all right duckie? You look a bit flushed."

Myriam rubbed the back of her neck. "It's just

a bit warm today," she replied, her eyes glancing briefly down at the canal and the lock below as she carried on walking.

Rose paused and looked back at the lock. She could see the young man still chatting amiably with Mr Dickenson yet, judging by the direction of his gaze, his attention was clearly elsewhere. Rose turned to follow her sister with a quiet, knowing smile to herself.

Five

Walking along the tow path, Myriam felt her spirits lifting. She'd always felt drawn to water, either the river or the canal. As a young girl she had spent hours just watching the ripples and reflections. She felt as though the water listened and then safely guarded the secrets of the many stories that had passed by. Walking along the tow path now, she watched the gentle movements of the water. She saw small bubbles rising up from the organisms that were hidden, living below the surface. The sights and sounds of the water soothed her thoughts and she could sense it listening to her silent story.

All the anxious feelings that had been building up over the recent weeks were pushed to the side as she breathed in the fragrant scents of the wild hedgerows and meadow flowers. She really hated living in the middle of the town. She had been born in the countryside and felt that the countryside was where she belonged. Today, this beautiful, sunny day, was just the medicine she needed.

They soon came to the place where they had arranged to meet Eliza and Mary. It was a large field that ran alongside the tow path. They knew the place because in the middle of the field was a giant, old oak tree. As they squeezed through the hedgerow Myriam could see that Eliza and Mary were already there, sitting on a blanket beneath the tree.

"You go ahead," called Rose. "I just want to

pick a few blackberries for us."

Myriam eyed the hedge and noticed that there were quite a few blackberries, already ripe and shiny, just waiting to be picked.

"Great idea," she waved, heading towards the tree. "Just don't be too long. I know what you're like, you'll wander halfway back to Banbury before you know it."

Rose laughed. It was true. She couldn't seem to stop once she started rummaging in the hedgerows for wild fruit. Usually, just when she thought she had collected enough then another ripe berry, barely out of reach, would catch her eye and she'd go after it.

Leaving Rose behind, Myriam excitedly made her way over to greet her friends. Mary had already seen her coming and was bounding across the field towards her. They met with a squeal of childish joy and hugged each other. Mary was just one year younger than Myriam and they both got on so well. Myriam, although fairly calm by nature felt enlivened in Mary's exuberant company. Laughing together they made their way over to where Eliza was sitting and flopped down on the ground next to her.

Eliza was completely different to her sister. Four years older and newly married, she always maintained a perfectly refined composure. It amazed Myriam how she managed to do this, as the sisters were farmer's daughters and both worked hard on the farm. Eliza managed to work in an incredibly ladylike manner, while Mary looked like she had been born in a stable and had lived there ever since.

It wasn't long before Rose joined them and they began their picnic. The four friends chatted comfortably together, catching up on each other's lives. After a while the conversation came around to the upcoming wedding.

"How are the plans coming on for the big day?" asked Eliza.

"Well, the dress was the last big thing to organise so now it's just a matter of waiting," replied Rose, taking a bite of some sweet, buttery shortbread that Mrs Price had made for them that morning.

"So, are you sure young Tom Watkins is *the one* for you Rose?" asked Mary mischievously.

"I certainly hope I'm sure by now!" laughed Rose. She took in a breath, looked brightly at them all and added, "He's a real good'un and I'm so happy when I'm with him."

Eliza and Mary smiled back at her, but Myriam felt an overwhelming urge to not make eye contact with any of them. She took great interest in picking a small fly off one of the blackberries.

Eliza leaned back against the warped, gnarled trunk of the old tree. "Do you remember those conversations we used to have? They would last for hours and hours. Just talking about our 'ideal' husbands."

Mary laughed, "Oh how we used to dream! I still do, I'll have you know. I just hope that he'll wait for me."

They all knew what she meant. Eliza and Mary's father, Mr Price, had suffered a stroke and as result he couldn't get around as well as he used to. The two sisters had almost single handedly run the farm for the last year. After Eliza married, she was able to continue working on the farm as her husband,

Andrew, worked as a farrier in the village, allowing her just to walk up the road each day from her new home. Mr and Mrs Price's ten-year-old son, younger brother to Eliza and Mary, would eventually take over all the farm work but for the time being, until he was old enough, it was up to the two sisters to keep everything going. For Eliza this meant that children of her own would have to wait. For Mary, who was set on marrying her childhood sweetheart, Samuel Haynes, it meant he would have to wait for her. She hoped desperately that he would. Although Mary and Samuel had never spoken a word to each other about their feelings, it was obvious to everyone who saw them together that they liked each other. The Haynes family had a farm of their own so Mary realised that it would be impossible for the pair of them to keep two farms running if her dreams ever did come true and they got married.

"Eliza definitely got the man she dreamed about," said Mary, steering the subject away from herself.

"He really is wonderful." Eliza was beaming.

"I must agree, he's pretty good," continued Mary. "He works all day shoeing horses and then carries on helping us at the farm when he's finished."

Eliza smiled at the thought of her husband.

"Let's hope Tom lives up to all my expectations then." Rose's eyes were still dancing. It was obvious that she had no doubts about it.

Myriam swallowed quietly, keeping her eyes low.

"Oh, Rose dear," said Eliza, starting to pack the picnic things away. "I have no doubt he will."

Myriam wished she shared her friend's confidence.

Six

That night, back in their room at the inn, laying on her bed and staring up at the ceiling, Myriam's thoughts went back to one of those conversations that Mary had spoken about.

She must have been about fourteen. It was the winter before her mother had died and it was bitterly cold. All four of the girls were inside the Evans' home playing games by a roaring fire, but they soon tired of the games and started talking about the subject of 'love'. It was their favourite thing to talk about as Andrew had just asked Eliza to start courting and she had said yes, with her father's approval.

"I always said I wanted to marry a handsome man," smiled Eliza.

"He is very handsome," agreed Rose.

"I don't care if the man I marry is handsome," said Mary. "But he'd have to be funny. If he didn't ever laugh, I couldn't stand it!"

Myriam added her thoughts, "I'm not too bothered what he looks like. I just hope that he's strong."

Rose looked around at them all. Eliza, who had the appearance of a serene angel. Myriam, dark haired and pretty. Mary, a bit lively but her blonde curls and infectious laugh made her the admiration of many. Rose then caught a glimpse of herself in the reflection from the window. She saw a short, overweight girl with a plain face that was surrounded by flat, lifeless hair.

"You'll all probably marry exactly the men you want to." She dug her fingernails into the palms of her hands. Her plump, pudgy hands.

Myriam wanted to reach out and gently squeeze her sister's arm but Mary continued talking.

"I wonder how you know it's love?" she pondered.

"I know I'm in love," replied Eliza.

Silvia Evans walked into the room at that moment. She stood behind Rose and placed a hand on her daughter's shoulder.

"Love feels different for each person," she said. All four girls looked at her and she smiled softly at them.

Myriam remembered her mother's little speech clearly. It was as though she could still hear her voice.

"All this talk of handsome men, funny men and strong men!" Her mother's voice was firm, yet soft. "Looks, humour and strength are very fickle things, girls. You need to look deeper. Look right into a man's soul if you want to find a really good husband. Find yourselves each a good man, and I mean a really good man. Not one of those who only says the right things, but one who does the right things too. Is he kind? Is he hard-working? Is he honest and true? Will he put your interests ahead of his own? Will others around you look up to him? Marry a man you can respect. If you can respect him, then you can love him deeply."

The four young women were silent, all of them taking in her wise words. She looked at each of them in turn and then her eyes rested on Rose. With her hand still on her daughter's shoulder, she gave it a gentle squeeze.

"Above all girls," she continued. "Above all, believe that a man you can respect is a man you deserve. Don't settle for anything less! Mr Evans, your dear father Myriam and Rose, is one of the most respectable men I have ever met. We are blessed with a happy marriage. I love him and I feel loved. I couldn't ask for more."

With that her mother had left the room and Myriam couldn't recall what happened next.

Pondering now over her mother's words, she pulled an image of her parents from her memory. They had been an unusual looking couple. Myriam's looks were very similar to her mother's. Her mother had been tall and slim with the same dark hair and attractive face. She had no doubt received much attention as a young woman, and yet she had chosen the love of Myriam's father.

Myriam remembered her father as a man who slightly resembled a teddy bear. He hadn't been blessed with great height and was quite round about his waist, but he had had a friendly face and such a warm, considerate manner that everyone had instantly warmed to him. Rose was so similar to their father. Myriam could clearly see that her mother's advice about the sort of man the girls should look for, had actually been a description of her own husband.

Myriam's thoughts moved from that evening beside the fireplace, listening to her mother's words and landed back at the lock. She recalled the young man who had been talking with Mr Dickenson. She had admired his strong arms. What was it her mother had said? *'You need to look deeper.'* Myriam wondered what was inside that young man's soul.

Then, with a sigh, Myriam's thoughts rested on Rose and Tom. Her recent anxious feelings weren't only about the future separation from her sister. That was a big part of it, but not the only part. Her unease stemmed from something her mother had said all those years ago. *'Don't settle for anything less.'*

Myriam would admit that Tom Watkins was kind, and it was clear to all that he loved Rose. But was he respectable? Could Rose really compare him to their own upstanding father? Myriam had her doubts. For sure, Rose was smitten. She was head over heels in love with Tom and Myriam just hoped it would last. She hoped that Rose wasn't just settling for the first man to offer her some admiration and affection. Myriam didn't know what was inside Tom's soul but she did know what was inside her sister's, and it was pure gold.

Seven

September 1837

To Myriam, it seemed like the morning of Rose's wedding flew past in a blur. She tried to grasp at it and savour it, but it escaped her. Before she realised, it was one o'clock and they were at the church.

St Mary's church, a beautiful, fresh-looking, new building, was directly opposite the Whately Coaching Inn. The two sisters had made the short walk from the inn to the entrance of the churchyard together in silence.

The morning had been full of noise and activity. Eliza and Mary had crammed with them into the small upstairs bedroom at the back of the inn and fussed over Rose's hair and dress. They had brought with them a small feast of sandwiches and cakes although neither Rose nor Myriam had been able to stomach eating much. Last minute nerves, coupled with overwhelming excitement, had caused Rose's insides to churn like a fork as it whipped up cream. Myriam felt light-headed and nauseous and kept praying for the strength to enjoy the day, for Rose's sake.

Finally, after much adjusting and re-adjusting, Eliza had announced that Rose was ready. She and Mary had then left to find their seats in the church, ahead of Rose's arrival.

Standing now, just outside the gateway to the churchyard, Myriam turned to face Rose and took her hand with one of hers, holding a small bouquet of flowers in the other. Rose's hand was shaking. Myriam paused, searching her sister's eyes for any hint of doubt. She could see nerves, mixed with sadness, but shining through strongly was excited anticipation. No, Rose did not have any doubts. Myriam smiled to herself. It was time to admit this was happening and let her go.

"Mother and Father would have been so happy today, therefore I'm determined to be happy too."

Rose squeezed her hand gently. "Thank you." She took in a deep breath, a breath of confidence, and turned to face the church doorway.

Mr Price was waiting just inside the porch. As their father's closest family friend, and in the absence of Rose's uncle, he had kindly offered to give her away. They walked over to him and Myriam thought she caught the shine of a tear in his eye as he held Rose out at arm's length to look at her.

"Look at little Rosie Evans, all grown up," he said and then pulled her towards him to give her a small kiss on the cheek.

Myriam was fond of Mr Price. Since his illness he had suffered a lot emotionally as he had learned to accept and live with his new limitations. She was impressed that he had always kept a positive attitude. He never burdened his family with the worries and anxieties that he must at times feel. He now took Rose's arm and looped it inside his own. He picked up the cane that he used to steady himself while he walked and nodded to Myriam.

"Well then girls, this is it." He motioned to one of the wedding guests who was by the door, waiting for the cue that they were ready. "Myriam, my dear, lead the way."

The doors to the church opened and Myriam heard the organist beginning to play. Inside, standing at the front by the vicar, she could see Tom waiting. He was fiddling with the cuffs on his shirt sleeves. He looked nervous too. Myriam locked her eyes onto the vicar, took a second to steady herself and then slowly began to walk down the aisle. It was the walk that she knew would deliver Rose to Tom.

Myriam was wearing a dress that she had saved from her mother's collection. She hadn't worn it before. It was pale pink with cream lace detail around the neckline and the hem. It was a beautiful dress and it fitted her perfectly, but no one was looking at Myriam. As Myriam walked past the guests, who were standing to welcome the small wedding party, she could see that all their attention was on Rose. Myriam smiled, recognising the admiration in their eyes. They were all seeing what she had seen a few weeks ago in the dress shop. They were watching a beautifully stunning bride walking towards her future husband. Nearing the front, Myriam's attention was drawn to Tom.

Tom looked completely overwhelmed. He was staring at Rose with the biggest smile on his face whilst gulping back lumps that seemed to be catching in his throat. Myriam watched as he grabbed a handkerchief from his trouser pocket and quickly blew his nose. Then Mr Price presented Rose at his side.

Shaking his head in disbelief, Tom touched her hand briefly before they both turned to face the vicar.

The sermon was short and simple. The vows were repeated without any mistakes and the rings were exchanged. There was only one more thing left to do. It was done quickly, like when a dressing is ripped off a wound; Tom and Rose turned to face their audience of family and friends and the vicar uttered those final few words.

"I introduce to this audience, Mr and Mrs Watkins."

Everyone clapped their hands, congratulating the newly married couple as they walked back along the aisle hand in hand. Myriam followed at the rear. Two words were swimming around in her head; 'Rose Watkins'.

And that was it. Just like that, the separation was done. Rose Evans was now Rose Watkins. Myriam realised that she was repeating that name over and over to herself. It sounded so strange. As she reached the door, everyone was gathered outside, waiting their turn to talk to the newly-weds. Myriam paused and looked at her sister. She really did look happy.

"Hey!" She felt someone grab her arm and turned to see Mary at her side. "Shall we leave everyone to it and head straight to the reception? See if we can have a quiet moment to ourselves before they all arrive?"

Mary, her oldest friend, knew best of all how Myriam was feeling. She was showing her a way out, a door she could quickly escape through and gather her thoughts before the celebrations for Tom and Rose

35

would begin. Myriam nodded and they quietly slipped past everyone, made their way around the side of the church and headed towards Parsons Street and The Flying Horse Inn.

<u>Eight</u>

Once away from the church and all the guests, Mary asked Myriam how she was feeling. She knew Myriam was really going to miss Rose.

"You know, I'm really happy for her," Myriam replied. "I truly am."

"Me too," said Mary. "She does deserve it."

"She really does," Myriam agreed. "I was worried about whether she was going to be happy enough with Tom, but seeing them today, I can see that he does really love her. I can't ask for anything more really, can I?"

"No." Mary shook her head. "You can't."

They were now outside The Flying Horse. It was a much smaller coaching inn than the Whately but the building was equally as old and atmospheric. Rose had made arrangements for a small meal of beef pie and mashed potatoes to be served for her and Tom's guests. She had also paid for a small group of musicians to play a few tunes so that everyone could have a good dance together. Myriam loved dancing and so was looking forward to it.

Myriam and Mary made their way inside. The clouds outside were heavy, threatening rain and although there were many lamps burning around the room, there was a lack of sunlight flooding through the windows to brighten the wooden, panelled walls. Despite this, it felt cosy and inviting. Small vases of flowers had been placed around the room and a large banner was hanging across the space between the bar and the seating area. Eliza had crocheted it with the words 'Mr and Mrs Watkins'. Everything looked lovely.

Myriam's nose was picking up scents of warm, gravy filled pastries. She realised that she was actually really hungry. She had hardly eaten anything all day and her stomach grumbled at her.

"I wonder how long everyone will be?" she pondered out loud, rubbing her tummy.

Mary responded by passing her something wrapped in a paper. "I slipped a sandwich into my purse earlier. Here you go, this should keep you going."

"Oh Mary, thank you," said Myriam between hurried mouthfuls of the cheese and ham sandwich. "I felt so sick earlier I couldn't face anything but now I feel like I might pass out."

"Let's get a drink and sit down while we wait for the others," suggested Mary.

They explained to the barmaid that they were part of the wedding group and asked if they could purchase a drink. She told them that a firkin of ale had already been paid for by the newly-weds for their guests, and served them both. Without protesting they said thank you, carried their ales to a table over by the corner and sat down to wait. Mary took a sip of the drink and she scrunched up her nose.

"I'm not really sure what the appeal is of this ale. The taste is so bitter."

Myriam took a mouthful, swished it around and then swallowed it quickly. "No, nor me. It must have been Tom who suggested it. I didn't think Rose drank ale."

At that moment the door opened and Tom, Rose and everyone else piled quickly into the room. Heavy rain drops began to hammer against the windows. Rose was laughing, slightly out of breath.

"Well, that was a bit of a dash but we made it just in time!" She let go of the lace train that she had been carrying and smoothed down the creases at the front of her skirt. Looking up, she saw Myriam and Mary sitting at the table.

"Well, there you both are! We were wondering where the pair of you had got to."

Tom eyed their drinks. "I see you've made a start without us." He clapped his hands together and then banged them down onto the bar. "Come on lads, we've got a whole barrel here with our name on it."

Tom passed the drinks around, being sure not to forget his new wife. Myriam watched as Rose took her drink and sipped it. For the briefest moment, a shadow of concern fell across her sister's face. Myriam spotted the small frown that appeared along her brow. Rose looked at the drink and then back at Tom. Tom, cup of ale raised high, was cheering to his bride. His eyes smiled at her and her frown quickly faded.

"Hip, hip hooray!" called out one of his friends and then the barmaid rang the bell to announce that the dinner was ready.

The food was delicious and Myriam savoured the tastes while she ate. The room was quiet for a while. Just the noises of clinking cutlery as everyone enjoyed their food. Tom and Rose were sitting together at a small table in the middle of the room.

Myriam had never seen someone eat and drink as fast as Tom did. She counted that he had filled his cup with his third helping of the ale and asked for extra mashed potatoes and gravy before she was even halfway through her meal.

Mr Price had noticed too. He leaned over to Myriam and whispered, "It's a good thing your sister works in the kitchen. I think he's a man who likes being fed."

Myriam agreed and laughed it off as a polite joke. But she wasn't sure she found it all that funny really.

The meal was soon over and everyone relaxed, letting the food settle whilst mingling and chatting with each other. It wasn't a very big wedding party. On Rose's side there were some old friends from Bodicote and a handful of guests from the coaching inn. Not everyone had been able to come, as some were needed to stay and work, but a few of the girls from the kitchen and Bill had been able to take the evening off to join them. Tom had his family there. His parents, two brothers and a sister; all older than him. One of his brothers and his sister were married so their spouses were there too. The Watkins were from Neithrop, a village outside the town. A few of Tom's friends from Neithrop had also come in for the wedding. They seemed a lively bunch, mostly factory workers who travelled into town each day for work.

Tom and his friends from Neithrop were making their way through the barrel of ale and their animated conversations were getting louder and louder. Myriam was pleased when the musicians arrived and the tables were cleared away for dancing.

Dancing was something she loved. Her parents had loved to dance and had often travelled into Banbury of an evening to attend a square dance at one of the halls or inns. They had taught the girls how to dance and it was something they both enjoyed. The musicians began with a waltz. This was something that Rose had chosen especially for her and Tom to dance to. It was to be their first dance together and she loved how romantic this new style of dancing looked. She had long imagined them in a single couple embrace, enjoying their intimate dance together.

Tom was deep in a conversation with one of his friends when Rose went and gently whispered in his ear. From the look on his face, it was clear that he didn't want to dance, and didn't want to leave the conversation he was having. Myriam watched as Rose took his hand and gently coaxed him towards the open floor. His face was set, annoyance written all over it. For an awful, brief moment Myriam thought he was going to refuse Rose's request but then his face softened and he walked with her to the middle of the room.

Tom clearly wasn't a great dancer and Myriam wasn't sure if it was due to his lack of ability or the influence of the ale as he swayed unsteadily to and fro with Rose in his arms. Rose however didn't seem to mind. She was dancing at her wedding with her husband and she was delighted.

They finished the first dance and another tune began. Others now joined them. Bill appeared at Myriam's side and asked her if she'd like to dance with him. Myriam accepted and they joined the others in a round dance. As they danced together Myriam smiled to herself. It was true, Bill did seem to like her. He wasn't that great at dancing but he was eager to impress her. He apologised each time he bumped into her or knocked her shin, or stood on her toes. He was a kind boy she thought, but that was just it; Bill seemed like a boy. She didn't view him as a man that she could look up to, who could care for her in the way she felt she needed. Bill was more like a friend. She was aware that he might one day expect more than friendship and was careful not to lead him to believe she felt more than she did. So as a third dance began, she steered him gently towards Mary and left them together. She knew Mary already had set her heart on Samuel Haynes but she could still have a little dance with Bill.

The country dances began and the heat rose as everyone in the room starting jumping and spinning around. The music and cheers from the dancers drowned out the noise of the rain that was still lashing against the windows outside. Tom was still dancing and seemed to be enjoying himself. He was laughing as he spun Rose faster and faster and she was crying out breathlessly with the excitement of the lively dances. Myriam danced and danced until she was too tired to dance any more.

Before they all knew it, it was time to go home and bid the new Mr and Mrs Watkins a long and happy life together.

Myriam held Rose tightly as they said goodnight. This would be the first time they would be spending a night apart. She kissed her sister gently and told her she loved her.

"I love you too duckie," Rose replied.

Myriam leaned in to kiss Tom goodbye. As her

cheek brushed against his, she caught a smell of stale ale mixed with cold sweat. It wasn't very pleasant.

"Goodnight Tom," she said moving back, away from him.

"Goodnight Myriam," he replied. "I promise I'll take good care of her."

Myriam nodded at him. "I'm sure you will."

<u>Nine</u>

June 1838

The first few months after the wedding were dark and lonely for Myriam. Rose and Tom had moved into a small accommodation behind the stables. Even though Rose was only living a stone's throw away from Myriam's own room, it was hard for them to spend time together. Rose worked early in the kitchen and Myriam worked late in the bar. They passed each other in the corridors and hallways but struggled to steal more than brief moments together. They rarely had opportunities to properly talk.

Added to the pain of Rose's absence from Myriam's life was the arrival, just three days after the wedding, of her new room-mate, Harriet Nichols. Harriet was brash and tactless. She lacked manners and concern for the thoughts and feelings of others. Self-assured and inconsiderate, she took over the small room they shared and trampled all over Myriam's fragile emotions. Harriet was the constant thorn in Myriam's life. Her slighting, scornful criticisms of Myriam's innocent and virtuous nature stung more than Myriam let on. The truth was that Harriet was jealous of Myriam. Despite Harriet's striking beauty, it was pretty, sweet Myriam who received all the attention from the customers. Harriet could flirt and smile and flutter her eyes at them as much as she liked but they were more intrigued by the mystery of quiet, pensive Myriam. The result was that Harriet disliked Myriam and so set out to make her feel miserable.

The winter months therefore passed by painfully and slowly. Myriam had never enjoyed the long, dark evenings and this year was no exception. Imprisoned inside the small room with only Harriet for company caused her spirits to sink low.

Her only source of pleasure was seeing that the sparkle in Rose's eyes continued. As the time passed and she watched her sister settle into her new life as Mrs Watkins, Myriam was relieved to see that Rose remained happy. It seemed to Myriam that she had worried needlessly about her sister's choice of husband. Tom was evidently looking after her and she was content.

Six months after the wedding, to Myriam's great surprise and immense joy, Harriet made an announcement. She informed everyone that she was getting married and moving away. She was marrying a coach driver from Oxford. Myriam was amazed that Harriet had settled herself enough to the attentions of *one* man and secretly felt sorry for the fellow who, in her opinion, had his head in the clouds. The news did though bring Myriam an instant feeling of relief. With Harriet's departure, a young, sweet kitchen girl called Josephine moved into the room. Josephine was polite and obliging. She showed thoughtfulness in her manners and ways. Conversations with her were of a pleasant nature, never a hint of malicious motives or implications.

Josephine moved in at the end of March. With the days getting longer, the skies brighter and buds appearing on the leaves, Myriam found her spirits rising. The dark, emotional moments she had felt frequently over the winter months were beginning to fade.

Myriam also took the opportunity of the better weather to spend time outside. She loved walking around the yard and the stables, watching the horses as they pulled at bags of hay and listening to their gentle snorts and the swish of their tails. Behind the inn was an extensive area of fields and scattered trees where she found time to walk, enjoying the sounds of birdsong.

Occasionally Rose was able to slip away and join her on those walks. It felt good to be together. Rose would chatter on about some funny thing that Tom had said or done and Myriam would listen to her happily. Rose had always been a chatterer. As a child she used to talk endlessly at mealtimes, giving their parents a minute-by-minute account of the days' events. Myriam loved listening to her. It gave her a feeling of nostalgic contentment.

By the time summer arrived, Myriam felt like her old self again. It had been about a year since she had felt this way. A year which had begun with waves of anxiety and apprehension, followed by the hopelessness of living alongside Harriet. But now, finally, her blue eyes were shining, her skin was glossy and fresh. Myriam was walking as she used to, with her head up, assured yet not pretentious. She gave the impression of being a young woman who once again had purpose in her life.

It was now the end of June and there was a buzz of excitement and activity all over the country. A year earlier, following the death of the king, eighteen-year-old Alexandrina Victoria had succeeded her uncle to the throne. The coronation of the young Queen Victoria was taking place at Westminster Abbey in London, and parades and celebrations were being held in towns throughout the whole of England. Plans were under way for a large procession to take place through Banbury. This would then be followed by sports, food and dancing. All the town's establishments were taking part, including the Whately Coaching Inn.

In the days leading up to the coronation Myriam was called into the kitchens each morning to help for a few hours. She enjoyed this because it meant that she could spend time around Rose. The plan was for establishments in the town to provide enough food for the over three thousand who were expected to take part in the parade and celebrations. Myriam kneaded dough for bread until her arms ached. The atmosphere in the kitchen was good, since everyone was looking forward to the celebrations.

The 28th of June and the day of the coronation started early for all the staff at the inn. Many who were travelling in from nearby villages would need stabling for their horses during the day so the lads out in the yard got all the usual jobs done as quickly as possible so they would be ready to receive the horses as they arrived. The breads and puddings that had been made previously were being packed up ready to take into town later that day.

At twelve noon the bells of all the churches in the town began to ring. Myriam and Rose rushed outside with the others to listen. It was a jumbled yet melodious sound. It gave Myriam goosebumps on her neck, even though the day was warm. Mr Hamilton had given everyone permission to attend the parade and the dinner, assigning a few to help with the serving. Rose would be helping but Myriam was not. Myriam ran to quickly change out of her work clothes and stopped to pick up her purse, popping a few coins inside in case there were any stalls set up with pretty things to buy. She made her way back out to the yard and walked with the others towards the town.

Myriam was used to seeing the town full of people on occasions such as Michaelmas but today was different. Michaelmas was a mostly business affair with a large market and trading of goods and skills. This gathering today was not commercial. It was a gathering of the people to welcome the Queen to her throne. The atmosphere was triumphant and jubilant.

Myriam, Rose, Josephine, Bill and the others made their way towards the procession. All the trades in the town had put together their own display to parade. Tom was driving the cart for the Whately Coaching Inn. They had dressed Mr Hamilton's personal mare with feathers and streamers of paper. Sitting atop the cart on bar stools, with a barrel of ale between them and shiny, pewter tankards raised high were two of the stable boys. They were only a few carts behind a procession of musicians playing a medley of national songs. Mr Hamilton's mare was a good horse but she was unused to the noise and jostling movements all around her. Myriam could see that Tom was having a hard job keeping control of her. As they passed by where the group from the inn were standing, he called out to Bill to remove the streamers from her head. Bill did so and Tom continued, hoping that she would calm down.

The most impressive part of the procession was

a large ship. The mainsail had been decorated with the words, *'Britannia rules the waves.'* The ship received cheers and applause from the hundreds of onlookers as it made its way through the town along with the rest of the displays.

Once the procession was over, Rose and Josephine made their way to where the food was, in order to help with serving. Myriam was left with Bill and another girl who worked in the bar. Mary had sent a message to the inn earlier that week to say that she was coming into town for the celebrations and would look out for Myriam. There were so many people that Myriam wondered if they would find each other, but she needn't have worried. Before long she saw a rush of golden hair as Mary pushed her way through the crowds and breathlessly arrived at her side.

"I thought I'd never find you," she gasped.

Myriam laughed. Mary was so unaware of others around her and what they thought. It was refreshing. Mary rolled her sleeves above her elbows and grabbed Myriam by the arm.

"I'm so hungry. We must go and get some food." She tugged at her arm and Myriam gave Bill and the other girl an apologetic shrug.

"Looks like I'm off," she said. "I'll see you both later."

Ten

Myriam and Mary found their way to where the dinner was being served and picked up a helping of meat, bread and pudding. There was a fast-flowing amount of ale available too but they declined. Banbury was overrun with ale houses and drinking establishments. Many of them were providing drinks for the celebrations and there didn't seem to be a shortage.

Myriam and Mary took their food and ate in a quiet area by the church. They then spent some time wandering amongst the crowds, catching up with people they knew. After a while they were drawn towards the sporting activities that were taking place just away from the town centre. A large crowd had gathered to watch and they pushed gently between the outside spectators, trying to get closer to see. When it was obvious they could make no further progress forwards, they stood on tiptoes to get the best view they could.

There was so much going on in a small area. Immediately in front of where they were standing were a few games of bowls. It seemed that another game with a ball was being played to their right. Over to the left, at the lower end of the field, was a lot of noise and commotion. This area seemed to be attracting many of the men and most of them appeared to have sampled a fair amount of the ale that had been available throughout the day. Mary could see what looked like boxing and cock-fighting taking place in that area. She tutted out loud.

"I don't know why men are drawn towards sports like that," she complained.

Myriam didn't respond so Mary glanced at her. She was frowning. Something over by the boxing was holding her attention and so Mary followed her gaze. Myriam wasn't frowning at *something*. She was frowning at *someone*.

Myriam had caught sight of Tom amid the groups of men who were watching the boxing. He must have returned the cart and Mr Hamilton's mare to the inn and then come back to join in the town's celebrations. He was with one of his brothers and some of his friends from Neithrop. She wasn't overly surprised to see him there. As Mary had just said, some sports appealed to some men more than others. What she was finding concerning though was the fierce, competitive way in which he was behaving. He was punching his fist into the air and yelling out loudly. He looked vehement and savage, as if he was being riled into behaving like a vicious animal by what he was watching. This wasn't the Tom she knew, the Tom who was now her brother-in-law. It made her nervous watching him.

Myriam was so caught up in what Tom was doing that she momentarily lost concentration on everything around her. Standing amongst the crowd, her mind became so distracted that she didn't notice the jostling and bumping of people passing by her. She didn't notice a small boy wearing dirty old clothes and no shoes. She didn't notice his hand slip inside her purse for a brief moment as he paused in his steps.

She didn't notice him pull his hand out and continue on his way.

But someone had noticed. A young man with strong arms and dark, mysterious eyes had been passing by and caught sight of Myriam. He'd only stopped to watch her for a few moments. His breath had momentarily quickened at the sight of her. He had wondered many times over the past months if he would see her again and now, here she was. As he watched her, he could see that something was holding her attention, she looked concerned. He wondered what it was that could have caused a frown of anguish to form across her pretty, delicate face.

Then he noticed the small boy wearing dirty old clothes and no shoes. He noticed his hand slip inside her purse for a brief moment as he paused in his steps. He noticed him pull his hand out and continue on his way.

"Hey you! Boy! Stop!" shouted the young man and chased after the boy.

Myriam heard the shouting and turned around to see a man running after a small boy. She felt inside her purse and suddenly realised that all her coins had gone.

"Oh Mary!" she cried, grabbing onto her friend's hand. "I think someone just took my money!"

Mary, eyes blazing, was about to leap into action and join in the chase when the young man came walking back towards them, dragging the small boy with him. Upon reaching Myriam and Mary, he instructed the boy to empty his pockets. Whimpering and sniffing back tears, the boy started to protest.

"You either empty them here in front of the

lady, or you'll empty them at the police house," insisted the young man.

Myriam hadn't really taken any notice of the man. Her eyes were fixed on the boy. She knew it was silly but she felt sorry for him. He looked so poor. The boy obeyed the young man and turned the pockets of his jacket and trousers inside out. Coins, watches and jewellery fell to the floor. Mary stooped down to pick it all up.

"You filthy little urchin," she scolded him. "You've been pinching off half the town today! Myriam, how much did you have in your purse?"

Myriam was still watching the boy. He could only be about eight years old. He was crying now.

"Myriam?" repeated Mary. "How much did you have?"

Myriam looked at the coins in Mary's hands and then back at the boy. She bent down so she was level with him.

"What you did was wrong, you know that?" she said to him. Her voice was quiet.

With his eyes fixed at his feet he nodded meekly.

"Do you have anything to say to me?" she asked him.

His eyes flicked and met with hers briefly before quickly returning to the ground again.

"I'm sorry Mam," he sniffed.

"Well, I've no doubt you are," she said. "Now tell me, and be honest mind, did your Ma send you out today to do this?"

The boy flushed red. He didn't respond.

"Never-mind," Myriam continued. "I expect she'll be angry if you go home with nothing?"

The boy nodded and again started crying.

"Well then," Myriam paused. She took two half-farthing coins from Mary's hand and held them out to the boy. "I want you to understand though that you still did wrong."

He nodded, staring at her in disbelief.

"So, take them, or I'll have them back," she urged him.

He took the coins and put them in his pocket and the young man released his grip on the boy's shoulder.

"Before you go," added Myriam. "You can apologise to this man for him having to chase after you."

The boy said sorry and then turned and disappeared into the crowd. Myriam stood up. Straightening her skirt, she began speaking.

"I just want to say, Sir," As she looked up to address the young man, she felt a flutter inside. Her stomach flipped and her tongue stuttered. She had met this man before. The man she was talking to was the man she had seen last year at the lock, the man with the strong arms and dark, mysterious eyes. Myriam swallowed. It was a dry gulp of nervous excitement. She composed herself and started again.

"I just want to say, Sir, that I'm extremely grateful for what you did. Thank you."

He attempted to say something in return but faltered. He had never felt so tongue-tied. She was mesmerising. Her eyes were so blue, like the jewels that were still sitting in the other girl's hands. Aware that she was waiting for him to speak, he gathered himself together to reply to her.

"It's not a problem Miss," he paused and glanced briefly at her friend. "Miss *Myriam* was it?" he asked.

Myriam blushed. "Yes. Myriam Evans."

He smiled. It was a warm, open smile. "I'm pleased to meet you Miss Evans." He dared to hold her eye contact for a moment longer.

It was Myriam who looked away first. Aware of her shaking legs, she focused her attention on the coins and jewellery still sitting in Mary's hands.

"What do you think we should do with all this?" she asked.

"If you'll trust me, I'll hand it to the police," he replied. "I'm about to return home. I can take it all to the police house on my way. Only if you trust me that is."

"I think we can trust you," she replied.

Mary handed him the coins and the jewellery. She hadn't said a word throughout the exchange but Myriam could see the amused look on her face and was trying to ignore it.

"Thank you again," said Myriam as he turned to leave.

He smiled warmly again and she flushed red. He was now walking away.

"Wait," called out Mary.

He stopped and looked back at them. Myriam felt sick. What was Mary going to do?

55

"You didn't tell us your name. Sir."

Myriam held her breath.

"It's Jim," he replied. "Jim Bailey."

Eleven

July 1838

'Jim Bailey'. That name kept floating round and round Myriam's thoughts in the days that followed the coronation. She couldn't get the image of him out of her head. The way he had smiled. That breathtakingly, open smile. The way he had looked at her. His eyes holding hers. Those deep, inky eyes from which she had struggled to look away.

Despite his forthrightness and the way he had handled the situation involving the little thief with solid firmness and assurance, she had detected in those eyes an element of shyness and vulnerability. Many would insist that this was a sign of fragility, and therefore a deficiency on his part. They would say those were traits of a weak man. But Myriam had seen no weakness. That glimpse of vulnerability had intrigued her. He was clearly a man of strength, both in physical ability and moral character. She wondered what would cause a man like that to be reserved, bashful almost. She was curious and he was now constantly in her thoughts.

Mary, of course, had noticed the attraction between them. Walking back to the inn moments after Jim Bailey had left them, Mary had made a simple comment.

"That was like watching sparks on a hot fire."

Myriam had blushed and behaved in a coy manner but she hadn't protested at the comparison. She had definitely felt the heat from those sparks as her cheeks had prickled from his attention.

Mary hinted to Rose that Myriam had met someone that day, but Myriam felt too nervous to discuss it. She felt that if she openly admitted what had happened, then they would laugh at her. Maybe she had got it wrong. Maybe she had imagined more than had happened. She was afraid that the attraction she had felt was just one sided. He wouldn't be the first kind man to stop and help a young woman. Maybe there was nothing special about it after all.

And so, Myriam kept her daydreams to herself and carried on with her normal activities.

Then, just a week after the coronation had taken place, he appeared in the yard at the inn.

It was a Thursday morning, just before noon. The air was damp and it was drizzling a little but it was warm. The rooms inside the inn felt stuffy so Myriam made herself a cup of tea and went to sit outside. She found a bench which had been placed against the side of a wall and sat down on it. The extended porch-way of the kitchen was providing her with cover from the misty rain. Rose was taking a short break and came out to join her. The ovens were going and it was hot in the kitchen. Rose sat and fanned herself gently with a towel.

Hearing the sound of hooves and the rumble of cart wheels, they both looked up to see Mr Dickenson's coal wagon entering the yard.

"Chef will be glad to see him," said Rose,

standing up to alert the lads that the delivery was there. "Mr Dickenson is late this week and we're almost out of coal."

As the wagon pulled in and the horse came to a stop Rose walked over to greet Mr Dickenson. A small fly had landed in Myriam's cup and was now drowning in her tea. She was trying to scoop it out without burning her fingers. Finally, she released the insect from the ocean it had landed in and looked up. Her teacup rattled against its saucer as she tried to steady her hands. The man climbing off the wagon wasn't Mr Dickenson.

Her heart was pounding and everything was shaking. She put the teacup and saucer down, afraid that she might spill its contents everywhere. He hadn't seen her yet. He was occupied, talking to Rose while unloading heavy sacks of coal. Myriam watched as his muscles flexed and strained with each movement. His attention was still on Rose and it looked as though she was asking him various questions which he was politely answering. Then the door next to where Myriam was sitting opened and two of the lads from the inn came outside, calling out to greet him good day. He looked over. Balancing a coal sack on one shoulder, he waved to them with his free arm. It was then that he caught sight of her. He stopped walking and paused, just for a moment. It was only a brief second. Two at the most. But it was enough for Rose to notice what was happening.

The shy, unsure smile on his face. The pink that was colouring Myriam's cheeks. Rose knew it all. Or at least she thought she did.

Rose waited until he had finished unloading

the wagon. The quick glances he kept making over to where Myriam was sitting didn't escape her notice. Myriam looked nervous, as if she might at any moment jump up and bolt inside, but for some reason Rose was confident that she wouldn't. There was something in her sister's eyes that told Rose she wasn't going anywhere just now.

When all the coal had been set down in the yard, Rose turned to him and asked if he would like a quick cup of tea. Glancing for the hundredth time at Myriam, he smiled and accepted. Rose then beckoned him to follow her.

Myriam stood up, realising that she had been holding her breath. Rose was coming towards her and he was following. She quickly let the air out of her lungs and gathered herself together. Approaching the doorway to the kitchen, Rose paused and spoke to Myriam.

"I'm just going to fetch a cup of tea for Mr err, Mr err." She realised that she didn't know his name.

Rose turned back to look at him, about to ask him what he was called. It was Myriam who seized the moment and spoke first.

"Mr Bailey," she quietly informed her sister, a nervous smile forming on her mouth as she stole a quick look at his also smiling face.

Rose cocked her head to one side and raised her eyebrows. Myriam was refusing to make eye contact with her.

"I see," she smirked. "I'll be back with your tea in a moment Mr Bailey." Rose disappeared inside and they were left alone.

There was a moment of nervous silence and

then Myriam remembered that it was raining.

"Here." She indicated towards the bench. "Sit under the shelter while you're waiting."

"Thank you," he replied and sat down.

She hesitated for a moment before sitting next to him.

"Thank you again for what you did at the coronation," she began. "I was, I mean, I still am, so grateful."

He was looking down. She saw him nod and smile. Then he turned and looked at her. Those eyes; she felt like he was searching her soul. After a moment he spoke.

"You were very kind to that boy."

"I felt sorry for him," she shrugged.

"Not many would have felt like that if they had been in your place."

"Maybe not, but I couldn't let him go home and be beaten for returning with nothing." The sky was dull and the clouds grey but her eyes shone such a bright blue. There was a gentle warmth in her expression as she was speaking. He found her mesmerising.

She blushed and he realised that he was embarrassing her. He looked away.

Myriam bit her lip and tried to think of something else to say.

"Mr Dickenson?" she enquired. "Is everything all right? I mean, I've never seen you delivering the coal before. Is Mr Dickenson well?"

"No, he hasn't been too well for a few days

now," Jim explained. "He couldn't get out for his deliveries and everyone was starting to get behind with their coal, so Mr Thomas said for me to give him a hand today."

"Do you usually work for Mr Thomas then?" Myriam knew that Mr Thomas was the lock keeper.

"Yes. I've worked for him for many years now."

Myriam was about to ask more questions but at that moment Rose rejoined them with a cup of tea for Jim.

As he sipped on the tea, Myriam studied his face. It was hard to tell how old he was. He was definitely older than her, but by how many years she wasn't sure. There was something about him that made her think that life hadn't been too kind to him. It wasn't that he looked sad. He just seemed to have an invisible load of responsibility over him.

Rose was talking, asking him what he did for fun. He shrugged, apologetically.

"I don't have a lot of time for fun," he replied, drinking his tea.

"Well, strictly speaking nor do we," Rose hastily informed him. "However, the first Friday of each month, which happens to be tomorrow..."

Myriam couldn't believe it but at that point Rose paused and gave him a wink. Her sister, a married woman had just winked at this young man.

If he noticed, he politely ignored it and Rose continued, "As I said, the first Friday of each month we both have the evening off and we tend to go into town for some dancing. You should join us. Tomorrow we'll be going to the Reindeer Inn, they always get a popular group of musicians there!"

He continued to sip on the tea while considering her bold invitation. He glanced at Myriam and she gave him a warm, albeit slightly uncomfortable smile.

"Well?" insisted Rose. "Do you think you'll join us?"

Jim shuffled onto his feet and looked awkward. Gulping down the remainder of his tea he then handed the teacup back to Rose. Myriam felt furious with her sister. *Why had she been so pushy?*

"Possibly, err maybe," he answered, hesitantly. "I'll have to see."

He thanked Rose for the tea, gave Myriam a quick, reticent smile and bade them both goodbye.

Twelve

Myriam felt deflated. Her stomach was in knots, and not the light fluttery ones she had felt when he had looked at her just ten minutes earlier. She didn't understand what had gone wrong. Well, she did; Rose had been too bold.

She picked up her own cup and saucer and thundered her way back inside and straight up to her room. Myriam, usually calm in the face of any storm, didn't often feel angry or tempestuous. Now though, as she slammed the door shut and threw herself onto the bed, she was surprised by just how annoyed she was. Especially as her vexation was directed towards Rose; someone who could normally do nothing wrong in Myriam's eyes.

She buried her head into her pillow and found, to her surprise, that she started to cry. It shocked her that her emotions were so violent over the whole thing. After all, she had only spoken to this man twice. Why did she feel so anguished about the way he had just left?

There was a meek knock at the door.

"Myriam, it's me. Can I come in?" Rose's voice was soft and quiet. It was clear that she felt bad.

Angry or not, Myriam would never ignore her sister or give her the silent treatment. She sat up, wiped her eyes and told her she could come in.

Rose closed the door and sat down on the bed

next to Myriam.

"I'm sorry if I scared him away," she apologised.

Rose took Myriam's hand and squeezed it gently. Myriam flinched a little. Rose had been too pushy, too insistent. But her intentions had been good and Myriam knew that.

"You meant well," she conceded.

There was a brief moment of silence. Rose wished she could go back and do it over again but differently.

"Was that the young man who helped you at the coronation?" she asked. "The one that Mary was telling me about?"

Myriam nodded.

Rose continued, "I recognise him. I think I've seen him before, by the canal."

"He said he works for Mr Thomas, the lock keeper," sniffed Myriam.

Rose handed her a handkerchief. "I think we saw him last year, when we were down by the canal. Yes, I'm sure he was the young fellow with Mr Dickenson. That was the day we bought my wedding gown."

"Yes." As Myriam confirmed what Rose was only just now remembering, Rose realised that her sister already knew this.

"He's very handsome." Rose looked intently at Myriam and saw that a fraction of a smile was cautiously released from her sister's face. "And he seemed very taken with you," Rose added. Myriam blushed but then the smile dropped.

Rose gulped back a small, nervous lump in her throat. She could now see that Myriam had been thinking about this man for longer than she had assumed. Rose hoped she hadn't spoiled everything.

"Look, just because he ran off quickly, it doesn't mean he's not interested in you."

"Then why did he rush off?" asked Myriam.

Rose looked at her crumpled face. Her eyes were swollen and her skin was blotchy.

"He seemed fairly shy. Maybe I just frightened him a bit. I do tend to do that. That's why Tom was the only one who would have me. I'm too outspoken for most men."

Myriam gave Rose's hand a squeeze. "No one could be frightened of you."

Rose stood up. "I need to get back to the kitchen but...are *we* all right? I'm really sorry that I upset you."

Myriam smiled. "*We're* fine. I know you didn't mean for it to end like that just then."

Rose turned to leave. She opened the door and walked out through it. Pulling it closed behind her she paused and then pushed it back open a little before leaning again into the room.

"He may still come to the dance though, you never know."

The following evening, after Jim had finished work at the lock, he made his way back to where he lived. It was in an area called Waterloo. Waterloo was away from the town centre, situated on the other side of the canal. It was a poor part of the town, but the houses were gradually being worked on and the area was slowly improving.

Jim arrived at his own house, turned his key in the lock and opened the door.

"Mother. It's only me," he called as he entered the house and closed the door behind him.

No response. There never was.

He hung his waistcoat and cap on the hook by the door and went into the small living room which was just off the hallway. His mother was sitting in her chair. She was so small and frail that it looked as if the chair was swallowing her. She glanced up as he entered the room and there was a brief glimmer of light from her eyes. She held her hand out to him and he went over to hold it. Stroking her bony, shaking fingers, he looked around the room. Everything was as he had left it that morning. Placing her hand gently down on the arm of the chair, he made his way through to the kitchen.

The fire in the bottom of the stove was almost out but the embers were still warm, so he stoked it up and added more coal. The heat had soon risen enough for him to heat up some stew that was left over from the previous evening. He had deliberately made extra so that he could be quick with everything today. While the stew was warming, he took the steaming kettle from the stove, filled a bowl with the water and took it upstairs. He washed away the dirt and grime from his day's work. He then dressed in a casual shirt and trousers and picked out a smart neck-tie to wear. Pulling the laces tight on his shoes, he realised his hands were shaking a little.

Back downstairs, he served the stew into two

bowls and returned to the front room where his mother was still sitting silently. He quickly ate his own dinner, trying not to scald his tongue as he slurped on the hot liquid. It tasted good but he found himself struggling to eat it. His stomach was flipping over with jittery flutters. Turning his attention to his mother, he saw that she hadn't touched her bowl. He reasoned that she would probably have spilled it had she tried. Ensuring her stew was now cool enough to eat safely, he patiently spooned it into her mouth. It was slow but eventually she had finished her own meal.

Back in the kitchen he cleared the bowls away and warmed a cup of milk. He took a small phial of tincture down from the top of the cupboard and added two drops of the herbal night remedy to the milk. Without it his mother wouldn't settle and sleep. She may be sitting in silence, staring into space but inside her poor head was a frantic overload of thoughts and worries.

After his mother had finished the warm drink, he gently scooped her up in his arms and carried her to her bedroom. Once he had settled her into her bed he sat in the corner of the room, reading a book. Glancing up every few minutes he saw that her eyes were still open, staring at him. Finally, after what felt like an age, she fell asleep.

Jim quietly left the room. He went downstairs, picked up his waistcoat and cap and exited the house. After closing the front door carefully behind him and locking it, he then knocked at the house next to his own. A woman opened the door to him. Numerous children were moving around inside.

"She's asleep now Kitty," Jim said.

"Lovely. Now off you go and enjoy yourself," Kitty replied.

"I won't be late," he assured her.

"You can be as late as you want!" she laughed.

"If there's any problem, anything at all, I'll be at the Reindeer."

"I doubt there will be. Now off you go." Kitty gave him a gentle push.

"I mean it Kitty. Anything at all, just send for me. I can be back here in five minutes."

"She'll be fine Jim. Now, go on will you!" she insisted.

He smiled at her. "Thank you Kitty. I'll see you later."

<u>Thirteen</u>

Myriam was at last beginning to enjoy herself. She had spent the first hour at the Reindeer Inn nervously watching the doorway in case he would walk through it. Her nerves had turned to disappointment as she had realised that he wasn't coming. She had even sat in the corner by herself for a short time.

It wasn't like her to sulk, although she wasn't really sulking. It was more a case of not feeling inclined to jump around like a giddy goat when her hopes that he would come had been dashed. Then Josephine had come along and, in her sweet, non-judgemental manner, had asked her why she wasn't dancing. It must have seemed odd to Josephine to see Myriam sitting by herself at the table in the corner. Myriam loved dancing so much that she was usually the last to stop, begging the musicians for just one more reel. Myriam could hardly explain to Josephine that she was upset because a man who had smiled at her a few times hadn't turned up to the dance, so Myriam gave herself a quick talking to and got up to join in the evening with her friends.

She was part of a four-couple quadrille. Myriam was partnered with Bill, and Rose with Tom. Josephine was with her cousin and there was another couple that Myriam recognised but didn't know personally. Myriam was laughing because both Bill and Tom kept forgetting the steps and turned into the wrong people. She was so involved in what was going on that she didn't notice as the door to the Reindeer Inn opened and someone anxiously stepped inside.

The noise and the heat of the room hit Jim as he walked in. The dark, oak panelled walls were filled with flickering lanterns and there was a comforting smell of warm bread mixed with sweet ale. The tables and chairs had mostly been removed with a few pushed to the sides of the room. It was a small space for dancing and it was full to capacity. There were so many people and so much activity was going on that he entered the inn unnoticed by anyone.

Jim stood and looked around. Almost instantly he saw her. She looked radiant. Her long dark hair was pinned back on her head. He could see that she must have taken time earlier to pin it carefully but even so, small strands were loosely falling around her face as a result of the lively movements. Her cheeks were flushed and her mouth was open, smiling widely. One of the fellows in the group had just turned the wrong way and bumped into her sister and she was laughing at him. She was wearing a simple dress, but it swished and flowed around her as she skipped about.

It was Rose who saw him first. Out of the corner of her eye she caught sight of him. He looked hesitant, like someone who was out of place slightly. She also noticed that, despite looking hesitant, something was fascinating him. Or rather *someone*. She could see that he was watching Myriam; enraptured by her. Distracted, Rose missed a step and bumped into Myriam.

Myriam tutted at her light-heartedly. "What's wrong with you? You're as bad as Tom and Bill," she chided.

"Nothing," replied Rose, nonchalantly.

Standing opposite her, Myriam saw the mischievous grin on her sister's face. She knew it wasn't nothing. She raised her eyebrows and mouthed a questioning, "*What?*"

Rose wouldn't reply. She just smirked at her and continued dancing.

The tempo of the dance was building. As the steps and turns got faster, Myriam's heart began to quicken and race. She loved this. The feeling of energy powering her feet and legs. The spins and kicks of movements in time to the music. With a crescendo the dance ended and they all applauded. She was gulping in air, trying to catch her breath. Her chest was pounding as the blood flowed quickly around her body. Then, looking up, she saw him.

Her heart stopped and the breath caught in her lungs. He was standing by the doorway looking directly at her. Apprehensively he smiled and waved. She felt the corners of her mouth turn upwards uncontrollably and waved back.

Rose was by her side and gave her a gentle nudge. "Well, go on then. Go and say hello."

Myriam walked over. Her breathing was still fast, but she wasn't sure if it was from the exertion of dancing or the sight of him. He looked so handsome. He was wearing a fresh, clean shirt with a dark green neck-tie. The light from the lanterns was playing with the shadows of his cap, making his jaw and cheekbones stand out more than usual. His eyes appeared darker too, against the flickering light. As she approached, he took his cap off, twisted it nervously in his hands and said hello.

"I'm sorry I'm late," he apologised, his eyes holding hers.

Myriam bit her lip. She felt so strange. She had never felt like this before. "You haven't missed too much," she replied. "It takes a while for everyone to warm up."

The next dance was beginning and Rose called out to them, "Myriam, we need a fourth couple over here."

Myriam looked over. Rose was now paired with Bill as Tom had made his way to the bar, a place he preferred to the dance floor. They were indeed a couple short for the set. She turned back to Jim. "So, are you here to dance, or to watch?"

She winced at her own words. They felt too blunt. He paused. There was a hint of fear in his eyes.

"I've not done a lot of dancing," he explained.

Myriam thought he was going to decline her offer. She braced herself for his refusal. However, he didn't refuse. Instead, he pushed his cap back onto his head and started walking towards the others. "But from what I saw, you're used to having people bumping into you, so it'll be all right."

She followed him excitedly to join the others. Brief introductions were made and Myriam couldn't help but notice the crestfallen look on Bill's face as he politely greeted Jim. For a moment she was distracted, feeling bad for him, but then the music started and the dance began.

They were dancing another quadrille. It wasn't the easiest to master, for someone unused to dancing.

The steps were varied, with criss-crossing of partners and places throughout. It was clear that Jim wasn't used to dancing nevertheless, he seemed to have a natural flair for it and picked up the sequences quickly. As the dance progressed, he made less and less mistakes. He felt himself relaxing, concentrating less on the steps and more on the company. Each time his shoulder brushed against Myriam's or he took her hands to spin her round, he felt a tingle as his senses reacted. She felt it too. The touches were brief, as they were part of the dance movements, but it felt like a fire was igniting between them with each one. She felt alive, her body and nerves overloaded with elation.

As each dance ended, they rolled comfortably into the next and the time passed by quickly.

Myriam had forgotten about the prolonged absence of Tom from their group until a bit of noise and commotion was heard from the bar. Someone tapped Rose on the shoulder and whispered in her ear. She disappeared from the group. Myriam watched as Rose followed the man to the bar, where Tom was standing. Or rather swaying. He was heatedly disputing something with another man and he looked less than sober. Myriam made a polite excuse and also left the group.

The barman was asking Tom to step outside but it was obvious that Tom didn't want to. Rose calmly walked up to Tom and lovingly leaned against him. She made a big pretence of yawning.

"Tom, I'm so tired. I don't think I can stay any longer. Can we go home?"

Myriam knew it wasn't true. Rose would never normally leave early. She must be trying to get Tom to leave quietly without a scene.

Tom, eyes fierce and cheeks burning, looked at his wife.

"Please?" she asked meekly and yawned again.

He softened and patted her gently on the head.

"Alsright, loove," he slurred.

Myriam felt her body tense. He *was* drunk.

Rose quietly led Tom outside and Myriam followed them. "Do you want me to come too?"

"No, you stay here and have fun." Rose looked embarrassed and slightly annoyed. It was the first time Myriam had seen her look like this.

Myriam nodded, smiling warmly to her sister and then Rose carried on up the road, leading an unsteady Tom towards home.

"Is everything all right?" Myriam turned round to see Jim standing outside the entrance to the inn. He looked concerned.

"Yes," Myriam replied brightly. "Let's go back to the others."

He could see the anxiousness behind her eyes. The joyful shine that had been there while they were dancing had been overshadowed by a cloud of worry. There was a bench on the opposite side of the road. He indicated towards it. "I'm quite warm, do you mind if we sit here for a moment so I can cool down a bit?"

Fourteen

Myriam was grateful. She hadn't really felt like going straight back inside. Sitting on the bench, she breathed in the night air. It was a warm summer's night, but it felt cool outside compared with the heat inside the inn. Myriam looked up. The sky was clear and she could see stars twinkling above her. The street was dark but with the light that was shining from the windows of the inn she could make out a lot. Two men were standing nearby, smoking pipes. She didn't like the habit, but the smell was sweet. She turned to look at Jim, sitting beside her. He had been watching her, trying to decipher her anxiety. She smiled at him as she noticed a look of genuine concern on his face. He seemed so kind.

"So Jim," she said. "Tell me about yourself."

He shrugged. "There's not much to tell. I work for Mr Thomas at the lock mostly and sometimes I help Mr Dickenson and others out, though not as often these days as Mr Thomas is getting older and needs me around more than he used to."

His voice was like velvet. So smooth and calming. She liked listening to it.

"How did you come to work for Mr Thomas?" she asked.

He shuffled on the bench slightly. She wasn't sure if she had asked something she shouldn't have. "Sorry," she regretted. "I didn't mean to be nosey. You don't need to answer that."

"No, it's all right," he assured her. "When I had only just turned thirteen, my father died suddenly. He worked in the weaving factory where he had a good job as one of the shift managers. One day though there was a bad accident. My father and two other men got caught in some of the machinery."

She noticed that his forehead was furrowed deeply. The memory was something painful for him.

"Anyway," he continued, "only one of them survived. My father and the other man didn't. It's just me in the family. My parents didn't have any other children, so I had to stop school and start working."

"I'm so sorry," she commented. There was a pause as she pondered over what he had told her. She hesitated briefly and then asked, "You went to school?"

"Yes. I loved it. I really wanted to study engineering."

There was a small moment of silence between them as he contemplated the career he might have had.

"So Mr Thomas took you on?" Myriam encouraged him to keep talking. She wanted to know more about him.

"Yes. Mr Thomas was a very close friend of my father's and he immediately stepped in to help. He has no family of his own and therefore no one to look after as such. He kindly pays me out of his own salary, which I'm not sure is very high. He's been like a father to me for years now."

"How long ago did your father die?"

"It will be eight years in December."

Myriam quickly did the arithmetic in her head. That would make him about twenty years old, soon to be twenty-one. She had turned eighteen only a fortnight earlier, so he was probably about three years older than her.

"How is your mother?" she asked. "It must have been a terrible shock for her?"

He let out long, deep sigh. "My mother has never been a well woman," he conceded. "As a boy I remember her frequently spending the day in bed. The doctor says it's something to do with her nerves, but I'm not sure I'll ever fully understand the issue that she has. Anyway, my father's death seemed to accelerate her symptoms. Her eyes no longer have any life in them. It's as though the spirit within her body is already gone. She's a tiny, frail woman who is barely existing. She's just waiting to die. It's such a waste of a life."

He let out another sigh. "That's why I was late arriving this evening. I had to get her dinner and then wait for her to go to sleep. She won't sleep if I'm not sitting by her side. It's like her body tries to drift off but then she'll snap her eyes open, checking I'm still there.

"That happens every night?" inquired Myriam gently.

"Yes. The doctor has given me some drops for her. I mix it in with her night drink. When she has eventually gone off it knocks her out completely, whatever it is. It's been a relief to me to have that medicine. She used to wake during the night crying and screaming before."

"The poor woman," sighed Myriam.

He smiled at her. She clearly had a caring heart. "Yes, she is a poor woman. The doctor doesn't think she'll live long. He says that the strain of her nerves will kill her soon, although he's said that for a while now. Whatever happens, I feel like I lost her years ago."

Jim straightened his back. It felt stiff already from the dancing. He realised that he had been doing all the talking.

"What about you?" he asked. "What's your story?"

"It has a certain similarity to yours."

Myriam looked at him. It was dark but she could make out the outline of his face against the light from the open door of the inn. He'd been so open with her. Now it was her turn.

"We grew up in Bodicote and our father was the doctor for the village. I had a very happy childhood. Then, four years ago, both mother and father were killed in an accident on the turnpike road from Oxford. I was fourteen."

"I'm sorry." His voice was strained, as if he was overcome by emotion.

"Thank you." He didn't say anything and so she continued talking. "We had nowhere to go so Rose enquired everywhere about work and lodgings for us. Eventually she secured us a place at the Whately and we've been there ever since. Rose made sure we weren't separated in those first few years. She was wonderful. I don't know what I would have done without her. She put my interests first in everything."

Myriam was shocked to realise that she was now choking up with emotion.

Jim lifted his hand and went to take hold of hers but stopped himself. He didn't want to be too forward or make her feel uncomfortable, so instead he took a handkerchief out of his pocket and gave it to her.

"Look at me, silly thing," she said, taking the handkerchief and wiping her eyes.

"Don't worry. It's clear that you love her a lot."

"She's just such a good person. It upset me to see her this evening, you know, when she left." Myriam now felt defiant. She strongly felt the need to defend her sister. "I've never seen Rose look embarrassed before. She's never had any reason to be. Until now."

Jim didn't respond. Myriam thought that maybe she had said too much.

The noise and chatter that had been a background lull got louder and closer as people began to exit from the inn. The music was over and people were leaving to make their way home. Bill and Josephine came out into the street.

"There you are!" cried Josephine, catching sight of them. "I thought you'd gone home already."

Bill approached them. "Is everything all right?" Poor, sweet Bill couldn't hide his disappointment that Myriam had been sitting outside with the new fellow for all this time. He also noticed that she had been crying.

Myriam gave him warm smile. "Yes. We were just getting some cool air."

"Well, you missed some of the best dances," tutted Josephine.

Jim stood up. "It getting late, I need to get back." He looked at Myriam. "Thank your sister for inviting me, I enjoyed it."

They all said goodnight and parted ways. Jim walked east, down Parson's Street, towards the canal while the others headed west, up the road in the direction of the coaching inn.

They had only walked a few steps when Myriam realised that she still had hold of his handkerchief.

"Wait a moment," she said to the others and ran down the road after him.

"Jim, hold on!" He stopped and turned around. She held the white cloth out to him. "I forgot I was still holding this. Thank you."

He was about to take it when a thought crossed his mind and he gently pushed her hand back. They both felt that same tingling sensation again.

"Keep it for now," he said. "Maybe you can come and return it to me at the lock sometime?"

He tried to keep his voice casual and carefree. He didn't want to sound too desperate to see her again. It was dark in this part of the street so he couldn't see her features clearly, but her eyes were shining brightly at him. She was smiling.

"Maybe I will."

Fifteen

It wasn't until ten days later that Myriam found an opportunity to go into town. It was a Monday morning, over a week since the night of the dance at the Reindeer Inn. Myriam had woken earlier than usual and so made her way into the kitchen to see if she could collect any fresh bread from the ovens. Rose caught her as she walked in and grabbed her quickly by the arm. Rose looked flustered and hot. Myriam could see that she was flapping around like a frantic chicken.

"Myriam, you're awake early. Tell me, are you busy this morning?"

Myriam, still sleepy from having only just woken up, squinted at her. It sounded like her help was required. She rolled her eyes and shook her head. "No, what do you need me to do?"

"Two of the girls are off sick today. Two! Can you believe it? Anyway, we have no one to go down to the butcher's and give them the order for the week. Would you mind going?"

Myriam had been expecting to be asked to spend the morning peeling potatoes and chopping carrots. She was surprised. "Is that all?" she asked.

"Yes, although while you're in town you could also pick up a few things. But we need the order to go in immediately!"

Myriam shrugged. "That's no problem. I don't

start my shift in the bar until noon anyway."

"Perfect," clapped Rose. "Here's the order." She handed her a piece of paper with scrawly writing on it. "It needs to get there by nine."

Myriam looked at the clock. It was eight o'clock. "All right. I'll go and get my things and set off. Can I please have a slice of warm bread first though?"

Rose wafted an apron at her. "Just go and get your things quickly. I'll make you something to eat."

Myriam ran back upstairs to change into her outdoor shoes. She looked out the window at the weather. The past few weeks had been so hot that it had felt quite uncomfortable at times but today was more overcast. It didn't look dark enough for rain, but she could see from the swaying of the trees that lined the back of the yard that the wind was blowing. Myriam decided to take her light, summer shawl with her in case she felt cold. Opening the drawer to take out the shawl, she noticed the small white handkerchief sitting neatly folded in the corner. Smiling to herself she picked it up and popped it into her purse and then made her way back downstairs.

Rose had a cup of tea and a warm slice of toasted bread, covered in sweet, sticky marmalade ready for her. Myriam almost inhaled the toast, gulped down the tea and then headed off into the yard. The urgency in Rose's face was pushing her out quicker than she could move.

Walking briskly, she made it to the butcher's well before nine and smiled to herself as she thought about her panicking sister. Rose had always been one to get flustered quickly when plans appeared to be going awry. Rose had given her a small list of a few other things that needed collecting. It didn't take long and Myriam was pleased it wasn't much else that was needed, as the basket she was carrying was small. With all the errands for the inn completed she made her way towards the canal.

She was surprised as she neared the lock to feel her heart start to pound violently inside her chest. She was sure that others around her must be able to hear it. Her hands felt weak as they carried the basket and she almost turned around and returned home. What if he hadn't meant it? She questioned herself. What if he wasn't really interested in seeing her again? Nevertheless, whether he had meant it or not, there was one thing she did know; *she* desperately wanted to see *him*. That thought gave her the motivation to keep walking in the direction she was going. She arrived at the canal and went along the side of the coal sheds towards the lock.

Nearing the lock, she could see that there was a narrowboat waiting to go through. Myriam paused for a moment, just taking in the scene. The boat was laden with heavy cargo. The boatman was on the other side of the canal guiding a strong looking cob pony around the lock gates. A woman, presumably the boatman's wife, was on the boat. It was a scene that warmed Myriam's heart. She loved animals and it appealed to her that animals and people could work together to accomplish great things. This way of transporting goods along the canal had always fascinated her. Strong, hard-working ponies, horses and even donkeys were valuable assets to their owners as they pulled tons of materials through the country's water system. The owners needed these creatures in order to earn their livelihoods and they loved their animals for it. To Myriam it seemed so harmonious.

She was so distracted by the activity that was going on around the boat and the pony, that it took a few moments for her to spot Jim. When she did her heart started racing again. He was working the heavy gates of the lock, pushing them open to let the boat in. He was wearing work clothes. They were old and slightly stained. The cap he wore wasn't like the smart one that he had been wearing at the dance. She thought he still looked handsome though, despite the appearance of his clothes.

Myriam made her way closer to the lock. The boatman was expertly guiding the boat into the small space. Closing the gate behind the boat, Jim looked up and saw her. A large smile instantly appeared on his face. Touching his hand to the top of his cap and nodding at her with a glint in his eye, he then held his index finger up and mouthed, "One minute," to her.

With the boat settled inside the lock and the gate closed, Jim jogged down to the front gate and turned the windlass to release the water. Myriam, still on the opposite side of the water to Jim, had followed him down to the front gate and was watching the water gush out from the lock. It was so loud, like the sound of a heavy waterfall.

"So, you finally made it." She almost jumped out of her skin. Jim was standing by her side. He had walked across the narrow lock gate to join her.

"Sorry," he apologised. "I didn't mean to frighten you."

"No, I just didn't hear you coming, that's all."

She looked at him. He was still smiling. A hint

of that shyness that she had seen on previous occasions was still there in his face but overall, he looked delighted that she was there. She was relieved. He had meant it; he had wanted to see her again.

He walked back towards the gate and beckoned her to follow him. Myriam looked down at the water. The water inside the lock was going down and the boat with it. It made the gate seem even narrower and even higher than it had just a minute earlier.

"I can't walk across there," she protested. "I'll fall."

"I'll make sure you don't," he said and gently took hold of her arm.

Tingling sensations waved through her but she was concentrating on her footing too much to notice. To her surprise, it wasn't as narrow as it looked and she easily walked across to the other side. The level of the water inside the lock now matched the level of the canal on the other side of the gate. Myriam stood back while Jim opened the gate and the boatman led the pony with its trailing load off down the tow path.

Jim turned his attention back to Myriam. He had been hoping she would come to see him and now here she was. He felt like a young boy, excited and nervous at the same time.

"How have you been?" he asked.

"I've been fine," she replied. "And you? Were you aching much after the dance?"

"Yes, I was," he admitted. "I might push heavy lock gates around all day, but that dance gave me a different workout." He smiled at her. "But I enjoyed it."

Myriam took the handkerchief out of her purse. "Thank you for letting me use it," she said, giving it back to him.

"Not a problem." He paused. "I was thinking that maybe..."

Myriam didn't get to hear what he was thinking as at that moment an older man came up from behind Jim and patted him brusquely on the back.

"Jim lad, there's a row of three fly-boats coming down. You'll need to fill this lock back up quick or we'll keep them waiting too long." He looked at Myriam and tapped his cap. "I'm sorry to interrupt Miss."

"You must be Mr Thomas." Myriam gave him a smile. "Don't worry Sir, I'll be going now."

"No, don't leave just yet," said Jim. "If you don't mind waiting, I should only be about twenty minutes or so."

Myriam nodded and Jim walked back to the top gate to refill the lock. Mr Thomas looked at Myriam. He wore a small frown across his forehead as he studied her face. After a moment though, his features relaxed into an open smile.

"So, are you the girl that got him to go to that dance the other night?"

She could see tufts of grey hair under his cap, wrinkles all around his face and his mouth missing most of his teeth. He seemed like a straight talking, no messing, yet deep down a soft-hearted man.

Myriam blushed. "Strictly speaking it was my

sister that invited him."

"Huh. But it's you that's come 'ere to say hello today, hey? Not your sister."

"That's correct Sir." She shuffled her feet nervously.

He winked and gave her a pat on the hand. "You seem like a nice girl. That boy needs a nice girl. Now, if you want to wait, you'd best stay out the way. There's a little spot to sit, just down the tow path there."

He indicated a few yards down the canal and Myriam saw a small bench set back against the hedge.

"Thank you," said Myriam and went to sit down.

It was a lovely place to put a bench. It was far enough away from the lock and the coal sheds to feel peaceful. Myriam pulled her shawl closer around her shoulders. She was glad she had brought it with her. The wind was gusty and when it blew, the air felt cool. Myriam sat down and allowed her thoughts to lose themselves in the sights and sounds of the water. The gusts of wind were creating small waves and ripples across the surface. It was calming to watch them. Two adult moorhens were swimming around, picking at small insects and flies that were floating on the canal. They were beautiful birds to watch. Covered in charcoal-black feathers with a flash of white on only the tips of their wings, they glided easily through the water. The red markings on their heads were distinctive and made Myriam think of a mourning widow wearing a bold and daring splash of rouge on her lips.

Over on the bank to the other side a small

movement caught Myriam's attention and she noticed another moorhen. This one's feathers though were duller, more of a grey than black. It was a juvenile. As Myriam watched the young bird scratching around in the dirt for worms and insects, she noticed that he wasn't alone. There were three of them in total. She smiled to herself as she watched the little family moving around. Then she heard a loud squawk, a sound like an alerted hooting. It was one of the adult hens calling. The three juveniles launched themselves into the water, swam quickly across the width of the canal and darted into a thick patch of reeds.

Myriam soon saw what had caused the panic. The first of the fly-boats was through the lock and coming towards her. The boatman greeted her as he passed by leading his horse. Myriam breathed in the sweet smell of the horse's hair. She loved that smell. Once they had passed, her attention returned to the moorhens. They were now hiding out of sight behind the reeds. Somewhere amid that small, green jungle of water plants there would be an old nest from which the juveniles would have hatched out of their eggs a few months earlier. When the adult had given the warning just then, they had all reacted so quickly to hide away. It had been an instantaneous flight reaction.

Myriam waited for them to re-emerge on the water. They took ages to come back out from their hiding place. Then, just a moment after they did, the second boat came along and, with another shrill hoot, they were all back inside the rushes again. It made Myriam think of her own life. There had been some moments when her flight reaction had been to hide away like those birds were now doing. She understood the safety and security they felt behind those reeds. No one could see them. It was as if they weren't even there.

After her parents had died, Myriam had wanted to hide. She had wanted for no one to talk to her, no one to disturb her. She had wanted to be invisible. Rose had not let her do that though. Rose had gently encouraged her to come out from behind her 'reeds' and to spend time with her friends. As hard as it had been at the time, Rose had known best. Although Myriam felt that the whole experience had changed her personality to some degree, she knew that she would be a much less confident woman now had it not been for that persistence from Rose.

Now though, she didn't feel like hiding away at all. She was enjoying her life. Rose was happy and so Myriam didn't feel any anxiety in that area. Josephine was sweet and easy to live with. And then there was Jim. Being around Jim made her feel positive and excited. There was still uncertainty about her life and the future, after all she barely even knew him. Yet, since she had met him, she felt hopeful.

Myriam was so lost in her thoughts that she didn't notice the remaining boat pass by. She was still staring deeply at the patch of reeds when Jim approached.

"Sorry about that," he said and sat down next to her.

She blinked and turned to look at him.

"Are you all right?" he asked.

"Yes. I was miles away. I was daydreaming about moorhens."

He looked at her quizzically, not

understanding what she meant.

"You can't see them now, they're hiding in the reeds," she explained. "I was watching them before though."

He nodded, not completely understanding the interest she had in the birds. However, her eyes were shining while she talked about them and he liked that.

"So, you met Mr Thomas then," he said, making the statement sound like a question.

"Yes, I liked him."

"He can be a bit grumpy. Some people don't get on with him."

"I got that impression," she admitted. "He has a kind face though."

"Yes, I suppose he does."

A small narrowboat was coming up the canal towards the lock. Jim waved to the boatman as he got closer and stood up. "I'm sorry, I'll have to go again."

Myriam noticed that he seemed disappointed. She felt disappointed too. He was easy to talk to and she wanted the conversation to continue. She also stood and picked her basket up from where she had placed it under the bench.

"I should be getting back anyway," she said, following him along the tow path.

"Thank you for coming."

"Thank you for asking me."

They were passing a bridge that went over the canal.

"I think I'll use the bridge to go back," she smiled. "Goodbye Jim."

"Bye," he replied.

She placed her foot onto the stone step, then stopped and turned around. He was still watching her. "What were you going to say? Just before Mr Thomas interrupted you?"

He looked unsure.

"You said that you were thinking about something?" she reminded him.

"Ah yes." He swallowed as he remembered. "I was thinking that maybe I could also come to the next dance. If you'd like me to, that is?" He had that shy look in his eyes again.

She smiled softly. She really did feel hopeful around him.

"Yes, I would like it," she replied.

<u>Sixteen</u>

October 1838

It was still early. Myriam had stirred when Josephine had the left the room to start work in the kitchens. While Myriam and Rose had shared the room together, she had taken for granted how quiet Rose had been each morning as she had dressed and gone to work. Josephine wasn't obnoxiously noisy, but she wasn't as aware of the sounds she made as she could be. She didn't seem to take notice of which areas on the floorboards creaked or how loud the door on the small wardrobe sounded as she shut it each time. Most mornings Myriam would stir slightly and then drift off back to sleep without any problem. Today though, she couldn't settle.

It was still dark outside so she fumbled for a match and lit the lamp. Looking at the clock she saw that it was six-thirty. Staring out the window she saw there was a faint glow of light on the horizon. The sun would soon be rising. Today was Tuesday. It was the usual day when the coal was delivered to the inn. Mr Dickenson normally arrived in the yard at around nine.

If she started now, she should have enough time to finish it.

Opening the bottom drawer of her small dresser, she pulled out a ball of dark green wool and some knitting needles. Connecting the two together was an almost completed scarf. Myriam hadn't done a lot of knitting before as she didn't really enjoy activities that kept her sitting still in one place for too long. However, she had wanted to make something for Jim and so had spent the previous few evenings knitting him, what she hoped would be, a special gift.

He had attended four dances in total now. Each one had been the highlight of her whole month. They had danced and laughed and sparkled in one another's company. Those around them could see their connection and each time a new dance began they assumed that the two who couldn't keep their eyes off each other would remain paired together. There had been no question otherwise. Although nothing had been said between them, Myriam felt that they were a couple. To those around them, it was certainly what they appeared to be.

They had also found opportunities to talk together. It had become their custom now to step outside at some point during the evening and talk. Myriam found that their conversations flowed effortlessly. She loved listening to his tales about the people on the canal and what other things he was doing as part of his work. And he was a good listener. He asked questions that drew her out and then really listened while she responded and told him her thoughts on different matters. She had never felt so relaxed in the company of a man. Each month she counted down the days and hours until she could see him again. She hadn't admitted it to anyone yet, but she knew she was falling in love.

Myriam put the finishing touches to the scarf, wrapped it carefully and then checked the clock; eight-thirty. Mr Dickenson would soon be there. She dressed and made her way downstairs, taking the small parcel with her. She had just finished eating some breakfast when she heard the hooves outside as the coal wagon pulled into the yard. Each week when the coal delivery arrived Myriam hoped that it would be Jim, as it had been back in July. Mr Dickenson though was a very healthy man and the illness that had prevented him from coming that day was a rarity. Jim had not delivered the coal since.

Today it was Mr Dickenson as usual. Myriam put her coat on and went outside. The warm summer was past, and dry, dusty leaves were blowing across the yard. Soon it would be winter when the days would be shorter. Myriam shuddered. She didn't relish the thought of winter. She much preferred the summer months.

Myriam waited patiently until Mr Dickenson had unloaded all the coal. When he had finished and was about to leave, she quickly skipped over and called out to him politely.

"Mr Dickenson, Sir. I was wondering if you wouldn't mind doing something for me?"

He was pulling the long reins over the back of his large cart horse and paused, turning to look in her direction.

"Miss Myriam. Of course my dear. What do you need from me?"

Myriam liked Mr Dickenson. He was probably about fifty years old. He had a wife and three grown up sons. Jim had told her that his sons had all moved away from the town to work in factories in different parts of the country. It fascinated Myriam that Mr

Dickenson always spoke to people as though he was older than he really was. He addressed everyone with a genteel politeness that made him sound beyond his years.

She held the small parcel out to him. "I was hoping that you could maybe give this to Jim Bailey for me?"

Mr Dickenson's eyebrows flickered. She noticed it and blushed.

He took the parcel from her. "That's no problem at all Miss. Do you have a message for the young man, to go along with the parcel?"

Myriam was momentarily taken aback. She hadn't thought of a message. Then she remembered something. This coming weekend was Michaelmas. She, Tom and Rose were going to meet Eliza, Andrew and Mary in the town to enjoy the fair together. She knew what message she wanted to give.

"Could you please tell Jim that we will be at Michaelmas this weekend. We will be meeting with our friends next to the bandstand at one o'clock. If he would like to join me, err I mean us, then he could meet us there if he likes."

"Of course, Miss, I shall pass that on." He noticed her correction and it made him smile. Jim had certainly been behaving differently the last few months and now he understood why. The lad was in love with this pretty girl. It all made sense to him now. Mr Dickenson climbed onto the wagon, flicked the reins against the back of his horse and drove out of the yard. He was smiling to himself, remembering the heady days when he had met his own dear wife.

Seventeen

It was Michaelmas. The traditional Michaelmas festival had already passed on the 29th of September, a fortnight earlier, but the town combined the Mop Fair and the Michaelmas celebrations each year during the month of October. The Michaelmas Mop Fair was always the biggest annual event for the town.

Myriam loved the Mop Fair. In the years past, the Evans family would join the Price family on their journey into the town for the occasion. She had happy memories of them as children, all bundled into the back of the Price's wagon with her father alongside them too, while her mother and Mrs Price would be squeezed up front on the seat with Mary's father as he drove them all. They were happy times. That was before Mr Price had become sick. He had been so lively and energetic, entertaining them all with riddles and games while they travelled. The fair was always held when the harvest was at an end. All the farmers were relaxed after the months of hard work and the Mop Fair was an opportunity for workers to trade. The fair was primarily a hiring event for workers in the area.

It had evolved into an occasion for entertainment too though. Stalls were set up with different foods and drinks for sale, and shows were put on for the audiences to watch. There were even travelling showmen and acts that journeyed from all over the country to provide diversion and enjoyment for the large crowds.

Myriam remembered vividly standing at the turnpike road one year a few days before the fair began. She recalled the dozens and dozens of wagons that had passed of various shapes and sizes. Strange noises and smells had hit her senses as the caravan of trailers passed by her, heading towards the town. That year she had delighted in watching the circus. Exotic animals had been paraded around a ring. She had been fascinated by the huge, but gentle elephants. Their large ears had flapped casually against their heads while they walked past her. One of the keepers had given her a piece of fruit to hold out and she had felt the warm breath of the elephant as he gently lifted his trunk and took the fruit from her hand.

Getting ready now for the fair, Myriam wondered excitedly what shows and displays would be on offer this year. She put on her warm jacket and placed a bonnet on her head. She didn't usually wear a bonnet but today she felt like it. It was pale blue and matched her eyes. She took her purse and secured it around her neck, tucking it into her jacket. The incident with the small boy at the coronation had unnerved her slightly and she knew that Michaelmas was a favourite target for pickpocketing thieves.

Rose and Tom were waiting for her when she got down to the yard. Rose loved Michaelmas just as much as Myriam did, but today her eyes didn't shine with their usual excitement. Myriam decided that she would try to find a moment later in the day to ask her if everything was all right. They made their way towards the town. It was early still, not yet noon. They wouldn't be meeting with the others for over an hour and so they took the opportunity to have a wander around and see what was on offer.

The Mop Fair was in full flow. They passed workers and traders all negotiating terms of employment. With the bulk of the agricultural work done for the year, many farm hands were seeking new employment and this was their place to obtain it. It wasn't just the land workers who were seeking employment, there were other tradesmen at the fair too. Many business owners were here to hire. They were looking for shoe menders, farriers, road pavers, boat builders, cooks, dressmakers and weavers. All were here to find work. They each wore a ribbon and the colour of the ribbon indicated whether one was looking for employment or had successfully secured a place already.

There was also a large market sale being held. Banbury boasted a big market most weeks and months but the Michaelmas market always broke the records. Hundreds and hundreds of cattle, sheep and other livestock were for sale. The animal pens stretched for yards and yards. To Myriam, all the animals looked very similar, but experienced farmers were examining them individually to see if they were of a good enough breeding and health to buy. Looking around, it seemed that most people were here for some sort of business purpose. However later, when the business side of matters was finished, there would be a lot of entertainment and celebration.

Rose and Myriam preferred to come to the fair early each year. They liked to enjoy the shows and events before it got too late. One year they had made the mistake of coming into the town later during the day. As the time had gone on the atmosphere had become more and more disorderly. Many men, and even some women, had been drinking since early in the day and were by this time quite intoxicated. Fights between rival village groups had broken out and the general ambience of the fair had changed. Neither of them had liked it. They heard that this was generally the situation each year and so had since decided to stick to a routine of arriving early and leaving before it got late.

Tom was hungry so they made their way over to a stall that was selling hot pies. Tom bought one for himself and a smaller meat filled roll for both Rose and Myriam. They were warm and the flavours were wonderful. Myriam could taste salt, pepper and rosemary which had been blended with the meat and rolled together within in the crusty pastry. It was delicious. They passed by a large tent which had been erected where outside was an advertisement of the production of a short play. It was some sort of murder mystery and showings were starting on the hour beginning at noon. Myriam said that she would like to return with the others later and watch it. She loved following a well scripted plot, acted out by talented people.

There was also an area with a few sports events taking place. It was mostly boxing, arm wrestling and weight-lifting. As they passed by, Tom whispered something in Rose's ear.

"No, I don't mind," she said and gave him a kiss.

Tom disappeared off to watch the boxing. It was a popular sport and quite a crowd had already gathered to spectate.

"I hope you don't mind," said Rose. "He said he will come and find us all later on."

"That's fine," shrugged Myriam. Eliza and Mary were her and Rose's friends. Tom didn't really know them that well. She supposed it made sense that he wasn't that interested in spending time with them.

Rose and Myriam made their way to the bandstand. Rose was quiet and Myriam wanted to ask her if everything was all right but before she had a chance to do so, they spotted the others. Eliza, Andrew and Mary were patiently waiting for them on the steps to a small flower shop. Myriam felt delighted to see them. It had been quite a few months since they had been together and Myriam had missed her friends, especially Mary. She realised that she hadn't yet told her about Jim. Mary would want to know everything. She always loved hearing all the details about any new gossip.

The five of them chatted for a few moments, catching up things in each other's lives. Myriam told them about the play and they all agreed it would be fun to watch it.

"We'll have to go and watch it soon though," said Eliza. "We can't stay too long. We just bought six new sheep over at the market. They are in a holding pen, but we'll need to load them into the cart and get home before dark if we can."

"Shall we go over there now then?" suggested Mary.

"Could we just wait here for a few more minutes?" asked Myriam, glancing distractedly about her.

They all looked at her. Myriam blushed.

101

"Myriam is expecting someone else to join us," Rose explained. She was smirking at them. "She has a new *friend*."

"She has a what?" exclaimed Mary and grabbed hold of Myriam. "And you never said anything!"

At that moment Myriam caught sight of Jim walking towards them and she quickly told Mary to hush.

As Jim made his way through the crowd of people to where they were all standing, Myriam noticed two things.

His eyes met hers and instead of sparkling and holding her own as they usually did, they quickly looked down. As his eyes fell to his feet, she noticed the sadness in them. Today they weren't dark and mysterious. Today they were white and bloodshot.

The second thing she noticed was his scarf. He was wearing one, but it wasn't the one she had made for him.

Myriam's stomach flipped over so fast that she was sure she was going to be sick. Something was wrong.

Upon reaching them he stopped. Myriam made the introductions and he politely greeted her friends. There was no warmth in his smile today though. After the introductions had been made, he looked at Myriam. Again, their eyes made contact for a brief second but then he dropped his gaze.

"May I speak with you alone for a moment?" he asked, but wouldn't look at her directly.

Myriam's face was pale as she nodded and followed him to a quiet corner across the street. She watched as he took a deep breath and began to speak.

"I'm afraid that I may have misled you in some way," he began. Myriam shook her head, confused. As he continued talking, she noticed that his voice was wavering. "I regret that I may have given you reason to believe that I feel more for you than I do. I'm sorry for this and for that reason, I can't accept this gift."

He reached inside his jacket and handed her the paper-wrapped parcel that she had given to Mr Dickenson a few days earlier. He was returning the scarf to her. Myriam took it from him. Her hands were shaking. He saw it and winced a little.

"I...I don't understand," said Myriam. She could feel a lump collecting in her throat.

"I'm sorry. I never meant to mislead you." He couldn't look at her.

Rose had been stood across the road watching and now made her way over to them.

"Is everything all right?" she asked. "Myriam?" Myriam shook her head. Rose looked at Jim. "What's the matter?"

"I'm very sorry." He turned to go.

"Wait. Jim?" called Myriam. He turned back around. Her eyes were stinging as tears threatened to fall from them. This time he looked at her. There was sorrow in his expression.

"Will you come to the dance next month?" she asked. She could barely get the words out.

He lowered his eyes and shook his head.

"I'm so very sorry. I just think it's best if we don't see each other anymore." His voice cracked. This time he walked away and disappeared into the crowd.

"Myriam, what's happened?" asked Rose, confused by everything.

"He said that he doesn't feel anything for me." Tears were now falling down Myriam's face. She pushed the parcel at Rose. "I'm sorry, I have to go home, I can't stay here."

Myriam turned and ran off through the crowd, back towards the inn.

Mary came over to where Rose was standing. She too had been watching the interaction between Jim and Myriam. "What's the matter? Are you going to go after her?"

Rose thought for a moment.

"No. Mary, can you go back to the inn and see that she is all right. There's someone else I need to go after."

With that, Rose stood as tall as she could and walked briskly in the direction of the canal.

Eighteen

Jim arrived back at the lock feeling maddened and angry with himself. The canal was quiet. Mr Thomas would most probably be inside the lockhouse, dozing peacefully in his armchair. Recently he had started the habit of taking a short nap after he had eaten his lunch. It was another sign that he was getting older.

Jim needed an outlet for his frustrated emotions. He saw a pile of logs that needed splitting and stacking, over by the small wood shed to the side of the house. He picked the axe up and began swinging it over his head. He was using so much force that the logs were splitting easily.

It had almost torn him in two when he'd looked at her face. That sweet, innocent face. Those kind, beautiful eyes. When she had spotted him coming towards her in the crowd her expression had been so open, so expectant. He hadn't been able to look at her, knowing what it was that he had been about to say. Then, as he had spoken, he had noticed her emotions change. How could he not?

He threw some of the split logs furiously onto the pile that he was creating. He had hurt her. He knew that for sure. She had looked so taken aback and her eyes had filled with tears. His words had been so unexpected to her. He'd given her no warning of the blow that he had been about to deliver. How could he have? He'd only recently realised himself that a separation between them was needed. He had realised it the day that Mr Dickenson returned from delivering the coal.

......

Mr Dickenson had come home that day and gone to find Jim at the lock. He had approached with a beaming grin on his face and was wagging his finger in a mischievous but friendly manner.

"Now it all makes sense lad!" he had said, still grinning.

"What does?" Jim had asked. He had no idea what the man was talking about.

"Your change of mood these last few weeks. The vacant, dreamy look that sometimes comes across your face. The constant cheerful whistling."

Jim had then thought back over the past few weeks. He hadn't noticed it but he supposed the man was right. He had been in a good mood recently. He still didn't understand what Mr Dickenson meant though.

"I'm not sure what you're getting at?"

"Ah, come on lad, don't be coy with me. You're in love! It happens to the best of us at some point." Mr Dickenson had handed him the parcel containing the scarf. "I'll tell you what; those Evans girls are good women and that young Myriam is a proper pretty little thing, not that it's gone to her head. She's so humble and mild. She's a fine young woman, that she is."

Listening to the other man's words, Jim had felt a fierce thud inside his chest. It was as if his heart had reacted to something unexpected and violent. Mr Dickenson had continued, "Oh, and she left a message for you. They'll be at Michaelmas and will be meeting with others at the bandstand at one o'clock so you can meet her there."

Jim had frozen. The colour had slowly drained from his face.

Mr Dickenson had been about to leave but he'd stopped and given Jim a friendly nudge. "Aww come on now, you didn't think you could keep it a secret forever did you? Those of us that have been there can spot the signs a mile away."

That was when Jim had realised that Mr Dickenson was right.

He was in love with her. It had crept up on him and he hadn't even noticed. He'd been so caught up in everything, so lost in the moments they had been spending together that he hadn't seen what was happening. He had fallen completely in love with Myriam Evans. And what was more, he had a feeling that she was falling in love with him too. Why else would she send a gift?

He had looked at the carefully wrapped parcel that he was holding in his hand and had known that he wouldn't open it. He *couldn't* open it. How could he possibly accept it? He would have to give it back.

He had then sat down on the lock gate and buried his head in his hands. How could he have been so blind as to what had been happening? He knew though that it had to stop then. Immediately. He couldn't let that beautiful, wonderful girl fall any deeper in love with him.

That was when he had decided that he would

107

go to the fair. He would go and meet her but only to return the gift and put an end to something that he should never have allowed to start.

He had rehearsed the lines over and over during the days that followed and knew by heart the words he wanted to say. They were words that he had convinced himself would be easy for him to say. Words that he had convinced himself would be easy for her to hear. But then he had arrived at the fair and he had seen her and all the words that he had rehearsed had escaped him. All he could do was say sorry and try not to look at her poor, bewildered face.

......

Jim bitterly threw another split log onto the pile. He was hot. Swinging the axe so fiercely was raising his temperature. He stopped to take his jacket off and then turned to hang it up on a hook by the front door to the lockhouse. Looking up, he saw Rose. She was standing, still as a statue, on the other side of the lock watching him. He had no idea how long she had been there.

"Jim," she called. "Can we talk?"

He knew enough about Rose to know that he didn't have a choice. She was here to talk whether he liked it or not. Putting the axe down he nodded and walked across the lock gate to where she was standing. He felt ashamed. She must hate him. He didn't know what she was going to say to him, but he was expecting the worst.

Rose had been watching him for a while. She had arrived at the lock only a few moments after him.

She had seen the fury and ferocity with which he had swung the axe. She had watched his shoulders heave as he had paused for breath and wiped hot, threatening tears from his face. By standing and observing him, Rose had gained an insight into what was going on with his emotions. It was clear to her that he was upset. It was clear to her that he was unhappy with the decision he had made regarding his friendship with Myriam. What was not clear to Rose was the reason for everything. She was careful with her words and adopted her softest tone possible.

She asked gentle questions and listened to him without interrupting. As he explained to her his reasons for his behaviour towards Myriam, she was able to build up an understanding of the situation.

When he finished talking and she had no more questions to ask him she took his hand in hers.

"My dear Jim," she said. "Thank you for explaining it all to me."

He looked at her. Defeat was written across his face.

"Do you see now, Rose?" he asked. "I can't see Myriam anymore."

"Yes. That is one solution to your problem," Rose conceded. "However, you owe it to her to tell her the reasons why."

He opened his mouth to object, but she wouldn't let him.

"You may think it is best not to tell her, but you underestimate my sister. You also have a moral duty to tell her the truth."

He closed his mouth. Rose was right. There

was no point in trying to argue.

"I think you should come with me back to the inn and tell her now."

He was about to protest as it was the last thing he wanted to do. But then he thought about Myriam. She was most probably crying in her room, not understanding what she had done wrong or why he had treated her like that. He knew that Rose was right; he had to go and talk to her again and he had to do it today.

Nineteen

There was the sound of footsteps coming up the stairway and a knock at the door. Mary got up to answer it but before she could, it opened and Rose stepped inside the room. Myriam looked up and Rose could see she had been crying a lot. Her eyes were swollen and red.

"I think you need a cup of tea, duckie," said Rose. "Mary, would you mind popping down to the kitchen to get one?"

Mary nodded. She was pleased that Rose was back. Mary hadn't really known how to comfort her friend. As Mary stepped out the room, she almost bumped into Jim who was waiting on the landing where Rose had left him.

"Oh, and take your time," Rose added. Then she went to the open doorway and beckoned Jim to come in.

He edged his way nervously into the room, his face filled with regret when his eyes rested on Myriam's grief-stricken face.

Myriam was shocked to see him walk in. She didn't understand what he was doing there.

Rose backed away. "I'll leave you both to talk."

"But Rose, you can't go. You can't leave us here alone, in my room!" Myriam was horrified that they might be seen together in her bedroom alone.

"I'll leave the door ajar and I'll be right

111

outside," Rose assured her. "And don't worry about me eavesdropping. I've already heard what he has to say."

Rose stepped out and pulled the door gently behind her so that it was almost closed, but not quite. Jim shuffled about awkwardly for a moment before he spied a chair tucked in against the dresser.

"Would it be all right if I sit down?" he asked meekly.

"Of course." Myriam could see that his emotions were strained too. As upset and hurt as she was, she felt sorry for him.

He took his cap off and unbuttoned his jacket. He felt warm. It was probably due to his nerves.

"Rose thinks it would be best if I explain to you my reasons for why we shouldn't see each other."

Myriam nodded. She was still confused and it was eating her up not knowing what she had done wrong.

Jim tried to smile at her. "Please let me tell you everything before you say anything in response."

"Of course," she replied.

"I remember the first time I saw you. You may not remember it, but I do." She nodded and he knew that she did remember it too. "It was a warm day. The sun was already hot and you passed by the lock. Your hair was hanging loosely around your neck and shoulders and I couldn't take my eyes off your sparkling blue eyes. 'Miss Myriam', Mr Dickenson had called you and your name lodged itself in my memory.

"I wasn't sure if I would ever see you again and then, months later, on the day of the coronation there you were. You were so fixated, watching something, that you didn't notice the boy stealing your money. I nearly didn't notice him either, I was so enchanted by you. Fortunately, as you know, I did see the boy and I brought him back to you and you were so kind. I'd never seen anyone speak so gently to a street urchin before. I knew then that you were someone special, Myriam.

"What an amazing few months it has been getting to know you, dancing with you and becoming your friend." As Myriam listened to him, her heart almost stopped. He was talking with her so openly and saying such wonderful things. However, there was still a tremble of hesitation in his tone. She sensed there was a big 'but' coming in this beautiful speech.

"I was so caught up in those moments with you that I hadn't realised just how deep my feelings had become." This was it; Myriam knew that something bad was coming. He was twisting his fingers apprehensively together. He was looking at the floor. She could tell he didn't want to say his next line. Whatever he was about to say next was going to hurt her.

"I came to the realisation earlier this week that I have fallen in love with you."

Myriam gasped and grabbed her mouth with her hand. Had she heard him correctly? Did he just say that he was *in love* with her? Jim reached out took hold of her hand. She felt a shiver but the usual fire between them wasn't there. His hand was cold. He looked at her and she searched his eyes for something, anything that would help her to understand what was going on inside his head. He had just told her that he loved her and yet his eyes were still so sad. As Myriam opened her mouth to ask a question, he released his hold on her hand.

"I haven't finished yet." He swallowed the lump that had formed in his throat. "I have fallen in love with you. I also suspect that you may feel similarly about me." She nodded. "But that's the problem," he sighed. "If I had ever thought that I would fall in love with you, or you with me, I would never have come to that first dance."

Myriam's thoughts were whirling. He had just told her that he loved her but now he was saying that he didn't want to love her. Was she not good enough for him? She had never gone to school like he had but her father had taught her to read, write and do basic arithmetic. Despite this, he must feel that she was below him in either intelligence or status.

Jim continued talking, "You see. I can't offer you a real life. At least not now. As terrible as this sounds; as long as my mother is alive, I cannot marry."

Myriam wanted to protest. He could see she did.

"Please, Myriam, let me tell you why I can't marry so that you can understand everything fully. As I've told you before, my mother is a very sick woman. She is a tiny, frail shell of a lifeless soul. There are two reasons why I will not marry while my dear mother, God bless her, is alive.

"Firstly, it would be unfair on you. Caring for my mother is an around the clock job. She requires attention each hour of every day. You would not be able to have a normal life as a wife. We would not be able to have a normal life as a married couple.

"Secondly, I can't marry for my mother's sake. Her nerves are in tatters. She lives as a woman sitting on needles, surrounded by eggshells. The slightest disturbance causes her great distress. If I was to introduce a new person to the home and that person was to then become my own wife, I fear that it would kill her. She dotes on me. Even if she liked you, the very fact that you would now be the other woman in my life would be more than she could bear. I couldn't do something that would tip her over the edge."

He stopped talking for a moment and looked at her. Myriam was trying to process all this information.

"So you see," he concluded. "I can offer you nothing, nor can I make you any promises and so it is best if we no longer see each other."

Myriam said nothing. Many thoughts were running through her head. She had been ready to protest everything until he had made that last argument. If he married her, he felt that it would kill his mother.

What was it her own mother had said to them all those years ago when they were young girls?

'Marry a man you can respect. If you can respect him, then you can love him deeply.'

She looked at Jim. He seemed exhausted. He was emotionally drained from the speech he had just delivered. As she looked at him her heart swelled with respect. He was willing to put his mother's health and interests ahead of his own happiness in life. This was a man she could respect. This was a man she could love. She had no doubts. This was the man she wanted to marry.

He too was looking at Myriam. Having finished with everything that he had wanted to say he was now waiting to hear what she thought.

"Jim." She smiled softly. He really did look weary. "Thank you for telling me everything and thank you for your frank honesty." He smiled. It was the first real smile she had seen him give all day. It filled her with confidence to tell him what she had decided upon.

"I shall wait for you."

His smile dropped. "No, you don't understand. I'm not asking you to wait. My mother could live for years, I wouldn't ask that."

Myriam shook her head. "It doesn't matter to me if your mother lives for one year, five years or fifty years; I will wait for you."

"I don't want you to do that. You deserve to marry someone and make him happy. I won't let you do that."

This time it was Myriam who reached out and took his hand.

"Jim Bailey, I'm able to make my own decisions and I choose to wait for you. No matter how long that may be."

<u>Twenty</u>

Almost forty-five minutes and one cold cup of tea later, Jim left the inn to go back home. Mary walked back through the town with him. Andrew and Eliza would need help to load the sheep into the cart and she had been a while at the inn already. Having seen Jim and Mary out, Rose returned upstairs to the room and sat down on the bed next to Myriam. Still looking exhausted, Myriam at least appeared happier than she had earlier.

"So, is everything settled between the two of you then?" Rose asked, trying not to pry but wanting to know what the outcome of the conversation had been. Myriam and Jim had both spoken in such soft tones that she had found it hard to make out everything that they had been saying from within the room.

"Yes. I think so," sighed Myriam. The emotional events of the day had taken a toll on her.

"Will you still see each other?" hesitated Rose. She wanted to know the answer but wasn't sure she should ask.

"Yes, sort of." Myriam puffed out her cheeks. "He was so certain that we shouldn't see each other but I insisted that I'm going to wait to marry him."

Rose smiled. Myriam gave the impression of being soft and compliant, but she was also extremely determined when she wanted to be. Rose could well imagine that Jim had stood no chance in winning that argument.

"What do you mean, *sort of?*"

"He doesn't want me to view us as 'courting'," she explained. "He's made it clear that I'm free to court and marry someone if I change my mind. For that reason, he said we're not to visit each other. I'm not to go to the lock and see him."

Rose raised her eyebrows. "He's very honourable, isn't he?" She was impressed with him.

"Yes, he really is," smiled Myriam. "He has though, agreed to come to the dances once a month and we will spend time together then. He feels that it is best if we have limited contact. In this way he hopes we won't be too sickened by the postponement of a courtship but that we will still be able to enjoy a few moments in each other's company from time to time."

"It all sounds very wise." Rose took Myriam's hand. "Do you think you can endure this? It may be a very long time until his mother passes."

Myriam closed her eyes and nodded. "I told him I didn't care if I had to live with a dependant mother-in-law, but he is convinced that if he were to take a wife then it would be too much for her to bear. As much as I want to be with him, I couldn't live with myself if she was to give up and die because of me. I don't want to wait, but I will, for her sake."

"That's very easy to say now but you may not feel the same a few years from now," warned Rose.

"I will feel the same!" Myriam insisted, before lowering her chin and conceding, "I just might not feel so patient about it."

Myriam let out a deep sigh. Her head was spinning with a range of emotions and sentiments that she was trying to understand. She felt elated and overjoyed that he had said the lovely things that he had to her. She could barely believe that this incredible man was in love with her. She wanted to lie on the bed and swoon about him, as most young women would if they had just had words of love expressed to them. On the other hand though, she felt heavy-hearted and despondent about the entire matter, clinging to a desperate hope and dream that she may not have to wait too long to be his wife.

Rose studied her sister's face, trying to decipher what her true feelings were. Myriam knew what she was doing and so changed the subject.

"I'm sorry that our day at the fair was ruined," she apologised. "I don't feel much like it but if you really want to, we could go back now and join Tom. Maybe we could still watch that play."

Rose looked over at the clock. Seeing that it was almost five o'clock she shook her head. "No, don't you worry. I don't feel much like it now either."

Myriam noticed that sad look in Rose's eyes again, the look that she had observed earlier in the day. "Is everything all right?" she asked.

There was a pause and then Rose replied, "No, not really." She looked away and then slowly shook her head. Myriam was perturbed to watch Rose blinking hastily as tears threatened to build in her eyes. This was so unlike Rose that Myriam knew something must be really wrong. She quickly thought back over recent days and weeks to pinpoint what it might be, but nothing sprung to her mind. It made her slightly uncomfortable though to realise that actually, when she stopped and thought about it, Rose hadn't seemed herself for a while and she just hadn't noticed it before.

"What's the matter Rose?" She was deliberately gentle in the way she spoke. Rose didn't like to appear vulnerable. She didn't find it easy to discuss emotions.

"It seems such a silly thing to get upset about. Especially after everything that has just happened today. It makes me feel selfish really."

"Never!" exclaimed Myriam and wrapped her arms around Rose as she gave in to the tears that she had been fighting to control.

Rose's shoulders shook as she let out a few uncontrollable sobs.

Myriam felt desperate. She had never seen Rose cry like this before, not even after their parents had died. "Please Rose, tell me what's wrong. I'd like to help."

"You can't help. No one can."

Rose took a handkerchief out of her pocket and wiped her eyes. "I should be grateful really. I have a good life."

Myriam didn't understand. "Please Rose. Will you tell me what it is?"

Rose blew her nose and nodded. "I don't think that I am able to have a baby."

She started crying again and Myriam hugged her. "Hush, hush. What do you mean? Do you know that for sure?"

"Well, I've been hoping to conceive for months

now, since right after the wedding to be honest with you, and nothing is happening. I want a baby so much! What if there's something wrong with me?"

Myriam frowned. She'd never even known that having a child meant so much to Rose or that her sister was set on starting a family so soon.

"I'm sure there's nothing wrong with you. Maybe you just need more time." Myriam had no idea what to say. What did she know about the matter? She was a little embarrassed by the subject really, but she couldn't let Rose see that.

"Don't you remember what father used to say?" continued Rose. "He used to say that some women have got something wrong with them, *mechanically,* you know? He said that some women just simply can't have children. What if I'm one of those women?"

Myriam was at a loss about how to respond. She felt out of her depth. This was a subject that she didn't really know anything about. All she knew was that for years Rose had been there when she had felt deep sorrow like this. Rose had comforted her and held her, letting her just sit in her arms and cry, despite the fact that Rose hadn't been able to come up with all the answers. This was what Myriam needed to do now. She had no idea how to fix the problem that was causing Rose all this anguish and pain, but she did know how to support her sister.

That's just what Myriam did. As the sun began to set and the small bedroom grew darker and darker, Myriam stayed there on the bed, holding her sister tightly. The rest of the town was outside taking part in the Michaelmas celebrations while Myriam gently allowed her sister to cry for something that she believed she was never going to have.

Twenty-one

Eventually, Rose settled and made her way back to her small apartment behind the stables to wait for Tom to come home from the fair.

Myriam felt like the day had stretched on forever. She was drained and felt sapped of all energy. Realising that she hadn't eaten for hours she made her way to the kitchen, quickly and quietly cut herself some bread and cheese and then went back up to her room. She lit the lantern and sat down to eat. Josephine was still down in the kitchen, cleaning up, and Myriam had sent word to Mr Hamilton earlier that she was unwell and wouldn't be able to work that evening. It wasn't a complete lie as she really did feel unwell. She felt sick with anxiety and worry, not only for herself but also for Rose.

While eating she thought back over what it was that Rose had said earlier. She had made reference to something their father had told them about women not being able to have children. Myriam could remember the conversation that Rose had recalled. It was memorable because he had just returned home from a call to one of the houses in the village. A woman, a friend of their mother's, had been giving birth and something had not gone as it should. Myriam could remember them all waiting for him to return. Her mother had been so worried about her friend and what was going to happen to her and the little baby. Usually the older women in the village managed all the births. Calling a male doctor to tend to a birthing mother was almost unheard of, unless something was seriously wrong. Eventually, her father had come back and told them that the woman and the new baby boy were both going to be fine. It had been a relief to them all.

"It's one of the most beautiful baby boys I have ever seen. That I will say," said her father. "Then, the ones that fight to live always seem to be the ones we think are special."

"Is it always scary when a woman has a baby?" asked thirteen-year-old Myriam.

"No, not always," he replied. Doctor Evans sat down and took off his boots. Myriam's mother placed a warm cup of tea and a plate of food in front of him.

"So, most of the time everything is easy?" Myriam was still curious.

Mr Evans thought about it for a moment and then he replied, "It's a very tricky thing, having babies. More often than not it goes just as God intended but there are some occasions when it doesn't. When that happens, I try my best to help. Most of the time I can do something to assist but sometimes I can't." He then paused.

Myriam remembered the glance that passed between her mother and her father at that moment. There was some secret between them that they hadn't told her and Rose. She still didn't know what it was but looking back and remembering the way that they had briefly looked at each other, she suspected that they had experienced 'something not going as God intended'.

Rose had been sitting quietly on the opposite side of the table but Myriam remembered that she had then joined in with the conversation.

"What is it that you can't help with father?"

Mr Evans put down his knife and fork. This was a conversation that required his attention. He'd long known that with two daughters, he would have to instruct them about the realities of life at some point. It might as well be now.

He smiled at Rose. "Well darling, sometimes the baby is too weak, or even the mother is. Or I arrive too late to help."

Rose nodded. "Is that all?" she asked.

He glanced at his wife again.

"No. There are other things I can't help with. Sometimes a woman can't carry a baby. Sometimes there is something wrong with her and I can't help."

"What do you mean?" Rose wanted to understand what could be wrong with a woman.

"Well, something inside just her isn't right, duckie. Something about her, you know, mechanically." He wasn't sure if he was answering her question very clearly.

"So, you mean she can't have a baby?"

He sighed. "A few things might happen; she might not be able to have a baby or she might conceive but then lose the baby quickly."

Rose nodded. She understood what he was saying but there was something else she wanted to know. "It is possible to know that something is wrong beforehand?" she asked.

He shook his head. "Not really. It's something you just find out along the way."

Rose frowned. "But you said that most times it's all right, yes?"

"Yes dear," he assured her. He could see this was something that worried her. "As I said, more often than not, everything is fine."

At that moment something occurred to Myriam.

"Father, I have another question," she said.

"Go on."

"Is it always the woman who has something wrong with her? What about the man?"

Her father had smiled and cocked his head to one side. She could remember him almost laughing at the idea.

"I'm pretty sure it's something wrong with the woman. I don't see how there can be anything wrong with a man that would cause any problems with childbearing."

Myriam now thought back over the last question that she had asked and the response her father had given. Her father was a doctor, and so he must have known about these things. It seemed so unfair to her though that all the blame for problems with childbearing should go to the woman. She thought of Rose, so sad and blaming herself for her inability to conceive a child. Poor Rose. Her sweet, unselfish, kind-hearted sister.

Myriam was tired. She turned the lantern down low, leaving a faint flicker of light for when Josephine would later come in. Myriam then undressed and got into bed. As she closed her heavy eyes and began to drift off to sleep, she said a quick prayer to ask God to please help Rose to have a baby.

Twenty-two

April 1840

It was a mild and bright morning. Warm rays of sunlight were awakening shoots and buds on all the plants and trees. Myriam loved this time of year. She was enjoying a walk in the fields behind the coaching inn. The winter that had just passed had seemed to last forever. It had been more temperate than normal and yet unusually wet. At times, it had felt that they had gone for days on end without being able to step outside other than to run out quickly for an errand, only to arrive back at the inn drenched through, with drops of water falling from soaking-wet coats and hats.

It occurred to Myriam that the wet months had now brought with them a blessing though. She could see that the mild, wet winter had helped the buds to grow easily. All they needed now was the smallest amount of light and warmth from the sun and they were ready to open and flourish into life. To Myriam's delight, the scenery in the fields was changing dramatically each day. Her eyes absorbed the fresh shades of green from the new leaves and the soft, creamy pinks from the blossoms as delicate flowers were blooming. Bees and small insects were even emerging to join the joyous, chirping birds whilst they held a springtime musical celebration.

In the eighteen months that had passed since that ground-shaking day of the Michaelmas Fair, Myriam's life had settled into a pleasant routine. Life at the inn continued as it always had. Josephine was still an agreeable room-mate and Myriam's work in the bar went on without disruption, albeit with the usual irritation of that one gentleman, but even he had seemed to be less of a bother recently.

Myriam had kept her agreement with Jim to not visit him at the lock. If she was honest, she had found it difficult at times. As the months went by, her feelings for him deepened and, more than anything, she longed to be near him. Their time together at the dance each month was becoming more and more special to her. She didn't waste a second during those evenings, but made the most the few, short hours they had together. Spinning around and laughing, they enjoyed the ease of each other's company. They were always certain to make time to have a moment to talk too, catching up what was happening in each other's lives. Myriam always wished they could talk for longer. She wanted to hear everything about him, not wanting to miss any detail of what he was doing although, she also knew that she had be careful. Their lives were not yet bonded together as she wished and to let herself become too consumed in him would only make it harder. So, she refrained from asking questions that pried too deeply and strove to keep the conversations light and cheerful.

Walking along now, her shoes damp from the wet, dewy grass, Myriam thought back over the previous few months. Everything had been uneventful for so long that the news she had received during recent weeks had caught her by surprise although, thinking about it, she should have noticed what was happening with the first revelation.

......

About a fortnight earlier, Myriam had finished her shift and was about to go upstairs to bed. As usual it was late and the clock had already struck midnight. She was wiping down the last of the tables in the bar and looked up to see Josephine appear in the room.

"I'd have thought you would have been asleep hours ago," said Myriam, surprised to see her. "Is something wrong?"

"No, everything is fine. It's just that I, well er...*we* wanted to tell you something." Josephine's voice was quiet. She looked round as Bill walked over to join them. He appeared to be both uneasy and excited at the same time. As he got closer, Myriam saw that Josephine then started to blush a little and when Bill opened his mouth to speak Myriam had already guessed what he was going to say.

"We haven't told anyone apart from our families yet," he began, looking apprehensively between them. He then stepped closer to Josephine and gently touched her arm, indicating that it was her turn to speak.

"You see, Myriam, we wanted to tell you first. You being my room-mate and Bill having known you so long now, it's...well it's very important to us to tell you." Josephine smiled nervously at Bill. Myriam smiled too. Why had she not seen until now what an adorable couple they made?

"What we're trying to say, is that you mean a lot to both of us," Bill continued. He now blushed a little as well.

It was true that at one time Myriam had meant a great deal to him and it was also true that, at that time, he had wished that he had meant a lot to her, but that was a long time ago now. That was before he had spent time with Josephine. He didn't hold those feelings for Myriam any more. Nevertheless, she was still an important person to him. He knew that she was in love with Jim, it was obvious. He didn't understand why the two of them weren't courting, or even married by now, and it wasn't his business to ask about the details, but he did want to make sure that Myriam wasn't upset in any way by his and Josephine's news. That was why he had wanted to tell her as soon as possible.

"So, we wanted you to hear it from us before others told you." Bill looked at Josephine again and this time he squeezed her arm gently. "The news is that I asked Josephine's father for his permission to court her and he said yes."

"And I said yes too!" added Josephine quickly, in case there was any doubt on Myriam's part about it.

Josephine was grinning and Bill, although anxious to see how Myriam felt, was smiling too. Myriam clapped her hands and beamed at them both.

"I can't believe I hadn't noticed, but I can see now how close you two have become." Myriam leaned forward and gave Josephine a warm hug. "I'm so happy for you."

Myriam looked at Bill. "You've got yourself a sweet, sweet girl in this one," she said nudging

Josephine gently. "I think you've made a good choice."

Bill was relieved. He hadn't wanted Myriam to be upset in any way and she wasn't. He nodded to her in agreement.

......

Walking beneath a large tree, Myriam smiled to herself as she thought about the two of them. Their news had been a surprise at the time, but she had quickly realised that if she had been paying more attention, then it would have been no surprise at all. Myriam was happy for them both. A couple of years earlier she had been aware that Bill had held feelings for her and it had troubled her sometimes that she didn't reciprocate them. She had worried that he would one day confess his feelings, thereby forcing her to refuse him and that he would then be hurt. Thankfully, he had taken note of the friendship that had grown between her and Jim and, although she had sensed his disappointment to begin with, it seemed that he had not taken it to heart but had found happiness in the company of Josephine.

Myriam paused in her walk to watch a bee that was collecting fresh, powdery pollen from the blossom flowers. The bee was working hard, focused on the task it was undertaking. She wondered how far from the hive it had travelled. They had hives over in the kitchen garden at the inn. Maybe it had come from there. If so, she would be able to enjoy honey from this particular tree later in the year. The bee, having collected what it needed, disappeared and Myriam's thoughts went back to the news that she had received just a week ago. On this occasion, unlike the news from Bill and Josephine, there had been no warning of what was coming. She, and Rose, had been taken completely by surprise.

......

The two of them had gone to the market together to collect a list of food items for the kitchen. Myriam liked this task and volunteered readily if someone was ever needed to go to the market. It was always an opportunity for her to see Mary. Myriam's work at the inn and Mary's distance from the town meant that they could go for weeks, sometimes even months, without seeing each other or having a chance to catch up properly.

Having purchased most of the things that were on their list, Rose and Myriam had decided to head over to the area where the Price family usually set up a stall and see if they were there. Most weeks, Eliza, Andrew and Mary would come into town to sell some produce at the market and so there was usually a good chance that they would see them. This week however, Mary was there with Andrew, but Eliza was missing. This was unusual. Eliza was the one who normally dealt with the customers since she had the more polite manner of them all and was quick with numbers for the costs and prices.

Rose and Myriam had greeted their friends and asked if everything was all right with Eliza. Mary opened her eyes wide, shrugged her shoulders and gave Andrew a meaningful look. He was hesitant and they waited patiently as he attempted to find the words which appeared to be eluding him. Myriam smiled to herself. Mary had no discretion. There was clearly a personal reason why Eliza was not with them, most probably one which Andrew felt uncomfortable to mention to them and here was Mary, putting him on the spot. Myriam suspected that it was Eliza's time for her monthly menstruation and that this was what was causing him to be so coy about how to respond. The poor man. She went to put him out of his misery.

"Andrew, let's not bother about what's wrong with her. Just give her our love, will you?"

He didn't respond. His mouth was open. There was clearly something he wanted to say.

"Andrew!" cried Mary. "If you don't tell them, I will!"

Now Myriam was confused. Maybe something was wrong with Eliza after all, although Mary didn't seem to be sad enough for it to be an illness.

Andrew finally found some words. "We erm, we...well, Eliza has some news. It's a shame she can't tell you herself really, but she didn't feel well enough to come into town this morning." He paused and Rose clutched hold of Myriam's arm.

"What is it? What happened?" Myriam asked Rose, jumping as she tried to see what had occurred to caused Rose to grab hold of her so tightly.

"Oh, nothing. I thought I just saw a rat." Rose was pale and she still had hold of Myriam's arm.

Myriam frowned at her. "There's enough rats running around those stables, I wouldn't have thought you'd be that worried by them."

Rose smiled weakly.

Mary was now impatient. "Enough about any rats. Go on Andrew, tell them!"

Andrew again began to speak. "As I was saying, Eliza wasn't feeling well this morning. You see, she keeps getting a bit sick in the mornings, that's what alerted us to it really." Rose increased her grip on Myriam's arm and she was about to tell her to let go, when it dawned on Myriam that Rose knew exactly what Andrew was about to say. As Myriam pieced it together and came to the same realisation that her sister had already come to, she felt moved to place her hand over Rose's while he continued talking.

"You see, the thing is, well... It seems that Eliza is with child."

He was smiling bashfully.

"I can't believe it, can you?!" Mary had been itching to jump in and say something. "Now I'll have to do even more of the farm work! Our Jacob isn't yet old enough to take it on. She could have waited a bit longer to have a baby!" She was pretending to be annoyed but Myriam could tell that her friend was secretly very excited.

"I can't tell you what a wonderful surprise that is to hear," Myriam responded, positively. "I know you hadn't planned for it quite yet, with all the farm work still on the go, but I'm so happy for you both. You must give Eliza our love and tell her congratulations." Myriam looked at Rose, who was doing her best to smile and nod in agreement. Her face was white though, and Myriam could feel her shaking as she still held tightly to her arm.

Mercifully, a customer approached at that moment, immediately followed by another. Myriam made polite excuses about needing to get back, explaining that it would be best to leave them both to serve people and then she quickly ushered Rose back towards the inn. With Rose still having failed to conceive, Myriam knew that their friend's happy news would be a hard blow for her dear sister.

They arrived back at the inn and Rose made her way towards her home. "Please tell the cook that I'm sick and unable to work today," she said, letting go of Myriam's arm and heading towards the door of her small lodging.

"Shall I come in and sit with you?" asked Myriam.

"No, thank you. I want to be alone."

......

She had seen Rose in the kitchen since that day, but Rose had avoided any conversation with her, presumably because she feared that Myriam might ask her how she was after the news of Eliza.

Myriam had worried frequently over the past months for her sister. For the most part, Rose was her usual self; happy, bubbly and smiling. However, at times, when she thought that no one was watching, Myriam had caught sight of the sadness that she was obviously feeling deep within. Rose had been married for well over two years now and still, she had failed to conceive. Myriam could see that as the time was going on, it was causing Rose more and more distress.

Her walk was now almost over and Myriam decided that she would need to find time to talk to

Rose about it. It wasn't good for her to bottle her feelings up in this way.

Myriam rounded the corner into the yard and saw that Mr Dickenson was there talking with Rose and Tom. He seemed to have arrived at the inn on foot, without his coal wagon, which was very unusual.

"Ah, here she is," pointed Tom and they all looked at her.

Mr Dickenson began to walk over.

Myriam knew immediately why he was there. Three evenings ago, it had been the night of the dance. It was the first time that Jim hadn't attended. He had sent word to Myriam to say that his mother's health was deteriorating and that he wasn't able to leave her that evening. Myriam had thought of little else since that night, wondering constantly how things were going. Now, here was Mr Dickenson, walking towards her with an anxious look on his face. She guessed that the worst must have happened and that Jim had sent Mr Dickenson to tell her the sad news.

"Miss Myriam," he said reaching her and holding out his arm, beckoning her to follow him. "Young Jim has sent for you."

Her stomach lurched. Surely Jim's poor mother had passed away. "Is it Mrs Bailey? Has she passed?" she asked.

"Almost, but not quite yet," he replied. There was an urgency in his voice. "Jim has asked that I fetch you quickly, Miss."

"Fetch me? To go there?"

"Yes. Can you come now?"

This was unexpected and Myriam wasn't sure

what it meant but she knew she had to go.

"Of course. I'll come with you right away."

Twenty-three

Over recent months, everything had been getting harder for Jim. Mr Thomas was ageing and, along with that, his health was deteriorating. The damp winter had stiffened the older man's joints and bones, making moving around something both painful and difficult for him. As a result, Jim had taken on almost all of the work at the lock. That in itself he didn't mind; he was young and healthy and it wasn't hard work for him under normal circumstances. However, his circumstances were far from normal. His mother's condition had been worsening and, particularly since the start of the new year, her health had gone significantly downhill.

It pained him to watch as she faded away from him. She had stopped eating, only drinking small amounts of warm tea and the occasional bit of watery soup. He had no idea as to what had brought on her sudden refusal to eat. Her nerves were certainly worse than he had ever seen them. Although her body had been shrinking each day, the trembling and shaking that she suffered had increased. Sitting silently in her chair, she would search the room with wild eyes, terror written all over her face. The dark evenings had been the hardest. Unsettled by the dancing shadows and the obscurity of winter light, she seemed to suffer fears and dreads, and he couldn't understand their origin.

The doctors had given him stronger medicines to try to settle her for sleeping. Each night Jim found himself sitting for longer and longer, waiting for her to finally give in and allow her body to rest. Kitty had been such a help over the past months and he didn't know what he would have done without the support he got from her.

Kitty Freeman lived next door with her husband, Luke, and their five children. Luke worked along the canal, at Tooley's Wharf. He was a skilled boat repairer. Kitty, besides running her own home and family, kept a regular eye on Mrs Bailey each day. Jim's mother easily became more agitated when presented with new acquaintances but Luke and Kitty had lived next door since Jim was a young boy and so it didn't cause any extra anxiety to have Kitty coming in and out. With five children of her own, what Kitty didn't know about looking after the sick and ailing wasn't worth knowing. She had a firm but gentle manner and, until recently, she had been able to get Mrs Bailey to do things that Jim had failed to persuade her to even consider trying.

During the past few months, with the extra work at the lock, Kitty had been Jim's lifeline. There had been times when she had left her oldest daughter, Marinna, to look after the other four children, giving them their dinner and putting them to bed, while Kitty had taken care of a highly disturbed Mrs Bailey. Kitty would light all the lanterns, make a cup of warm, sugary tea and then sit with the older woman, gently stroking her hands while singing soft tunes of soothing melodies. Kitty was the only other person who could calm the poor, fractious woman. Apart from Jim, his mother wouldn't settle down with anyone else.

Jim had most appreciated Kitty's help on the nights of the dances each month. Those brief few hours spent with Myriam had been his only source of joy for so long. He had savoured each dance and each opportunity to take hold of her outstretched arms, to spin her round and to watch the light sparkle in her beautiful eyes. Her bewitching, open smile always had the same effect upon him; it forced a smile upon his own face. His face, which had become etched with frown lines and furrows caused by worries and concerns, would react to her warm, encouraging glances and looks. Being in her company filled him with a momentary distraction from the reality that was waiting for him at home. She would always ask after his mother and he always found a way to give a short, polite reply and then steer the conversation in a different direction. He wanted, for that one evening each month, to forget his problems and be fully lost in Myriam and her world.

And Jim found that losing himself in a world with Myriam wasn't a difficult thing to do. The more time he spent with her the more enchanting he found her to be. She took his breath away for so many reasons. Her beauty was undeniable, but he had come to discover that she had so many other qualities too. She was kind and caring yet determined and quite unafraid at the same time. He had no doubts that one day, when the time eventually would come and they could marry, that Myriam Evans would be an incredible woman to have as his partner in life.

Jim hadn't found their extended courtship an easy thing to deal with. Falling in love with Myriam and yet not being able to share his life with her was something he found extremely difficult to cope with, especially as he knew that she had the capacity to provide him the emotional support he desperately felt he needed at times. Some evenings he would sit, watching his mother and waiting for her to fall asleep, wishing that he had Myriam beside him, to hold his hand and soothe his own anxious thoughts. But at the same time, the deteriorating condition of his mother reinforced to him that his decision not to introduce Myriam into the family had been the correct one. Everything until now had been handled so delicately that he felt content. He was confident that he had done the right thing by his mother.

During the last few days though, there had been a marked change. On Friday, the night when he was unable to attend the dance, his mother had been more agitated than he had ever seen her. She had been shaking and trembling as usual, her eyes glaring and darting about wildly, but then she had begun to cry out loudly. Her words had been indiscernible but the sounds she made had sent chills through him. That was when she had tried to get up. Her body too weak to support itself, she had failed, and as she attempted again and again to move, she had put herself in danger of falling. Kitty had immediately come over to help Jim. However, with both of them unable to calm the woman down, the doctor was sent for. He had sedated her heavily and finally she slipped into a deep sleep. Leaving them a strong potion to continue administering, the doctor had told Jim that he felt this really was the end for her now. In his time, he had noticed that just prior to giving in and letting go of their hold on life, many of his patients would let out a last fight and surge of energy in a similar way. He told Jim to prepare himself for the worst over the coming few days.

Jim and Kitty, between them, had not left Mrs

Bailey's side since that evening, three days ago. She remained sedated and, for the first time in what seemed to Jim like a lifetime, she looked peaceful.

It had been Kitty's idea to send for Myriam. Over those past few days Jim had spoken about her to Kitty. He had told Kitty how he wished it had been different and how he wished that he could have her support at this time.

"You should ask her to come," Kitty had said.

"But I couldn't. It would kill mother."

Kitty had reached out and taken hold of his hand. "Jim, your mother is almost dead," she had whispered. "Don't you think that it would be nice for her to meet the girl you love, before she goes?"

Jim had thought about it. Kitty had made a good point and at this stage it couldn't really make anything any worse.

As he waited now for Mr Dickenson to bring Myriam to them, he felt nervous. He hadn't even told his mother about Myriam for fear of what it would do to her. He also felt unsure of what Myriam's reaction would be to the small, frail woman he had lived with and taken care of for so many years; the pitiable woman who was his mother.

There was a gentle knock at the door and he knew it was her. His mother, sleeping peacefully in the armchair, didn't flinch or react to the noise at all. Jim got up to answer the door and Kitty gave him a warm smile of encouragement.

Jim opened the door and there stood Myriam, wide-eyed and beautiful as ever but he could see concern written all over her expression as she smiled at him. He then realised that she must be nervous too. She had never been to the house, never met his mother and now he had sent for her all of a sudden. Yes, he could see that she was extremely anxious, her face was pale and her lips appeared dry as she pinched them together tightly.

"Thank you for coming," he said and beckoned for her to step inside the doorway. It felt so formal, it was odd.

"Of course," she replied, looking around. "Mr Dickenson was very urgent about me coming right away." The hallway was bare, she noticed. Just a stairway and two doors leading into other rooms. "Mr Dickenson said there isn't much time?" She searched his eyes as he nodded sadly and then dropped his gaze. He turned around to face the doorway nearest to them.

"Mother is in the sitting room," he whispered. "She's sleeping but the doctor says that she can hear us."

At that moment the door to the sitting room opened and Kitty appeared. She greeted Myriam with a friendly smile.

"Jim, I'll go into the kitchen and leave you three together for a bit."

"Thank you Kitty," nodded Jim.

Kitty smiled again at Myriam and made her way through to the kitchen, closing the door gently behind her.

"She seems lovely," said Myriam. Jim had told her about Kitty and how she helped to care for his mother. Kitty was just as Myriam imagined. She looked sensible but had a kind manner. Myriam sensed she was a woman who had seen a lot of life and knew how to deal with its ups and downs.

"She has been so good to us," confirmed Jim. He took Myriam's hand. She noticed how cold his hand felt and gave it a gentle squeeze. He smiled in response to her encouragement and took a deep breath. "I sent for you because the doctor has said that mother really doesn't have long left." He was still whispering and Myriam could see the watery glaze of threatening tears in his eyes.

"I sent for you because Kitty made a point that I hadn't considered. She said that it would be nice for my mother to meet the woman that I love before she goes. Until now, I have been convinced that her meeting you would only cause her more distress but I've come to realise that at this stage it may actually bring her a measure of comfort."

Myriam swallowed. This really must be the end for Mrs Bailey if Jim was making this decision. She knew just how strongly he had felt until now that she could not possibly meet his mother for fear of what it would do to her nerves and therefore her health.

Jim continued, "She has been sedated by the doctor, but he said that she can hear us so feel free to talk to her; only if you want to though." He rubbed the back of his neck. "You may find it odd, so you don't need to. It won't make any difference either way. I just thought that if you...you know, if you felt you wanted to, then...well, then you can."

He was fumbling for words and Myriam felt so deeply for him. She gave his hand another squeeze.

"Shall we go in to see her?"

He smiled and nodded, grateful for her calm manner. Releasing her hand, he opened the door to the sitting room and stepped inside. Myriam followed. The room was warm. The fire had been lit and hot embers glowed softly. Everything about the room felt cosy. There was a small couch and two armchairs. The window faced south and sunlight was streaming in through the glass. In one of the armchairs sat a tiny, sleeping woman who Myriam guessed was Jim's mother. Although sleeping, the woman's face was strained with anxiety and worry. Years of terrors and fears were ingrained in the lines on her forehead. Myriam felt sad for the poor, helpless woman. Next to the armchair was a small, cushioned stool. Myriam pointed to it.

"May I sit there?" she asked.

Jim nodded and as Myriam went to sit down, he leant over his mother and took her hand.

"Mother." He spoke softly so as not to startle her.

Mrs Bailey opened her eyes and briefly looked at him before closing them again.

"Mother, there is someone here I want you to meet. Her name is Myriam and she's become very special to me. I thought it would be nice for the two of you to meet each other."

There was no reaction from the sleeping woman. Jim stepped back and sat in the other armchair. Myriam, settled on the small stool, reached over and took hold Mrs Bailey's hand. Holding the bony fingers inside her own, she gently stroked the frail, paper-thin skin. Studying the woman's face,

Myriam could see a likeness to Jim's; the strong cheekbones, and angular jaw. She suspected that years ago, Mrs Bailey would have been a handsome woman.

"It's lovely to meet you, Mrs Bailey," she began. "You have a beautiful home. This room reminds me of my own home where I grew up. We had a fireplace with a very similar mantelpiece."

Jim sat back and watched her. He needn't have worried. Myriam was taking this in her stride, as she did most things. She really was quite incredible.

Myriam continued talking. She kept her voice quiet and her tone peaceful. "I live at the Whately Coaching Inn now. Well, I actually work there. Anyway, my room isn't nearly as homely as this room is. I can see that Jim has worked hard to take care of you both. You have a good son Mrs Bailey, I thought you might like to hear that. People think well of him. That's something you should be proud of, as you raised him to be so good." Myriam paused, not sure how much she should say.

"I would like you to know, Mrs Bailey that I think a great deal of your son." Myriam glanced at Jim. She wondered if maybe she was saying too much but he didn't seem to mind. In fact, he was smiling. She raised her eyebrows and he nodded, encouraging her to keep talking.

"I've actually become quite fond of him." Myriam felt a desire to let this dying woman know that her son would be taken care of and loved after she had gone. "I don't want you to worry about him. I want you to know that I'm going to take very good care of him."

Overcome with emotion, Myriam looked down and swallowed as tears threatened to escape from her eyes. She glanced across at Jim and tried to gather her thoughts but there was something strange about his expression. He was concentrating on his mother. Turning her attention also to the woman, Myriam could see what it was that he was looking at. A small smile had appeared on Mrs Bailey's face. It was barely noticeable but definitely there, an upturning of the corners of her mouth into a definite smile. Myriam looked at her hand as she felt the thin cold fingers gently squeeze against her own. If she wasn't mistaken, Mrs Bailey was acknowledging what she had just said.

"Thank you," whispered Myriam and the woman again gave her hand another light squeeze. She hadn't imagined it.

Jim had seen the movement of Mrs Bailey's hand and he joined Myriam next to his mother. Kneeling on the floor in front of her armchair, he took hold of her other hand.

"Mother, I want you to know that Myriam is a good girl. She really is. I wish you could have got to know her more, as I have. You would like her, I'm sure of it."

Mrs Bailey briefly opened her eyes and gave both their hands another squeeze. Then she closed her eyes and released her grip, falling back into a sleep again.

"We should let her rest," said Jim. His eyes were red. The moment had been very emotional for both of them. He couldn't believe that his mother had as good as blessed his choice of wife. He hadn't ever even imagined it would have happened.

"I should get back. I'll leave you both together." Myriam knew that this was something big for Jim. He had spent so long being afraid of this moment and now it had passed and in a way that he never thought it would.

They left the room and stepped out into the hallway. Jim opened the front door for her.

"I would walk you back, but I don't feel I can leave her," he apologised.

"Of course you can't. You need to be here." She looked at his face. The face that she had come to know so well. The face that dominated her thoughts each day. She longed to hold his face in her hands and to stroke his head and soothe all his concerns away, but it was not the time for them yet. Soon it would be, although it saddened her to think of the loss he was about to experience. Soon though, she would be able to comfort him as she desperately wanted to. She smiled at him and looked deeply into his eyes, willing him to read all the thoughts and feelings that she had in her head and heart for him.

"Thank you for sending for me," she said. "I'm so glad that you did."

"Me too." He lightly touched her fingers. "It means so much that you were able to meet her, and her you."

"I know," she nodded. She turned to leave. Walking only a few steps she turned back. He was still at the door, watching her.

"Will you be all right?" she asked.

"I think so," he replied with a small shrug.

"You know I love you."
"Yes. I love you too."

Twenty-four

Mrs Bailey died two days later.

Jim sent word to Myriam and she immediately went to see him. He was at home, waiting for her when she arrived. The door was ajar and calling out 'hello' she let herself in. Kitty and Mr Dickenson were with Jim and they were all sitting together in the front room. It was a bright, fresh day and the sunlight was streaming through the windows, as it had on Myriam's previous visit. It struck her again what a beautiful room this really was. Mr Dickenson stood to greet her and then made his excuses to leave. He had come to pay his respects to Jim but felt uncomfortable lingering longer than was needed.

Myriam turned her attention to Jim. When she entered the room, he had been reading quietly to himself from a small, well-worn notebook. He now put it to one side and looked up at her. His eyes were red and tired but the smile that broke out on his mouth at seeing her extended into his eyes too. He had been waiting for her to come. The loss of his mother and all the sadness that came with it was one thing but now, he knew that everything would be all right. From now on he would have his precious Myriam by his side. With her support he was confident that he could overcome any challenge that faced him.

He stood up and took her into his arms. Holding her close against him, he breathed in the

151

sweet smell of her hair. With her head turned sideways against his chest, Myriam allowed a single tear to drop, to fall down her cheek and soak itself into his shirt. She had never been this close to him before and it caught her breath to be held so tightly by him. Her emotions were spinning, as were his. His grief at the loss of his mother was transmitting to her and she felt it too. Myriam hadn't known Mrs Bailey but this poor woman, who had just lost hold of her grip on life, was the mother of the man she loved and it pained her to know that her life was now gone forever. It also pained Myriam to think of the distress that this loss would cause Jim. She thought back to the day her own parents had died and the complete and utter sense of loneliness that she had felt at that time; the feeling of being an orphan. Jim, although an adult, would surely be experiencing similar feelings.

Jim had indeed been struggling to make sense of his emotions that morning. When Myriam had arrived, he had been reading from an old journal of his mother's. He was reading words that she had written years ago, from a time before he had even been born. It was strange, peering into the thoughts of a woman that he thought he had known so well and yet, from her expressions, realised how much she had changed from the young woman who had written them all that time ago. There was a time, he now knew, that had existed before her nerves and anxieties had got the better of her thoughts. The sadness he had felt at the moment of her death was now replaced by a mourning for that other version of his mother, the version he had never had the opportunity to see or know. At that moment, Myriam had arrived and now here she was, leaning against him whilst he held her tightly, fearful of ever letting her go.

They had both held back their feelings for so long for fear of not being able to endure the unknown length of time that they would have to wait, that the emotion of this moment and all the possibilities that were now open to them overwhelmed them both. No words were needed, they both knew exactly how the other was feeling and so they remained standing, embracing one another and allowed the stormy sea of sentiments to settle within them.

It was Myriam who remembered that Kitty was there. Self-consciously she pulled away from Jim and smiled sheepishly at her. Kitty though, was both discerning and reasonable. She wasn't shocked by their intense display of affection. Giving Myriam a warm smile, she said hello.

"Shall I make us all a pot of tea?" she asked, moving to get up from her seat and go into the kitchen.

Indicating for her to stay seated, Jim replied, "No, it's all right Kitty, you stay where you are. Myriam, sit down please, I'll go and get us all a drink."

He left the room and Myriam sat down on the couch next to Kitty. The armchair where Mrs Bailey had been sitting when Myriam had visited two days earlier remained empty. It didn't feel right for any of them to sit there.

Before Myriam had barely sat down, Kitty reached out and grabbed hold of her hand. She did so in such a warm and friendly manner that Myriam felt instantly at ease with this new woman.

"I'm so pleased that Jim has you, dear," she whispered.

Myriam looked at her. Kitty had an open, kindly face. Her eyes were green and twinkly, as if they were constantly taking in their surroundings and processing everything quickly in order to give an appropriate response. She bore the marks of a busy housewife and mother. Her clothes were simple, and practical. Her fair hair was wildly sticking out in all directions, making her appear amiable and sincere. On first impressions, Myriam was drawn to this woman. She smiled in response to her kind sentiments.

Kitty continued, "He has spoken so much about you over the recent few weeks and I'm delighted to finally have a chance to meet you properly, although, I do wish that the circumstances were not so unpleasant."

Despite Kitty's excitement at meeting Myriam, she was clearly bearing her own grief for Mrs Bailey.

Myriam responded by giving her hand a gentle squeeze. "Jim told me that he doesn't know how he would have coped without your support during the past few months. He has praised you so highly. I understand that you have known the family for a long time, this must be very difficult for you."

"Yes, it hasn't been easy and now I feel very sad indeed," she conceded. "I think that the hardest part is knowing how altered she was from the woman that she used to be. I mean, ever since I first met her, she was always a bit *fragile* but nothing like she was since her husband died." Kitty looked at the open doorway. They could hear Jim moving about in the kitchen. "That poor young man, he's dealt with a lot so far in his life."

There was a brief pause as both women reflected on the uncertainties that life presented one with at times and then Kitty patted Myriam's hand gently. "But it does warm my heart and rest my mind to know what a lovely young woman you are and to see how much you two care for each other. He'll be just fine now, of that I'm sure."

Myriam smiled, but before she could reply Jim returned to the room carrying a tray with a pot of tea and three teacups on it. The three of them sat and talked companionably while drinking the warm tea. Myriam asked about Kitty's family and listened as Kitty talked enthusiastically about her children and all their antics. Jim remained quiet. He appeared to be listening to them both, although as his eyes stared into the distance, it was clear that he was far away in his thoughts.

After a while, Myriam glanced at the clock and saw that it was time she made her way back to begin her shift at the inn. Standing to go, Jim got up to see her out. Kitty, ever insightful, picked up the tray.

"I'll take these things to the kitchen and wash them. It will give you a moment of privacy." Although her words were direct, Kitty's manner was subtle and she politely left them together.

Jim took a forceful, determined step towards Myriam. He had been so distant while they had been sitting, drinking tea and yet now his expression was anything but distant. His dark eyes looked at her intensely. As he reached out and took hold of her hand there was something about the earnestness of his grasp that caused her stomach to flip over and her heart to pound violently inside her chest. Myriam hadn't experienced a reaction this strong to him since the night of their first dance together.

He was looking at her so ardently that she found herself starting to blush as the skin on her face and neck heated up in response to him. Then she gasped as he dropped down onto one knee. Still looking deeply into her eyes, he began to speak.

"Myriam. My dear, beautiful, enchanting Myriam. Many months ago, I told you to forget about me and to carry on with your life. I told you to go and find love elsewhere. I felt I had nothing to offer you and it was true, I didn't. But you refused my request. Instead, you bravely and loyally vowed to wait and then, while I gave you nothing, you gave me everything."

Myriam was shaking, she felt like her heart was about to explode out from inside her.

Jim gulped back an emotional lump from his throat and continued, "Since the day we met, you have become the reason I get up each morning. We have spent so much of our time apart and yet you have been constantly with me, ever and always in my thoughts." He gently tapped his temple to give emphasis of how much he had thought about her. "I didn't want to do this now, not today when I should be grieving, but I feel I must. I feel that I owe it to you. You've waited too long already and I don't feel that it's fair to make you wait any longer."

He took in a long, deep breath and then whispered those words that she had at times thought she would never hear.

"Myriam Evans, will you marry me?"

Twenty-five

The funeral service for Mrs Bailey was held three days after her death. Myriam had awoken to a typical mid-spring day. The air was mild and breezy, and clouds kept rolling along above the town. One moment it was pouring with rain, the next there was a burst of sunlight and the sky shone the colour of crisp, sapphire blue.

Waiting in the yard, wearing her black bonnet, Myriam noticed the sky darken as another set of rain clouds rolled in. She went over to shelter by the stables and waited for the others to join her. Tom, Rose, Bill and Josephine were all attending the funeral. None of them had ever met Mrs Bailey but they all felt that it was important to give some support to their friend, Jim.

A tall, chestnut mare with a small white star on her head was eating from a bag of hay in the stable next to where Myriam was standing. Inquisitive about the new arrival beside her, the mare left her meal and looked out over the stable door at Myriam. Myriam loved horses. They were her favourite animals. She admired their trust in the humans who owned and worked with them. Naturally creatures of flight, with a timid, nervy nature they could face dangerous situations and unknown fears with courage and complete confidence in the rider or driver who was guiding them. As Myriam stroked the soft, velvety nose of this horse she felt that it was similar to Mrs

Bailey. She had been a nervy creature of flight by nature and yet her complete trust in Jim and her reliance on him had been incredible. Myriam thought of Jim, he would most probably be on his way to the church now. He was to arrive along with the undertakers and the coffin. Still stroking the mare and gently running her fingers though the silky mane, Myriam said a small prayer for Jim, asking God to give him the strength he needed to get through this day.

The others joined her in the yard as the raindrops began to ease off in their intensity. As a small, sombre group they made their way across the road to the church.

Saint Mary's church was large inside. It had been built to serve the whole town and the small group who had gathered for the funeral barely filled the front few pews. Leaving the others a couple of rows back and sitting down at the front next to Kitty, Luke and the two oldest of their children, Myriam looked around at those who had gathered for the sad occasion. Jim, who had started work at the lock when he was thirteen and then cared for his mother, didn't have any of the usual close friends. By his own admission, he had told Myriam that other things had become more important than maintaining friendships with those he had played with and gone to school with as a boy. However, Myriam could see that despite this, Jim was well thought of and respected by those he did come across in his daily life. Many of the canal people were there. Myriam knew that, like her own friends who had come along, they hadn't known Mrs Bailey but they too were here to give their support to Jim. Seeing them confirmed to Myriam something she had realised a long time ago; Jim was a good man. People respected him and wanted to support him.

The vicar stood up in the pulpit and indicated to everyone that the service was about to begin. The doors opened and the undertakers arrived with the coffin that contained poor Mrs Bailey's lifeless, small body. At the front, walking determinedly with the coffin resting on their shoulders, were Mr Dickenson and Jim. As he walked, Jim kept his eyes fixed on the floor of the church aisle beneath his feet. Running down the centre of the aisle was an ornate, iron grating and his feet followed it, leading him past the rows of empty pews. Nearing the front, his eyes flickered up and met with Myriam's. He blinked, gave her a brief smile and then focused his attention back on his own steps.

Jim hadn't realised how hard it would be to carry the coffin containing his own mother but it felt like the right thing to do. She had cared for him as a little boy. She had fed him, cooked for him and lovingly washed and fixed his clothes. In recent years, things had been turned upside down and he had been the one to take care of her needs. Today was his final deed towards her, his final act of love for the mother who had loved him.

Placing the coffin on the stand in front of the alter, Jim and Mr Dickenson took a seat on the front row. Jim gave Myriam's hand a light squeeze as he sat down next to her. He was so grateful that she was here by his side today.

The sermon wasn't too lengthy. The vicar didn't dwell on Mrs Bailey's later years. Instead, he focused on the time around Jim's childhood and the life they had as a family back then. He read a few

Bible verses in an attempt to comfort the small congregation but they didn't really make a lot of sense to Myriam. She remembered thinking the same thing at her own parents' funeral. Death left so many questions and she always found that they remained unanswered by the meaningless words of vicars.

The service was over and they made their way out to the churchyard to lower the coffin into the ground. There was an interval between the rain showers long enough for the sun to shine brightly while they all stood around the grave. Throwing a flower onto the coffin, Myriam could feel the rays of sunlight lifting the spirits of everyone a little, including those of Jim.

Tradition was that following the funeral a small reception was held, with food and drinks for family and friends of the deceased but Jim had decided not to abide by this. His mother had always been a private person and so was he. All in attendance had businesses to run and work to do so he took a moment to thank everyone for attending and then it was all over.

With most of the funeral guests gone, Myriam asked him what they should do for the rest of the day.

"I think I'll go back to the lock with Mr Thomas. It does me good to be working, stops me thinking too much," he said.

She nodded. She had come to realise over the past few days that staying busy at work was what he wanted to do. "Will you come to the inn later do you think?" she asked.

Each night since his mother had died, Jim had come to the inn after work and sat by the bar. He had ordered a meal and enjoyed being in a room of people. Although Myriam was working, they were able to talk a little together when there a few quiet moments between orders from customers and it had meant that he wasn't at home spending the evenings alone.

"Of course," he said, smiling warmly at her. "I'll see you later."

Myriam and the others made their way back to the inn. It was now almost noon. Mr Hamilton had given Myriam permission to only work the evening shift that day, due to the funeral, and so she had a few hours before she was expected in the bar. She felt tired, the previous few days had been emotionally exhausting. Thanking the others for their support she went up to her room, hoping to have a small sleep before starting her shift. Lying on the bed, with a blanket pulled up around her, she was just drifting off when there was a quiet tap on the door.

"Myriam, it's me," hissed Rose.

Myriam smiled and sat up. "Come in," she called.

Rose came in carrying a long cardboard box. She placed the box on top of the chest of drawers and then sat down at the end of Myriam's bed.

"How are you holding up, duckie?" asked Rose.

Myriam nodded. "I'm just tired. I think it's all the emotion."

"Well, you've had plenty of that this week," agreed Rose. "What with meeting a dying woman, being proposed to and then attending a funeral, it's no wonder you're feeling worn out."

The day of Jim's proposal, Myriam had rushed

161

home to tell Rose the news. Rose was delighted for her sister. She had worried so much over the past eighteen months that Myriam's determination to wait for Jim would ultimately cause her pain and disappointment but now, she could see that all was going to be fine. She could also see that her and Jim had formed such a strong bond during this time that she had no doubt that they could get through the grief of Mrs Bailey's death together.

"Now duckie, speaking of proposals and weddings, I have something for you." Rose got up and retrieved the box from where she had left it and placed it on the bed, between them. "I've saved this for you."

"What is it?" asked Myriam.

"Open it and see." Rose was smiling, her usual twinkly smile.

Myriam took the lid off the box. Inside was thin wrapping paper. She peeled it back to reveal a beautiful white gown. Giving Rose a quizzical look she gently lifted the gown out of the box and held it up. Myriam knew instantly what it was.

"Mother's wedding dress," she exhaled, emotion catching in her throat.

"Yes," confirmed Rose. "I saved it, as I thought that one day you might want to use it. There's no pressure though. If you want to buy your own then that's perfectly fine, but I just thought that with your height and shape being so much like hers that you might..."

"Of course I want to wear it!" interrupted Myriam. "I never even knew you'd kept it. It would be so special to get married to Jim wearing this."

Rose smiled. "That's what I'd hoped you'd say."

"Thank you so much."

Myriam jumped up and hugged her sister, holding her tightly. She felt Rose let out a deep, heavy sigh and it reminded her that there was something she had been meaning to ask her about. Pulling away and carefully folding the dress back into the box she planned her words delicately.

"Rose, may I ask how you are?"

Rose tried to look as though she didn't understand the question, so Myriam gently probed a bit further.

"It's just that we haven't had time to talk together properly for ages and I was wondering how you are and well, how you've been feeling since we were told Eliza's news."

Rose gave in, she had been avoiding Myriam since that day at the market, but she knew that she couldn't hide from this conversation forever. She also knew that it wasn't fair to shut her sister out. They were so close to each other.

"I took that news badly," she conceded. "I'm trying not be selfish. I'm trying my best to be happy for her but it's so hard when I've wanted it for so long."

Rose wouldn't look up as she twisted her fingers together.

Myriam took her hand gently. "I know we haven't talked about it for a long time, but I guess that you're still trying for a baby?"

Rose nodded. "And even so, nothing is happening. I wish I knew what was wrong with me."

She looked deflated. Myriam could see that the burden of being unable to produce a child was weighing her down.

"Do you feel pressure from Tom?" she asked.

Rose looked up, shocked by her question. "No! Tom has tried to tell me to forget about it for a while, to stop putting myself under obligation to have a child. The problem is, I don't feel under obligation, as if it's some sort of duty I have. Tom is such a sweetheart! He says he loves me whatever; children or no children. I just feel this intense *need* to have a baby. I can't describe it. I desperately want to be a mother!"

Myriam didn't understand the sentiments that Rose was describing. She had no maternal feelings and wasn't sure if she ever would but her heart still suffered for her sister. She could see that the pain it was causing her was eating into her spirit. She hoped that it would only be a temporary situation and that soon the baby that Rose longed for would come.

There was one thing that Rose had said that did lighten Myriam's concerns. Rose had said that Tom had assured her of his love for her; baby or no baby. Myriam had always had her doubts about elements of Tom's character and she still did, regardless of what Rose had just said, but it did settle her mind to know that he wasn't pressuring his wife. Despite the questionable decisions that Myriam felt her brother-in-law made at times, it comforted her to know that he really did love and care for Rose.

Twenty-six

June 1840

Myriam woke, on the morning of her wedding, as the sun was rising. She looked at the shadowy hand on the clock. It was only quarter to five. She turned over to try and continue sleeping. There were still eight hours between now and the ceremony and she had tossed and turned so much all night that she felt it was imperative that she sleep for longer. It was no good though, her eyes blinked open and refused to allow her to drift off. Giving in, she sat up and stretched out her arms. Her body was tired and stiff, but her mind was alert and her thoughts were dancing inside her head.

Rose had insisted that she have a drink of warm milk with rum added to it the night before to try and help her to sleep. She had taken the drink and gulped it down quickly, unused to the flavours of burnt wood and molasses. The bitter concoction had failed to do what it was supposed to though, and she had struggled to settle into a deep sleep all night. She had flitted from dream to dream, all of them equally bizarre and confusing in their content.

The last dream that had awoken her had been the most peculiar of them all. No doubt prompted by talk throughout the town, and indeed the whole country, of the attempted assassination of Queen Victoria and her husband, Prince Albert just a few days earlier, Myriam had been dreaming that she and Rose were riding together in a stagecoach which was being driven by Tom. Tom had whipped the horses up into a frenzy, shouting that there was no time to lose if they were to collect the wedding cake in time for the guests to eat it. Since the royal wedding earlier that year, sketches and artist's renderings had appeared in the papers and on posters everywhere of the extravagant cake that had been prepared for the occasion. It was so big that Myriam had wondered at how one could even attempt to bake a cake so big that four men were required to carry it. In her dream, Rose had been pleading with Tom to slow down when suddenly Jim had jumped out from the side of the road and shot a gun, firing wedding cake all over them. The shot from the gun had caused her to jump and brought the dream to a swift conclusion. She was now fully awake.

Her mouth felt dry and she quietly slipped out of bed to pick up her glass of water. Josephine was still asleep. She was taking the day off for the wedding and had not yet stirred, no doubt enjoying her rare opportunity to sleep on for longer.

The long, low rays from the early morning sun were casting soft streams of light into the room which settled on the wardrobe in the corner. Her mother's dress was hanging against the wardrobe door, ready for her to put on later. Myriam smiled as she watched the delicate material shimmer and shine in the early-morning light. She couldn't believe that it was finally the day when she would become Jim's wife. By the time the sun would set that evening, she would be 'Mrs Myriam Bailey'. Her stomach fluttered at the happy thought.

Quietly putting on a robe and a pair of slippers she left the room and padded softly down the stairs, heading towards the kitchen in search of a cup of tea and something to eat. Opening the door to the busy kitchen of the coaching inn, she was hit by pleasant smells of warm bread and the sound of eggs being cracked into a large bowl. The staff in here worked hard, getting up early to ensure the breakfasts were ready for the guests who were eager to continue with their journeys.

She was surprised to see Rose in the corner, leaning over something that she was preparing. Rose had also taken a day off work for the special occasion and therefore Myriam was curious about what she was doing in the room at this early hour of the day. Rose and Tom had a small kitchenette in their place so she didn't need to come to the main kitchen for their personal meals. Rose had her back to Myriam and so didn't see her as she approached and leaned over her shoulder, peering nosily at the creation on which Rose was working.

"What are you up to Rose Watkins?" asked Myriam, staring at the pile of cakes and ribbons which were spread out across the table surface.

Rose jumped out her skin and spun around screaming, "What are you doing here?! You should still be asleep." She spread her arms out to hide what was behind her. "You didn't see anything did you? I wanted it to be a surprise."

Myriam had seen a lot of delicious, fruit-filled Banbury cakes. They were her favourite and she could feel her mouth watering just thinking about them; but she had also seen a lot of mess and disorganisation. If she was careful with her words, she could be truthful and not spoil the evident surprise that Rose was lovingly preparing.

"All I could see was a lot of ribbon and mess," she replied, shrugging.

Rose didn't look convinced. "Are you sure that's all?"

Myriam wasn't going to lie so instead she answered with a question of her own. "What are you up to?"

"Never you mind! It's none of your business." Rose flapped her arms at her, pushing her away from where she was working. "Why are you awake anyway? You don't need to be up for hours yet. A bride needs her beauty sleep you know!"

"I just can't sleep," Myriam responded with a frustrated shake of her head. "I had such a fitful night too. In the end I thought I'd just get up and get on with the day. I'm hungry so I came down to get some food. I wasn't expecting to see you here." Myriam added the last sentence with a mischievous raise of her eyebrows.

Rose flapped at her again. "Stop fishing. You'll have to wait and see what I'm doing. I saw Cook mixing up eggs and I think there may even be sausages on the stove so go and get yourself some food and get out of here."

Myriam grinned, "All right, I know when I'm not wanted. I'll go." She turned to leave.

"Hey," called Rose and reached out her hand to grab her.

Myriam turned back to face her. Rose stepped

forward and reached out, taking hold of her face with both hands.

"Happy, happy wedding day my little duckie."

Rose rarely showed emotion, but Myriam could see that her sister's eyes were watery with sentiment.

"Thank you," she replied, leaning forward and giving her a gentle kiss on her soft, rosy cheek. "Will you come up later and help me dress?"

"Of course."

By noon, Myriam was almost ready to get into her gown. The morning had been very different from the morning of Rose's wedding almost three years earlier. Myriam had been specific in her request to have *'no fuss made'* and so none had been. Unlike the day of Rose's wedding, when the room had been full of girls and their chatter, hairbrushes and powder brushes, the morning had passed calmly and quietly. Myriam was a private young woman and, as much as she loved her friends dearly, she had wanted this time of preparation to be peaceful. She had wanted it to be a moment of reflection. Josephine had kindly gone to get herself ready elsewhere and so it had just been Rose and Myriam together in the room. They had talked happily with each other while fixing one another's hair and applying small, subtle amounts of rouge to their faces.

They hadn't shared so much time together in this way since before Rose had married and for Myriam, it was the perfect start to what she hoped would be a perfect day. The sunlight was still pouring in through the window and the little attic room was now feeling warm under the summer heat. Gently dabbing beads of perspiration off her forehead with a handkerchief, Myriam suggested that she dress into the gown and then make her way downstairs to try and cool off a bit before they walked to the church.

Agreeing with her suggestion, Rose helped her into the long, lacy dress and fastened the buttons at the back for her. The dress fitted Myriam perfectly, no alterations had been needed. As her sister turned around to face her, Rose wiped the tears that were now falling from her eyes.

"Come on, no tears Rose, not today," said Myriam handing her a clean handkerchief.

"They're not sad tears, honestly. Although it is sad that mother and father can't see you. They're happy tears. You look so beautiful and I'm just so happy for you."

Myriam gave her hand a squeeze. "Well, if that's it and we're ready, I think I need to go downstairs. It's just too hot in here now."

They both made their way outside to the yard. Tom, Bill and Josephine were just leaving to walk over to the church. Tom whistled at the sight of them both. Myriam with her hair expertly pinned and her veil floating in front of her face looked every bit the beautiful bride. Rose had bought a new dress. It was pale pink with cream sequins and she also looked particularly attractive. Rose waved her arm at Tom, hissing at him to keep moving and leave them in peace but she couldn't help but blow him a small kiss too.

Rose and Myriam waited for a few moments in order to allow the others enough time to cross the road and enter the church before they too set off towards Saint Mary's. Leaving the yard and coming around the front of the inn, they found Mr Hamilton waiting for them. He had come to see the bride off.

"Young Myriam, you've been a pleasure to employ. You will be missed." He took her hand and kissed it in a very gentlemanly manner.

"Thank you, Sir," replied Myriam, a little taken aback by his words of endearment. "I won't be far away. If you ever get stuck, you can call for me."

"No, no." he waved his arms. "You go and get on with your new life. I appreciate the offer all the same."

Myriam nodded and smiled at him. "Very good, Sir. In that case then, if you'll excuse me, my new life is waiting for me just across the road there!"

Twenty-seven

Jim had arrived at the church nearly forty-five minutes earlier. He knew that he was ridiculously early but he had just been pacing around the room at home and so he thought he might as well pace around the churchyard instead.

It had also given him time to stop and leave a couple of fresh flowers at his mother's grave. The headstone had not yet been placed there but he knew where it was. He had found the grave and left the flowers neatly in the spot where the headstone should be, telling her that today was his wedding day and that he hoped she was resting well. He wasn't one for sitting in a churchyard, talking to dead people, but it felt important to say a few words and to not just silently drop the flowers and leave.

After a short wait outside by himself, Luke, Kitty and their five children arrived and he made his way into the church with them. He had been inside this building a few times over the recent years for weddings, christenings and, of course, funerals. He thought of the range of emotions that those who had sat on the pews had felt during those times and felt certain that surely no one had experienced the same feelings that he was going through right now. They were feelings of immense relief that this day was here, tinged with a sadness at the events which had led up to and allowed this wedding to take place. He almost felt guilty that he was so happy at the prospect of his marriage to Myriam. He conceded to himself that the mix of feelings he had were extremely hard to work out.

Before long, the other guests arrived and now it was just Myriam and Rose that they were waiting for. As the vicar indicated for the organist to begin playing and asked the small group of wedding guests to stand, Jim obediently stood and then closed his eyes and took in a deep breath.

Myriam was inside the church. She was walking unescorted down the aisle, with Rose walking just a few steps in front. Mr Price had offered to give Myriam away, as he had Rose, but it had been her choice to walk alone. Jim would be alone and so she felt it was best if she were also. It would be just the two of them together in everything from now on.

Jim's eyes were still closed. He was silently and slowly counting to ten, gently exhaling with each count.

Myriam was now half-way down the aisle. Her eyes flicked to the side and she briefly caught Mary's beaming smile. The wedding party was small, but it was made up of the people who mattered to Jim and Myriam the most. They had both decided that they wanted the day to be simple and without any excess pomposity or ceremony. The most important thing for them was the marriage, not the wedding.

Jim reached the number ten in his head and opened his eyes to look at her. The small amount of breath that was left in his lungs was taken away from him. She was resplendent and dazzling. He thought that she was beautiful every time he saw her but today she looked radiant.   Her eyes, those eyes that mesmerised him every time he looked at her, were now fixed on his own. Seeing that he had opened his eyes and was now looking at her, her mouth opened into a wide, happy smile. As she neared the front of the church and came to where he was standing, he took her hand and pulled her gently towards him.

Standing beside each other, listening to the words of the vicar, Jim wouldn't let go of her hand. Myriam could feel him shaking a little and it touched her to see how emotional he was. Soon, they were saying their vows; pledging their devotion and love for each other in front of family and friends. Then it came to that final moment of the service; the singular moment that they had both at times felt would never come. They turned to face the small congregation and the vicar introduced them as 'Mr and Mrs Bailey'.

Jim was shaking and, despite the cool temperature inside the church, Myriam flushed hot with emotion. They walked up the aisle to the door and almost fell out through the doorway into the brilliant summer sun.

Knowing they had only a brief moment before everyone would follow them, Jim gently placed one hand on the small of her back and used the other to delicately pull her chin up towards him. Lowering his head down, he leaned towards he and gave her a soft, lingering kiss.

She felt a quiver run through her body as his warm lips brushed against hers and then she held her breath as he pressed them onto her own. His fresh smell and the sweet taste of him was intoxicating, causing her to feel exhilarated and heady.

Since the day of his mother's death and his

proposal to Myriam, Jim had insisted on being respectable in everything. He had maintained that they would refrain from any displays of intimate affection until they were married. Myriam had wondered what it would feel like to kiss him for the first time on their wedding day. She had never been kissed by anyone and so had nothing to compare this with, but for her it was heavenly.

She had no time to dwell on it too much though, as now everyone was arriving to join them outside the church. They pulled away, both blushing a little, and greeted their guests. Everyone then made their way happily down the hill to the Three Pigeons Inn, where Myriam and Jim had hired a room and arranged for a meal for everyone.

It really was a small wedding party. With the Prices and Andrew, along with Mr Thomas, Mr and Mrs Dickenson, Bill, Josephine, Luke, Kitty and their small tribe the total was twenty-two including Tom, Rose, Jim and Myriam. Despite being a small group, it was exactly what Jim and Myriam wanted. The room at the back of the inn, away from the road, was light and airy. It lacked the large, wooden panelling which was so popular in most of the town's establishments. The bare, stone walls and added benefit of many windows, meant that plenty of natural light filled the room. This was the main reason that Myriam had wanted to have their wedding meal here. It felt like a happy room.

Sitting at a long table and looking at everyone gathered around, Myriam felt that everything was perfect. Each and every person who was with them in that room meant something special to them and had in some way added to and enriched their lives. She

175

looked at old Mr Thomas, being helped to fill his glass with water by Mr Dickenson. Those two men had become Jim's surrogate family over the years, both of them providing him with the advice and guidance he had needed as he had grown into a young man.

Myriam watched the Prices. Mr Price was ensuring that his wife was sitting comfortably while Mary slapped her brother's hand as he reached for a sugar lump from a small table that was tucked behind him, in the corner of the room. Then there was Andrew and Eliza. Eliza was now showing a small, neat bump that carried their growing baby. She looked elegant as ever and Andrew was attentively helping her to find a comfortable position at the table, one that wouldn't place unnecessary pressure against her stomach. That whole family meant so much to Myriam. They had known her since she was born and helped her through the saddest time of her life. She loved all of them dearly.

Myriam then allowed her attention to focus on Bill and Josephine. What a sweet couple they made. Bill was whispering something in her ear and she was giggling in response to his words. Myriam thought back on all those evenings at the inn, with Bill working on the other side of the bar. They had shared mischievous looks, both of them privately entertained by the antics of the various customers that had passed through over the years. She was happy that Bill and Josephine had found each other. Josephine had been such a delight to live with, never causing fuss or difficulties but instead she had been easy going and accommodating.

A small commotion across the table caused Myriam to look at Luke and Kitty. They had been good friends to the Bailey's over the years and had recently been Jim's lifeline. Myriam smiled as the two youngest children squabbled over where they were sitting and Kitty stood up to calmly rearrange her children's seating positions. The sweet, fifteen-year-old Marinna, was strategically placed between the two younger ones and peace returned. Myriam had already warmed to Kitty in the short time that she had known her and was glad that they would now be neighbours.

Lastly, Myriam's eyes rested on Tom and Rose. Tom was trying his best to not look disappointed that no ale was being served. Apart from a small glass of wine with the meal, Jim and Myriam had decided to keep the alcohol consumption down on this day. Tom, with his impetuous ways and impatient nature had a good heart. He was sitting with his arm around the back of Rose's chair, chatting amicably with Luke. Casting her eyes from Tom to Rose, Myriam became aware that Rose was looking back at her. She sensed that Rose had been watching her for a while. Her eyes were twinkly and her rosy cheeks creased as she smiled at Myriam. Dear, faithful, loving Rose. Myriam would never find words to express her gratitude for the way that Rose had taken care of her since their parents' death. She loved her so much that at times it hurt. Even now that she was married to Jim, she knew that nothing would ever come between her and her sister, they had been through so much together.

The staff at the Pigeon Inn indicated to Jim that the meal was ready and so Jim stood up to address everyone. Taking hold of Myriam's hand, he thanked them all for being with them on their special day. He mentioned the absence of those they had lost to death but emphasised how everyone around the table was filling that hole for them. He didn't find it easy to talk in front of a crowd and so kept his words brief and succinct, still managing to convey the gratitude they both felt.

Once he had sat back in his seat the meal was presented. A large cut of pork had been slowly roasting all morning and now fell apart as Jim carved it for everyone. They all helped themselves to potatoes, vegetables and jugs full of gravy. The clinking of silver cutlery against porcelain plates indicated everyone's enjoyment of the meal.

After everyone had eaten and the food had been washed down with a glass of sweet wine, Rose got up and left the room. Myriam suspected that it was now time for her to reveal the little surprise she had been working on that morning in the kitchen and she was correct. Rose returned carrying a large platter upon which she had carefully and delicately arranged a stack of Banbury cakes into a pyramid, decorated with ribbons.

"I know you both didn't want fuss and so had decided not to bother with a wedding cake, but I wanted to do something," Rose explained. "I know how much you love Banbury cakes, Myriam, duckie, and so thought I'd create for you a Banbury cake, cake!"

Rose was so excited with her efforts that it looked as though she might drop the fragile invention. Tom jumped up and carefully took it from her, placing it in the centre of the table. Everyone marvelled at the ingenious idea and Myriam was delighted. It was true, she did love a good Banbury cake.

It felt like the afternoon had passed by in a blur and before Myriam knew it, the meal was over. Everyone had sat for a while, chatting together and enjoying the company, but now it was time to leave. They had only booked the room until six o'clock, not wanting a big, musical celebration that extended late into the night. This seemed to the others as an odd decision, especially as Myriam loved dancing, but everything had been planned in a way that wouldn't dishonour the loss of Jim's mother. Jim and Myriam knew that they were probably being overly sensitive, but they just didn't feel comfortable with it any other way.

They said farewell to their guests and then began to walk towards home; Jim's home in Waterloo. In the days leading up to the wedding Myriam had moved her things into the house that would now become her new home. She was excited at the thought of running her own household and looking after her new husband.

The walk home took them along the canal. As they set off from the inn, Mr Thomas, Mr and Mrs Dickenson, Luke, Kitty and the children walked alongside them. Soon though, the slow pace that was set by Mr Thomas was too leisurely for the lively youngsters and so Luke and Kitty walked on ahead with their bouncing children and it wasn't long before Jim and Myriam lost sight of them. Mr Thomas urged Jim and Myriam to go on ahead also, but Jim refused and instead insisted on supporting the old man all the way to his small lockhouse. Once there, they said good evening to the others and continued their walk together, just the two of them.

It was a beautiful, warm evening. The sun

would not set for another couple of hours yet and therefore, activity on the canal was still in progress. The yards that lined the bank beside the town had closed for the day but the boats were still moving, trying to make the most of the long daylight hours to cover as much distance as possible. A boat was coming towards them carrying a load of timber. The boatman passed through the town regularly and knew Jim. He let out a long sharp whistle at the sight of Jim, all dressed up in his smart suit with his pretty new bride alongside him.

"You kept that girl quiet, never said a word to us about getting married. You crafty thing!" called the boatman as the boat got closer. Myriam blushed and the boatman touched the top of his hat apologetically. "Beg your pardon, Miss, I didn't mean to embarrass you. You look mighty pretty though, and I've never seen young Jim looking so handsome. He brushes up well!"

Jim laughed and waved at the man, not stopping to engage him in conversation. There would be plenty of time over the coming weeks and months to introduce Myriam to everyone. Today though, was about just the two of them.

They crossed the canal, pausing on the bridge to look into the water. Midges were hovering in the air and small insects were skating across the surface, their long, threadlike legs splayed out to distribute their weight evenly. A few small fish were rising, causing ripples to disperse across the water, from one bank to the other. As Jim and Myriam leaned over and looked down, they could see their reflection looking back at them. It was blurry, being caught in the motion of the unsettled water. Jim closed his arm around Myriam and squeezed her side gently.

"Let's go home, shall we?"

That night, laying in her new bed with Jim's strong, loving arms wrapped around her, Myriam felt as if she were the happiest woman in the world. He was sleeping and his slow, deep breaths whispered against her ear. She loved him so much and now, finally, they were together. As her eyes became heavy and she allowed them to close, she fell into a deep, peaceful sleep. There were no fitful, strange dreams about gunshots and wedding cake. Instead, her dreams were filled with happy images of their flickering reflection on the canal and the sensations of his amorous touches and generous kisses.

Twenty-eight

May 1841

Myriam loved her new life as 'Mrs Bailey'. She felt that she couldn't be any happier. Jim was an affectionate, attentive husband and she took pride in being a busy, industrious housewife. During the first few weeks after the wedding, Kitty had spent much time at the house helping Myriam to make it her home. It wasn't that Myriam wanted to change everything about the way the house had been before, when Jim had lived there with his mother, but she felt that it was important to make it *their* home as they began the new phase of their lives together.

Kitty had helped Myriam to wash the walls in Jim's bedroom, apply oil to the door and hang new curtains. Old Mrs Bailey's room was undeniably the better of the two bedrooms but it hadn't felt right to Myriam that they use that room for themselves and so she had turned it into a sewing room. Located upstairs, directly above the front room, it benefited from the light of the sun in the same way as the room below did. Myriam had become very proficient at sewing, thanks to Kitty's direction and instructions. In time, she had redone all the cushions and made new covers for the couch and the two armchairs downstairs. The furniture now felt like it was new and that it was theirs.

She was also enjoying cooking. Working in the

bar at the inn and waiting at tables, Myriam had not had much opportunity during her life to cook meals. During the first few months of her marriage, Rose had come to see her each week, staying long enough to teach her a new recipe each time she visited. With added tips and prompts from Kitty next door, Myriam was keeping Jim well fed and content.

Jim was still working hard at the lock. Mr Thomas was getting more and more frail as time went on and he could no longer do many of the duties. Most days the old man walked out as far as the lock gate and passed the day in conversation with people while Jim took care of everything. There was a lot for him to do to keep the canal moving.

Water levels need to be checked and recorded and tolls collected, but those were the simpler jobs. Other tasks included controlling the traffic on the road. As each boat passed through, it was important that the lift bridge was raised so that they could keep moving. It was hard to stop or change the direction of the boats suddenly once the horse had been hitched up and had begun to pull the load through the water. If Jim wasn't alert, the bridge would be down and there would almost be a collision as the boat struggled to be halted in time. The road could be busy at times, especially on market days, with carts coming in and out of the town from all around, and Jim found he was at times running about all over the place trying to keep everything moving smoothly and everyone happy.

He looked forward to going home to Myriam each evening. For so many years he had returned home to a cold, quiet, lifeless house. There had never been any real conversation with his mother, and he had now come to realise just how lonely those years had been. Since the wedding though, he was happy to return to a warm home at the end of a hard day on the canal. Smells of delicious food would hit his nostrils as he opened the door, often accompanied by the pleasant sounds of her happily singing to herself. Their home was filled with love and contentment. Their evenings were spent talking together or sitting in the front room, quietly listening to the comforting crackle of burning logs in the fireplace.

Jim was open with his displays of endearment and Myriam responded to him with generous kisses of her own. If anyone ever passed by and peered in through the window during the evenings, they would more than likely see a young couple who were most certainly in love, often dancing together to their own made-up songs in the comfort of their own home.

That's not to say that life wasn't without challenges. Jim was often tired and he worried greatly about the long-term health of Mr Thomas. The old man refused to accept that he was getting older and weaker and wouldn't talk about his future at the lock. Myriam walked along to the lockhouse most days and took care of tasks inside the house. She enjoyed this. She loved to be outside, and walking by the canal each day allowed her to feast her eyes on the bushes, ferns and creatures that lived there.

Once at the lockhouse, she would spend an hour or two doing little jobs to help Mr Thomas. Having never married, Mr Thomas was a true bachelor. It was evident to Myriam that he had never learned to cook and his meals apparently comprised of bread with some sort of meat or cheese to accompany it. Hence, Myriam took it upon herself to bring Mr

Thomas leftovers each day from the meal she and Jim had eaten on the previous evening. Placing it in a pot inside the stove when she arrived each day allowed it to heat up slowly and then, when Mr Thomas came in each evening, he would have a warm meal ready for him.

The inside of the little lockhouse had been neglected and was disorganised and dirty when Myriam had first begun her visits. Gradually though, over time, she had sorted and organised Mr Thomas' things and cleaned the entire house thoroughly. He hadn't said much in response to her hard work. He was a stubborn old man, set in his ways and reluctant to accept help, but she could see from the expressions on his face that he was grateful to her.

Myriam liked Mr Thomas. She had never known either of her grandfathers and she found herself viewing the grumbling, cantankerous old man as a sort of grandfather figure in her life. Beneath his crotchety exterior she could see that there was a kind, sensitive soul.

One day, late morning, Myriam had finished washing Mr Thomas' bed linen and was hanging it outside to dry. The sky was overcast but the clouds were not heavy as though full of rain. The air felt warm and she knew that despite the lack of direct sunlight, the sheets would soon dry. Mr Thomas was standing by the lock, leaning on his walking stick. Myriam guessed that there was a boat in the lock due to the fact that Mr Thomas was shouting down into it. The top gate was open, allowing water to rush in and fill the lock and the noise of the falling water was loud. It was often hard to hold a conversation nearby when the lock was either being emptied or filled. A few minutes passed and as the water level inside the lock rose, Myriam saw that there was indeed a boat inside. The long narrowboat slowly appeared above the side of the lock and she could see that Mr Thomas was in fact talking with a young woman. Her husband, the boatman, was just the other side of the upper gate preparing their horse. The sight of boatwomen and children was becoming more common on the canal. Entire families were now sometimes living inside the small living spaces aboard the boats. Myriam wondered at the life they must have, living in such a tiny space, sleeping at a different mooring spot each night. She admired those women.

Once the boat had exited the lock and continued up the canal towards Cropredy, Myriam asked Mr Thomas if he would like to take a short walk with her. She was aware that his old joints pained him and were often stiff and sore, so she encouraged him to accompany her on short walks at times to try to help him to keep his limbs moving as freely as possible.

Taking hold of his arm to help steady him, Myriam led the old man slowly down the tow path towards the little bench that she had sat on the first time she had visited Jim. It had become one of her favourite places. Reaching the bench and first ensuring that Mr Thomas was comfortable, she then sat down next to him.

"That young woman just told me that she has only been married for two weeks," he commented, referring to the boatman's wife whom he had been talking with at the lock.

"What a strange home in which to start off a

married life," said Myriam. Mr Thomas only made conversation if he felt like it, so she usually kept her responses short. If he wanted to talk with her, he would add more words.

"She looked like a robust young girl and seemed to me to be enjoying the whole experience."

"I wonder if it feels a bit like an adventure at first," pondered Myriam.

"Living on a narrowboat or getting married?" asked Mr Thomas. He had a good sense of humour and Myriam smiled at his dry remark.

"Both, I imagine."

"Hmmm. Well, I've never experienced either so I couldn't really comment," he returned, and she detected a hint of regret in his tone.

A moment of silence passed. The waters were still; something which was rare along the canal. From behind the reeds appeared a moorhen and Myriam smiled to herself. She hadn't seen them so much recently. She was watching the bird peck around against the bank just beside her when another small movement over by the reeds caught her attention. Four tiny black dots of fluff appeared. Baby moorhens. That was why she hadn't seen the adults much recently, they must have been sitting on the nest, guarding their eggs. The small babies were making little chirping noises and swimming about all over the place. The parent bird was picking out insects from between the murky rushes and then feeding them to the little ones. It was enthralling to watch. Mr Thomas had spotted the small birds too and he was also watching them, clearly intrigued.

"It's nice to see how that adult looks after the

young'uns," he said.

"It's beautiful," she replied.

"I've made arrangements for both you and Jim." The statement caught Myriam by surprise and she turned to look at him. He was still watching the moorhens.

"What do you mean?" she asked.

"Just that after I'm gone, I've made sure that you'll both be just fine."

She placed her hand on his. "Come now, let's not talk about that."

"Facts are facts, my dear." He now looked away from the birds and faced her. "I'm getting older, there's no point in denying it. Besides, I've always regarded Jim as the boy I never had."

Myriam nodded.

He lifted his hand from under hers and gave it a little pat before picking up his walking stick, placing it firmly into the ground and leaning his weight against it in order to stand.

"Not a word to Jim though. This is our little secret," he said as she helped him to his feet.

Myriam frowned. She didn't keep secrets from Jim. They were open with each other about everything. Mr Thomas saw her expression and tapped his nose.

"Our secret," he insisted and she nodded reluctantly.

Twenty-nine

Something that Myriam loved about being Jim's wife and not working at the inn was that it gave her time to do some of the things she wanted to do. She now found that she had time to visit Mary. Every few weeks, she would walk along the tow path to Bodicote and spend the day at the Prices' farm.

The day after Mr Thomas had made her vow to keep his secret, she tidied away their breakfast things, packed her work apron and gloves into a small, cloth bag and then put on her boots. Once she was ready, she headed off to the farm.

It was overcast, as it had been the day before, but the air still didn't feel cold. In fact, Myriam found herself getting warm as she briskly walked along and so she forced herself to slow down a little. She loved walking along the tow path. Once away from the town it was less busy and, apart from passing donkeys or ponies with their owners, each pulling a floating load through the water, there were very few people to meet. It gave her moments to think and to reflect on things. It also gave her a chance to feed her hungry eyes on the rural views. The countryside had been so much a part of her childhood and she found at times that she longed for it desperately.

Often, as she made these walks away from the town, she felt like a greedy little child in a sweet shop. She was aware now of how her senses rapaciously grabbed at the sights, smells and sounds that were on offer. She could feel her eyes feasting on the soft tones of green along the hedgerows. She always found it to be such a calming colour, soothing for one's soul. Her ears tuned in to the melodious bird songs and distant bleating of lambs, searching out their mothers amid fields full of grazing sheep. She breathed in deeply and inhaled the fragrant scents of kingcups, forget-me-nots and wild roses. Myriam savoured these walks and never took them for granted.

In time, she crossed the canal at one of the swing bridges and began to climb the hill that led towards Bodicote. Passing the Haynes' farm, she waved to the family from across the field. They looked busy in the distance, doing something with the crops. Having grown up in the village, she knew most of the families, and remembered playing with Samuel Haynes and his sisters when they had all been young children. Their farm bordered onto the Prices and soon she reached the boundary and was on Mr Price's land.

Crossing a field full of ewes with their young lambs she stopped to watch the small, woolly animals. They were adorable as they bounded around on their spindly legs. A group of about a dozen lambs had gathered together around a large stack of hay and were jumping and kicking about in excitement. Myriam would have stayed and watched them all day if she hadn't heard Mary shouting out to her from the farmyard at the other side of the field.

Mary had been waiting for her to arrive and was happy to see her. Myriam could see though that her friend looked tired.

"How are things?" she asked as they made their

way across the yard towards a large shed.

"Well, I'm glad the lambing is all finally over!" Mary replied. "It's the first year without Eliza around to help, but it went well. Jacob was more useful than I thought he'd be."

Eliza had given birth to a baby girl at the end of the previous year. She was a pretty little thing with dark eyes and dark hair, like her father. They had named her Emeline and Myriam thought that it suited her well. During her expectancy period and now with her little baby to look after, Eliza had not been involved in the work on the farm for many months. Her original plan was to leave Emeline with her mother while she returned to help Mary, but Emeline had not been well in recent weeks and as a result Eliza's return to work was somewhat delayed.

"I'm glad that Jacob was useful. Let's hope it continues," remarked Myriam, pulling her apron and gloves out of her bag. "Now, you've got me for the day so what can I start doing?"

Mary smiled and linked arms with her friend. "I do love you, Myriam Bailey. You're made of good stuff!"

"I mean what I say too! What can I do?"

Mary hesitated. She felt bad asking her friend to work when she was here for a visit but by the look on Myriam's face, she could see that she did indeed mean it.

"Well, if you insist on helping, I haven't had a chance to clean the shed since we finished lambing and put all the sheep out to the fields. It's a big job but I think that with the two of us we can just about manage it."

"Of course," said Myriam and started walking towards the shed.

There was a lot to do inside the large shed which had been used to house the ewes while they gave birth to their lambs. The floor was covered with soiled straw and the air inside the shed was dank and dusty. The smell that hit Myriam's nostrils as she stepped in through the doorway caused her nose to react and she sneezed instantly.

"Sorry," apologised Mary. "I did try to warn you."

"It's no bother, my nose will settle in a moment," replied Myriam.

The two of them worked together companionably, loading barrows with the mucky, grimy straw and then wheeling them across the yard to the large soil heap they had for stable droppings and soiled animal bedding. It didn't take as long as Myriam thought it would, and before long all the dirty straw had been cleared from inside the shed. It still smelt bad inside though and Mary said that they should wash the stone floor. Her father had taught her that in order to keep the animals well and to prevent any illness, everything should be kept clean. He wouldn't approve if she didn't maintain the high standards that he had set on the farm.

They stopped quickly for some lunch, after which they began to fill some buckets with water. Once hot water from the kettle that had been sitting on the stove had been added, and a bar of soap had been vigorously rubbed into the warm liquid, they were soon ready to continue. The buckets were hard to carry and splashes of water sloshed out over the edges. Pouring the soapy water over the floor, they then took a broom each and started to scrub the stony surface. Until now, they had been working so fast that there hadn't been much opportunity for conversation but now they slowed a little and began to talk.

"Do you think Jacob will soon be ready to take over the farm work?" Myriam asked, thinking back to what Mary had said earlier about him helping with the lambing.

"He's certainly getting more useful but there's a lot more he needs to learn yet," replied Mary. "He'll be fourteen at the end of the summer. I think father wanted me to keep running things until Jacob is at least fifteen. That will be another eighteen months or so still."

Myriam nodded. She admired Mary and the way she worked tirelessly to keep the farm running. She was quite incredible for a young woman.

"Have you seen much of Samuel recently?"

Mary blushed and nodded. "A bit."

"Have you two had any sort of conversation yet about how you both feel?" Myriam probed.

"Well, yes we have actually," Mary admitted, pausing to lean against the handle of her broom for a moment. "He's told me he likes me. It was very sweet. He was all embarrassed and coy. I told him that I'd been waiting for him to say something and that I felt the same."

"I'm sure you did!" Myriam laughed. Mary was extremely forthright, and Myriam could well imagine her informing Samuel that she knew what he had been going to say. "I'm glad you both know where you stand with each other now anyway."

"Yes, and we've agreed that as soon as Jacob can take over everything here, then we'll get married."

"It all sounds perfect and simple."

"Yes, I suppose it is," agreed Mary. "It doesn't make it easy to wait though, does it?"

"No," said Myriam, remembering how difficult she had found it to wait for Jim. "It doesn't." Myriam paused for a moment, reflecting on the deep emotions that surrounded waiting for something that you longed for and desired. She decided to change the subject. "How are Andrew and Eliza getting along with Emeline?"

"Oh, not too bad, although it's been difficult I think, with Emeline not being too well the past few weeks. She such a gorgeous little thing. I love her so much."

Myriam smiled. It was clear that Mary doted on her new niece.

Mary looked up from the spot on the ground that she had been brushing. "I'd have thought Rose would have had children by now. Do you think she will soon?"

Myriam gulped. Caught off guard by Mary's direct question, she coughed and poured more water onto the floor.

"I err, I suppose...well, I just don't know." she spluttered. She had no idea how she could answer the question truthfully without revealing Rose's personal business.

Mary realised she had made a mistake and quickly sought to correct it.

"I'm sorry, that was none of my business to ask.

You've no need to answer. Please ignore me."

Myriam was grateful. Mary might be forward and brash, but she was also honourable. If she in any way sensed that she had stumbled across an intimate secret she would in no way pass it on. Myriam had said nothing, but she knew that her flustered response had actually told Mary everything. She was confident though that she could trust her friend not to say a word to anyone.

They finished brushing down the shed floor and Myriam decided it was time to make her way back home. They had both worked hard and felt tired, but it had been a good day spent in each other's company.

Thirty

June 1841

Bill and Josephine's wedding was held in the middle of June, on the longest day of the year. For Jim and Myriam, it felt like the longest day of their lives.

Myriam had been feeling unwell during the week leading up to the wedding. Kitty's two youngest children had both been sick with fevers and vomiting and therefore Myriam presumed that she had caught something from them. She had first been ill while eating an egg sandwich and as a result she hadn't been able to stomach the smell of cooked eggs all week. Her sense of taste seemed to have been affected also, as she had gone completely off the flavour of tea and was drinking a hot stew of steamed nettles instead.

Jim was feeling especially worn out. With Myriam being unwell he had taken on a lot of the tasks that needed doing in the home along with his usual work at the lock. The summer days on the canal were always the busiest and the longest. Boatmen wanted to keep moving with their loads for as long as the daylight allowed them and this meant that Jim didn't return home until late most evenings. He was also growing increasingly concerned about Mr Thomas' overall physical condition. The old man was getting less and less able to move around and it troubled Jim to leave him outside unattended.

The morning of the wedding Jim left the house early, at first light, to see to the important tasks at the lock. One of the younger lads from Bridge Wharf was going to assist Mr Thomas while Jim attended the wedding. Jim had been in half a mind to not go at all, but it meant so much to Myriam that they be there together and he didn't like to disappoint her. Jim left Myriam asleep in bed. She had not vomited during the previous two days but had still complained about feeling tired and nauseous. He was aware that it took a bit of time to get over a sickness, but this seemed to be lingering on. He was concerned about her and hoped that she would wake up this morning feeling a bit better.

Myriam woke about an hour after Jim had left and weakly sat up on the side of the bed. She felt terrible, although not as bad as she had earlier in the week. Hopefully she was over the worst and would now be able to regain some of her strength. Making her way into the kitchen she was pleasantly surprised to hear a growl from her stomach. Finally, she was feeling like she wanted to eat something. Pondering about what to make for breakfast, she decided on a slice of bread with marmalade. She may be feeling a lot better than she had in previous days, but she didn't want to risk cooking any eggs.

Returning home to get dressed into his shirt and tie, Jim was pleased to find Myriam sitting in the front room wearing a pretty dress, ready to leave for the ceremony. She looked pale and her hair appeared dull but at least she was feeling up to going. He knew that she had been very excited for her two friends and had been anxious that she might not feel well enough to attend the wedding. Having washed and changed, he took her hand and helped her up from where she was sitting, giving her a gentle kiss as he did so. She smelt sweet and fragrant. It was a scent that he felt was particular to her, and he loved it.

"Are you sure you feel well enough to attend?" he asked softly.

"I still don't feel particularly wonderful, but I do feel a bit better than I did. Besides, I really don't want to miss this."

He nodded and together they made their way to the church.

It was a beautiful day. The warm, midsummer sun was shining brightly. The town was busy as they made their way through, and Myriam held on to Jim's arm while they walked together. She hadn't felt too ill while sitting quietly at home that morning, but now, after only a few minutes of walking, she was quite exhausted. She didn't want to say anything to Jim, but she felt that she may have made a mistake in her self-assessment and left the house before she was really well enough to do so.

They arrived at the church and greeted everyone. Myriam tried her best to smile and engage in conversation. In truth though, she was greatly relieved when they finally sat down and the organ began to play, although the sound was hurting her head which had begun to ache not long after they had left the house.

Josephine looked radiant. Her bright smile flashed and beamed at everyone as she walked down the aisle, arm in arm with her proud father. Bill stood at the front of the church with a wide smile of his own bursting from his face. They really were a perfect couple together.

To Myriam's dismay, she was unable to concentrate on the ceremony. Her head was pounding and her stomach had begun to twist and cramp inside her. She felt incredibly uncomfortable and wished she had stayed at home. Jim didn't know what was wrong, but he could tell that something wasn't right as Myriam held on to his hand, squeezing it tightly, trying to distract herself from the pain that she was in.

Once the vows had ended and Bill and Josephine had been announced to the congregation as husband and wife, everyone stood and followed the newly-weds outside. Myriam however didn't move. Still holding on to Jim's hand she looked at him.

"I think I need to go home," she said, grimacing.

Myriam wasn't sure how she made it home, but she was glad that Jim had been there to help her. Her stomach was still cramping, causing her to wince in agony. Making her way down to the little outhouse at the bottom of the garden, she lifted her skirt to relieve herself. Seeing the spots of red blood on her underclothes she breathed a sigh of relief. It all made sense to her now. The spasms and griping were because she had started menstruating.

Returning to the house she explained the situation to Jim and then got into bed, wrapping herself up in a blanket. It was a warm evening, but she wanted the comfort of the blanket around her. Jim came and lay on the bed next to her. He had been concerned by the amount of pain she was in and was solaced a little to know the reason for it, although he still remained worried. He knew that some months she suffered more than others from the pain of menstruation. This though had been the worst reaction he had seen her have, and so, as she drifted off to sleep, he lay beside her gently stroking her head, hoping that she would awaken later feeling much better.

Thirty-one

Jim woke up with a jump. Someone was banging on the front door downstairs. He looked around. It was dusk and he was on the bed next to Myriam. He realised that he must have fallen asleep too. The banging continued and Myriam was now awake also.

"What's going on?" she asked.

"I'm not sure," he replied, lighting a lamp. "I'll go and see who it is."

He made his way downstairs to see who was wanting to speak with them so urgently. Myriam sat up. She felt drained. There was still a dull ache across her front but the sharp, stabbing pain she had experienced earlier had subsided. Moments later Jim returned, running up the stairs and from the panicked look on his face she could tell that something was wrong.

"It's Mr Thomas," he said, picking up his jacket and putting it on. "He's fallen outside the lockhouse and Mr Dickenson has sent for a doctor."

He paused and looked at her.

"How are you feeling now? I don't have to go, if you need me..."

Myriam interrupted him. "I'm fine. The cramps have stopped. Of course you need to go."

He leaned forwards and stroked her face. "I was so worried about you earlier, but if you're sure the

201

pain has gone and you'll be all right?"

"Honestly, I'll be just fine. Now go, quickly!"

"I don't know how long I'll be."

"Just go," she insisted.

He gave her a kiss and left, pausing only to light a small lantern to carry with him to the lock. It was now almost dark outside and getting late.

Myriam sat for a while on the bed thinking about poor Mr Thomas. He used a walking stick, but it wouldn't have helped him if he had lost his footing and slipped. Jim had said that he was outside the lockhouse, she hoped that he hadn't fallen against anything hard there.

Sitting on the bed and thinking about what was going on by the lock, Myriam was suddenly hit by another wave of cramps. Similar in intensity and ferocity to the ones she had felt earlier, it caused her to double over at the pain. It was now dark outside and not wanting to walk down to the outhouse alone, she lowered herself to the floor and pulled the bedpan out from under the bed.

Jim arrived at the lockhouse to find a small crowd of people gathered around. He pushed his way through to the front. Mr Dickenson was kneeling on the ground, leaning over Mr Thomas while talking softly to him. The old man was still lying on the ground where he had fallen, just outside the lockhouse. His eyes were closed.

"Is he...?" Jim asked.

Mr Dickenson looked up and Jim could just about make out his face against the dancing shadows from his lantern. He looked anxious and concerned.

"He's breathing but I can't get any response from him."

Seeing no blood or obvious injury, Jim took a quick look around. There was a coal bucket tipped over beside them, along with Mr Thomas' walking stick. He must have fallen while bringing in coal for the stove.

"Should we try to carry him inside?" The hot, summer sun had set and it was a clear night. Jim could feel the air cooling quickly now that the heat from the sun had gone. He was concerned that Mr Thomas would get cold if left out here on the ground.

"The thought had crossed my mind, but I wondered if we should wait for the doctor first," replied Mr Dickenson.

"I'll get some blankets from inside then."

Jim opened the door and went into the lockhouse. The stairs were off the side of the kitchen, at the back of the house. Making his way up, through to Mr Thomas' room, Jim saw that there was a kettle on the stove. One of Myriam's pots was there too with the contents of a meal still inside. The kitchen was a mess, there were dirty pots and plates everywhere. Without Myriam's help this past week, the tasks inside the house had been ignored. Jim quickly collected a few blankets from upstairs and returned outside.

The doctor had just arrived and was dispersing the crowd, firmly telling them all to go home. He placed his lantern on the ground and then bent down to examine Mr Thomas. He first lifted Mr Thomas' head, no doubt looking for any injuries. Next, holding the old man's wrist and taking out his pocket watch, the doctor counted his pulse rate. After a while he stood up.

"I see nothing obvious that I can treat from where we are. It's my guess that he has had a nasty bang on his head and that is why he is now unconscious. We need to get him inside but, rather than take him into his house, I'd feel better if we were able to somehow get him to my home. I have all my instruments and medical books there. I feel it would be a better thing to have him at mine."

"And what then? Will he come round soon?" asked Jim.

"To be quite honest, I'm not sure. My main concern presently is that his heart rate is weak and slow. Regarding his consciousness; at this stage I just don't know."

Jim rubbed his hands together, they felt cold and clammy. "My friend here has a coal wagon. Do you think we can we take him to your house safely in that?"

The doctor nodded and Mr Dickenson hurried to prepare his horse.

Kitty let herself into Jim and Myriam's house and called out. On his way to the lock, Jim had stopped by and asked her to keep an eye on Myriam while he was gone. Kitty had tapped gently on the front door in case Myriam was asleep. Getting no reply, she had been about to return home when she thought she heard a distant groan, as if someone was in pain. Peering through the keyhole she had seen a flicker of light from upstairs and guessed that Myriam was in fact still awake and that something wasn't as it should be.

Hearing another groan, Kitty climbed the stairs while carrying her lantern carefully in one hand. She opened the bedroom door to find Myriam sitting on the floor, leaning against the bed. Beside her was the bedpan and Kitty made an immediate assessment of the situation.

Helping Myriam back into the bed, Kitty wrapped the blanket around her. Myriam was pale, and clearly in a lot of pain.

"I'll be back in a moment," she assured her, before heading down to the kitchen.

The coals in the stove were still warm and the kettle too. Taking the kettle from the stove, she filled a cup with the warm water and added two spoonfuls of honey. Opening a cupboard door Kitty reached into the back and took out a small bottle. '*Opium tincture*' - she had hoped it would still be there and it was. Kitty had helped Jim so often to mix up the medicines for his mother that she knew exactly where to find what she needed. She added a few drops to the cup and took it upstairs to Myriam.

"Here, drink this," she urged.

"Thank you," Myriam smiled weakly, her face wincing from the pain. She took a sip. "It's sweet, what is it?"

"My secret invention to soothe pain," smiled Kitty, stroking her hair. "A warm, honey tea. I'll be back in just a moment. I want to check something downstairs."

Kitty returned to the kitchen and gathered a handful of towels and a bowl of warm water. Her intuition told her that these would be needed later.

She left them at the top of the stairs, just outside the bedroom door, and rejoined Myriam.

"How are you feeling?" she asked.

"I feel terrible."

"Jim said that it's your menstruation?"

Myriam nodded. "It's painful sometimes, but I think that this is the worst it's ever been."

"Hopefully the honey tea will help a bit."

There was a moment of quiet. Kitty wanted to choose her next words carefully.

"Last week you were sick. Do you know what it was from?" she asked.

"The same as your two littl'uns I think; vomiting, nausea, fatigue."

Kitty pursed her lips together. "It seems that my two were both sick because they had found an old ham sandwich in their room and eaten it. I'm not sure that you would have done that."

Myriam heard her but she was groaning again with another wave of cramps. Once they had subsided a little, Kitty spoke again.

"Is it later than usual, this month's menstruation?"

"I have no regular pattern so I couldn't really tell you. I've tried to keep a record over the years but it's never the same. It arrives when it arrives. I can't predict it."

"Do you remember when it was last, before now?

"I think it may have been a long gap this time." Myriam thought about it. "I'm sorry, I'm not sure when it was. Why are you asking?"

Kitty reached out and held her hand.

"I'm asking because I think you may be with child."

Myriam looked at her confused. "With child?"

Kitty nodded.

Myriam looked down at the bedpan. "But...?"

Kitty sighed, there was no gentle way to say it. "I'm sorry dear, but I think that you may be losing the baby."

Losing the baby. Myriam tried to understand those words but she couldn't. Surely you could only lose something that you had, or at least something that you *knew* you had. She didn't know that she had a baby, so how could she lose it? Her stomach tightened again and she groaned. Myriam squeezed Kitty's hand.

"Will you stay with me?"

"Of course I will," soothed Kitty.

Jim and Mr Dickenson waited outside the doctor's home all night. They sat on a hard wooden bench, inside a small woodshed which was attached to the side of the doctor's house. The shed was dimly lit by the lantern that they had brought with them. It was quiet inside the shed, except for the occasional hoot of an owl, or call from a hungry fox.

Jim remembered visiting the same house years earlier to see the man who had been in the accident with his father; the man who had survived. It had been a cold, dark wintry night and the whole town had felt as if it was frozen. That night there had been a lot

207

of noise. The injured man himself had cried out as his body had reacted to the necessary treatments that the doctor had administered to him. His family had been outside weeping and crying. Jim still couldn't remember why he had felt the obligation to visit that man on that fateful night, but he could remember distinctly the strong feeling he had had that it was the 'right' thing to do under the circumstances. Those noises had haunted him for weeks afterwards.

On this occasion though, sitting with Mr Dickenson, Jim thought that everything felt calm. That summed up Mr Thomas he supposed. Mr Thomas had always been a peaceful, quiet man. That's what Jim had found so pleasant about him. Underneath his blunt and surly exterior, he was very tranquil to be around. It was so opposite to Jim's life at home with his mother; a mother who flapped and fussed and fretted about everything.

Mr Dickenson was struggling to stay awake and his head kept dropping as his muscles relaxed and failed to support its weight. Finally, as the sun was beginning to rise, the doctor came out to speak to them. Jim could already read from the doctor's body language and facial expression what the news was. He didn't need to hear the words. He allowed the doctor to say them though. Mr Dickenson would need to hear them.

Mr Thomas had died. The cause of death was a suspected internal bleed on his brain which had been caused by the impact of his fall. The doctor asked them if there was any next of kin that needed to be informed. Jim shook his head.

"No," Mr Dickenson sighed. "He had no

family."

The doctor nodded, understanding the situation.

"I'm sorry for your loss."

Jim swallowed and lowered his eyes.

Thanking the doctor for his help and efforts, they left and walked silently back towards the lock. Mr Dickenson lived behind his coal shed. His wife would most probably still be awake, waiting for him. Reaching the canal, he put an arm around Jim's shoulder.

"Will you be all right lad?"

Jim nodded. "Don't worry about me, I'll be fine."

"Your young lady will be waiting for you."

Jim thought about Myriam, most probably sleeping still. Hopefully she would regain her strength now after not feeling well all week. It would be good to let her sleep a bit longer and not disturb her just yet with the sad news.

"I think I'll just pop into the lockhouse and make sure everything is as it should be inside," said Jim.

"Do you want me to join you?" asked Mr Dickenson.

"No, no. I'll be just fine," replied Jim. "You get on back home and get some sleep. I'll come by later on today."

"All right then, if you're sure," said Mr Dickenson and they parted ways.

Thirty-two

Jim picked up the bucket from where it still laid on the ground outside the lockhouse. He put the scattered pieces of coal inside and carried it around the back of the house to the garden. The sun was rising, giving him some light to see well enough for what he was doing. The coal store was beside the back door. After placing the bucket down, he opened the back door and walked into the kitchen. It really was a mess inside.

He began to clear things away. His mind and thoughts were numb. He didn't know how he was supposed to feel. Mr Thomas wasn't his father, but he had been more like a father to him than his own ever had. Mr Bailey, Jim's father, had worked long shifts at the factory and never been home much to spend time with his young son. Jim remembered asking him if they could do things together such as to go for a walk or to the market, but his father had never been able to answer him, except to tell him to stop bothering him, and to ask if it wasn't enough that he was working hard to take care of them all.

Clearing things away from the table and the top of the cold stove, Jim thought back to his days at school and how his friends would talk excitedly and proudly about their fathers and the things they did together. Jim had always sat quietly in the corner, listening jealously to their chattering, hoping they wouldn't ask him to add stories of his own. On one occasion he was asked to join in with them and he remembered making up a story about how his father had taught him to catch fish in the Cherwell river. It was the only occasion in his life that he had ever told a lie and, although the reaction of his friends had made him feel pleased at the time, he had felt regret later for giving in to the pressure and allowing himself to be untruthful.

The long-suppressed, bitter feelings of resentment that were now storming inside of Jim were causing him to become more and more heavy-handed as he stacked dishes and piled pots onto the shelves. Unaware of the rage that was building inside of him, he began to stomp around as he moved about the kitchen. His breathing was getting quicker and his heart was starting to pulsate faster within his chest. Leaning into the pantry to stack some dishes on the bottom shelf, he stood up quickly and hit his head heavily against the low doorway. Yelling out in fury and vexation, his hand reached out, took hold of a plate from the middle shelf and he launched it angrily at the floor.

The plate hit the flagstone floor with a crash and the porcelain china shattered into tiny pieces across the floor. Shocked by the noise and by his own level of emotion, Jim stepped backwards, out of the pantry, and sat down wearily on a chair. His head was throbbing. Leaning forwards, he held it for a moment in his hands. Why was he so angry? He was allowing himself to become enraged at something which had long since passed. They were memories he thought he had dealt with a long time ago; he thought he had moved on.

Another memory then came to Jim, and as his

mind unravelled and he relived the past sights and sounds, he began to understand the real reason for his frustrations.

Jim's father had been dead for about three months when Mr Thomas approached Mrs Bailey and told her that he would like to employ her young son as his assistant. Jim had already left school and had started working in the factory, on the machine line. Mr Thomas had known Jim's parents for years and he had always had a soft spot for the young boy. The wages for a boy in the factory were low and Mr Thomas was offering a fair rate. An agreement was made immediately.

When Jim had begun working at the lock, he had been a sullen, resentful young lad with a quick temper that was easily lost. Mr Thomas, unruffled and yet always firm, was patient with the boy and never too quick to judge. He consistently showed Jim love and kindness, generously giving him the attention that he could see the boy needed and craved. Jim came to admire and care for Mr Thomas in a way that he had never imagined he would. As his mother became more and more fragile, he leaned more and more on the support and direction that Mr Thomas gave him. In time Jim's own temper diminished and he developed the same calm approach that Mr Thomas had to things.

One day though, about two years after Jim's father had died, Jim woke up to find his mother in a bit of a nervous state. Her health problems were beginning to worsen and she was difficult to pacify. He arrived at the lock late for work. Mr Thomas, not knowing what had happened at home that morning, chastised Jim in his usual churlish manner. It was a manner that Jim was well used to, except that on this day it wasn't received well. Jim launched into a rage and began to stamp and pace about. Allowing his anger to get the better of him, he threw the windlass angrily onto the ground. It bounced against the stony surface and hit a pony which had been tethered nearby while the boatman was closing the lock gate. Spooked and frightened, the pony broke free and then bolted off down the tow path with ropes flapping around its legs. The ropes got tangled up and pulled the poor animal down to the ground, breaking one of its legs in the process. A shot gun was found and the pony was dispatched.

From the recesses of his memory, Jim could still see the disappointed look on Mr Thomas' face as he chastised him later that afternoon.

"Allowing a moment of anger to control you will cause weeks, months, even years of sorrow," said Mr Thomas in a firm, unyielding tone. *"And the good name and reputation you've worked hard to build will be torn apart in seconds,"* he added.

Fifteen-year-old Jim nodded sheepishly. He loved Mr Thomas like he had never loved anyone and he knew that his outburst had caused him sorrow as well as embarrassment and expense over the whole incident.

"I'm sorry Sir," Jim felt like crying. *"I wish I could go back in time and change it."*

"We can never go back," stated Mr Thomas, plainly. *"But we can move forward and learn and improve. Will you learn? Will you improve?"*

Jim looked at him. His red, bloodshot eyes were desperate. "I will, I promise I will!"

Mr Thomas patted him on the head. He loved the lad as if he were his own.

"Just promise you won't lose your temper again. An animal's life is bad enough, don't ever have the regret of losing something more precious."

Jim had vowed that day that he wouldn't lose his temper again and he had faithfully kept that promise. Until now.

As Jim remembered the promise he had made to the man who had cared for him as he would his own son, Jim allowed tears to fall from his eyes. He allowed himself to cry for the old man. Mr Thomas had taught him so much and helped to shape him and train him into the man that he now was. Jim wasn't sure how life was going to continue without him.

Once his eyes were dry and the pieces of broken china had been swept up from the floor, Jim made his way outside. The canal was now awake and alive with activity. Two fly-boats were already coming up towards the lock. It struck Jim as somewhat cruel that life continued on, regardless of who was in it. At the same time, he reflected on what a merciful kindness it was to be able to continue as normal no matter what happened or who came and went. Life outside the lockhouse would continue today as it always had. Passers-by would comment on and console each other over the loss of Mr Thomas but nothing would come to a halt and that, he supposed, was how things should be.

Opening the gate for the first of the two fly-boats Jim considered whether he should first go home and see Myriam. It seemed to him that he'd missed his chance though, as boats were now arriving from all directions and the movements across the swing bridge were building in volume too. He had asked Kitty to check on her when he had left last night, and she had been looking much better than she had done earlier that day. Confident that everything was fine back at home, he decided to stay at the lock until later in the morning when things would get quieter. Hopefully he would then have a better chance to slip home to see her and to also get some food and a change of clothes.

By the time the sun had begun to rise, Myriam's ordeal was over. Kitty had stayed with her and it had surprised Myriam how quickly it had all happened. Having cleaned the room and prepared Myriam some food, Kitty then sat in a small chair in the corner of the bedroom and waited for Myriam to fall asleep. Her eyes were closed but Kitty could hear that her breaths were still light; she had not yet drifted off. Kitty hoped that Jim would soon be home. Myriam had not shown any emotion over the situation, and Kitty felt that maybe she was waiting for Jim to return before she allowed herself to contemplate what had just happened to her.

Jim didn't get a chance to leave the lock until mid-afternoon. He would have been there longer if Mr Dickenson hadn't come over and insisted that Jim let him look after everything for the remainder of the day while he go home and rest.

Wearily, exhausted both physically and

emotionally, Jim opened the front door to his home and went in. The house was quiet. There was no movement downstairs. He called out and heard the floorboards in the bedroom creak as someone walked across them. Kitty appeared at the top of the stairs and made her way down.

"Kitty?" He was surprised to see her. He hadn't expected her to be in the house. "Is everything all right?"

She touched him gently on the arm. "Myriam is just resting, it's good that you're home."

He sighed in relief. It had been a difficult day, losing Mr Thomas so suddenly. He was glad that Myriam was well and just resting.

"Thank you Kitty."

She smiled and made her way to the door. "I'll leave you both."

Jim went upstairs and made his way into the bedroom. Myriam was sitting on the bed. She was still pale, but she smiled when she saw him.

"You're home," she said with an inward sigh of relief. She had so many confusing feelings that she wanted to explain to him and she was pleased that he was now there.

He sat on the bed and took off his cap. His back was turned to her. She watched as he ran his hand through his hair and then rubbed his neck. She could tell that he was tired.

"How is Mr Thomas?" she asked. "I hope he wasn't hurt too badly."

His hand stopped moving and she saw his back stiffen.

Jim turned to look at her and she knew then that Mr Thomas wasn't all right.

"I thought that someone would have come to tell you," he said. The tears were building again behind his eyes.

"No." She shook her head. "I've not heard anything."

Jim opened his mouth and tried to tell her that Mr Thomas had died but the words wouldn't come out. Instead, all he could do was lay down on the bed next to her and cry. As she wrapped her arms around him and held him tightly, she began to cry tears of her own. Tears that were for another life which had been lost that day.

Thirty-three

Myriam didn't tell Jim about the miscarriage that night. He was so upset about Mr Thomas that she felt it wouldn't be the right time to tell him what had happened to her in his absence.

She didn't know how he would feel about the prospect of a baby, or what was in reality the loss of a baby, but she was certain that he would be upset that he had failed to be there when she had needed him. She had come to appreciate that Jim felt a strong sense of duty to give support to those close to him when it was needed. He would feel guilty for leaving her alone and would no doubt condemn himself for running out to see to Mr Thomas. As a result, Myriam decided to wait for a better time to tell him about what had happened to her.

They had never really talked about having a family. It was something Myriam assumed they would do at some point, but during the first few months of their married life they were just happy to be together. Babies hadn't even been thought of because they were so content as just the two of them.

In the days that followed that long painful night, Myriam pondered her own feelings. Her emotions were in turmoil. She hadn't been aware that she had been carrying a child and so she struggled to understand the feelings that had been stirred up within her. Between feelings of listlessness and sorrow she found that the overriding emotion she felt was that of guilt. Her thoughts kept turning to Rose and how her sweet sister had struggled for so long to conceive a child. Myriam had apparently done so without any effort, planning or preparation. It was true that the baby had been lost, but Rose had never even got that far. Myriam felt that life was so unfair sometimes.

The days went by and Myriam regained her strength and a funeral was soon held for Mr Thomas. Before she knew it, a week had passed and she had still failed to find a time that felt right to tell Jim about the baby. Seven days had gone by and it now seemed too late to mention it. He was getting on with things at the lock and appeared to have dealt with his grief for Mr Thomas. She was now reluctant to bring the subject up. Maybe it was better to just carry on and forget it had happened.

Almost two weeks after Mr Thomas death, Myriam was at the lockhouse. She had decided to spend a few hours each day sorting out Mr Thomas' things. They had heard nothing about what would happen with the lock and the house and although Jim was continuing with the work as usual, he had confided in Myriam that he was beginning to ask around for other work as he felt certain that a new lock keeper would soon be employed. Myriam was in the kitchen packing away crockery when she heard the front door open and Jim called out to her.

"I'm through here, in the kitchen," she replied, standing up and stretching her back.

"There are two gentlemen from the canal company here," he said. "They've asked to talk with me privately so we're just going to sit in the front room."

Jim showed the two men into the room and explained that Myriam was in the kitchen dealing with Mr Thomas' possessions.

"Please, ask your wife to join us if she is here," commented the older of two men and Jim asked Myriam to come through and sit with them.

Myriam greeted the visitors and then sat down on a small chair beside the fireplace. The two men were wearing matching jackets, no doubt some sort of canal company uniform. Myriam notice that the younger of them had some paperwork in his hand. The other man, who was older and seemed to be the more superior, began to speak. He addressed Jim directly.

"We would first of all like to offer our condolences for your loss. We are aware that you are not related to the late Mr Thomas, but we understand that you were close to him nevertheless."

Jim nodded.

"Now, for the reason for this visit." The man nodded at his colleague who passed him a document from the handful of paperwork he was holding. "As you know, Mr Thomas took up employment with the canal company to be lock keeper at the Banbury lock back in 1806. When he took you on as his assistant he did so with the company's consent and full permission. Two years ago, Mr Thomas wrote to inform us that his health appeared to be deteriorating and to also notify us that you were more than capable of looking after all the work for the foreseeable future. Based on this, we made the decision to leave everything as it was, here in

Banbury, as the arrangement that Mr Thomas had with you was working well and everyone was benefiting as a result."

The man paused and opened the document he had been holding. Jim waited for his next words. He knew that they would be employing a new lock keeper and so expected that the document was some sort of notice, informing him that he would need to clear the house and hand over all the canal records. The man's next few sentences came as a surprise to Jim.

"As well as informing us about the changes in his health, Mr Thomas also wrote to request something of us. He recommended to us that upon his death, the position of lock keeper here in Banbury be transferred to yourself. He requested that the appointment be made formally at the time of his recommendation and put in writing so as to guarantee your continued employment after his absence. This, Mr Bailey, is that confirmation."

He stood up and handed the piece of paper to Jim. Jim opened it and looked over it carefully. It was just as the man had said. The document outlined the terms of employment and listed the duties he would have. It stated the annual salary he would receive and also included the agreement to live in the lockhouse. Jim blinked and looked up at the man.

"I never knew anything about this," he said, trying to take it in.

"Mr Thomas insisted that this be kept confidential until after he had passed."

"He told me," Myriam whispered quietly and all three of them looked at her.

"You knew about this?" asked Jim.

"Well, no not exactly, but he told me that he had made arrangements to look after us. He made me promise that I wouldn't say anything. I didn't understand what he meant when he said it, but this must have been what he was talking about."

"The crafty old beggar!" laughed Jim and stood up to shake the men's hands and to thank them.

"Not at all," they replied. "You've already been doing the job for years now. You even continued these last few weeks despite having received no news from us. You're the obvious choice for the new lock keeper. Even if Mr Thomas hadn't made this agreement, we'd have been approaching you with an offer, I dare say."

The two men left and Jim turned to Myriam with a look of disbelief on his face.

"I can't believe it, can you?"

She shrugged and smiled. "He was so fond of you. He wasn't going to leave you without employment."

Jim looked around at the room they were in. It was a small room, not as big and airy as his mother's. The entire house was a lot smaller than the one they had in Waterloo, but it had a little character of its own.

"Do you think you'll like living here?" he asked, stepping forwards and pulling her into his arms.

Myriam thought about the past few weeks and the other secret that she was still keeping from him. Was now the right time to say something? No, he was happy now. They had something new to look forward to. Myriam realised that she had somehow missed the 'right moment' to tell him about the miscarriage. She made a decision there and then that she wouldn't tell him. It didn't matter now anyway. She looked around the small lock keeper's cottage; it was lovely. They had enjoyed living in their house in Waterloo but there were painful memories stored within those walls – for both of them now. This cottage would be a new start. It would be a new little place to make their own and to call home. She rested her head against his shoulder and breathed in his smell.

"Yes," she replied. "I think I'm going to love living here."

Thirty-four

September 1841

Myriam opened the door to the hen-house to let the five clucking chickens out into their run. It was an area at the bottom of the garden that had been fenced off to stop them from getting into the vegetable beds. Chickens were useful birds, but they made a mess if left alone to roam wherever they pleased.

Jim and Myriam had moved into the lockhouse during July and had been busy making it their own. Myriam loved the new garden. It was a lot bigger than the garden they had left behind with the house at Waterloo. It stretched out, away from the house. At the far end of the garden, where Jim had built the chicken run and hen-house for her, Myriam could hear the faint babble of running water from the Cherwell River, which flowed only a stone's throw away from their hedgerow. She loved the soothing sound of moving water, and this far end of the garden was her favourite part.

It was a bit late in the year, but she had managed to plant out one of the three vegetable beds. She was looking forward to filling all of them the following year with lots of sweet, home-grown produce. Out here, behind the house, Myriam could forget that she was in the middle of a busy town with a bustling, active canal right outside the front door. In her garden she was able to transport herself back to her childhood and the happy days of her village upbringing.

Jim was content with their new home too. He was initially concerned about the emotions it might stir within him to live in the house that had belonged to the man who had meant so much to him. However, to his relief, he found that living in Mr Thomas' home gave him a sort of solace and contentment, helping to soften his grief.

It was particularly beneficial for Jim to be able to step outside the front door and directly into his workplace. It meant that he was able to spend more time close to Myriam during the day. She would prepare his lunch and bring him cups of tea. He enjoyed her constant company, knowing that she was never too far away from him.

Myriam was also getting to know some of the regular boatmen and their families who passed through the town. She found them all to be likeable, friendly people who were grateful for any kindness that was shown to them. So many tended to look down on the canal people, distrustfully labelling them as 'water gypsies'. Myriam could see that this was due to ignorance on the part of others, as they were, in fact, humble folk, generally quiet and unassuming. During the late summer, Myriam had spent hours picking various fruits and berries from the hedgerows alongside the canal. After taking them home and washing them, she had prepared dozens of jars of jams and jellies which she was now selling for a small fee to the boatmen and their wives. It gave her a sense of accomplishment and also provided her with an excuse to interact with the mysterious women who lived on the canal. Myriam was curious about the lives that these travelling women must live. It seemed so earthy and adventurous, and most certainly not without many hardships and discomforts. She admired the boatwomen and was grateful for the privilege to be a small part of their lives.

Leaving the chickens happily pecking around in the dirt for small bits of food, Myriam went back into the house and collected her basket and money purse. Putting on a hat and wrapping a shawl around her shoulders, she made her way outside through the front door. The hot summer weather was now behind them and winter was coming. A cool breeze cast ripples across the water and leaves floated through the air, some landing gently on the surface of the canal. Myriam looked up at the sky and smiled. She disliked the onset of winter and its long, dark nights but at least today the sun was shining brightly. As long as the days remained bright like this, she would be happy.

It was still early and Jim was busy with the swing bridge on the road. Keeping everything moving above and below the bridge was a juggling act at this time of the day. She decided not to disturb him. He knew she was heading to the market so he wouldn't be surprised to find her not at home later on.

Myriam arrived at the market and set about purchasing the few things that she needed. It was quieter than usual as Michaelmas was only about a month away and so a lot of the animal sales were being saved for the fair. The potato harvest had started too, meaning that many of the farmers were busy getting in the crops, and so had not made the journey into town. This was true of the Prices. Myriam found their usual place and was surprised to see only Mrs Price and Eliza standing at the stall. Eliza held Emeline in her arms. Mary and her brother were no doubt busy in the fields.

Myriam went over to say hello. She had been so busy since the move to the lockhouse that she hadn't found time to walk out to Bodicote and so hadn't seen the family for many weeks.

"Well, just look at you," gasped Myriam, taking hold of Emeline's little fingers and stroking them gently. "Haven't you grown?"

Myriam couldn't believe the difference in the little girl from when she had last seen her at the beginning of the summer.

Eliza smiled and lowered Emeline to ground.

"*Yes, Auntie Myriam*," responded Eliza using her best baby voice. "*I've grown a lot. Look I can even stand up by myself now!*"

Emeline clung onto the leg of the market stall to steady herself and stared at Myriam with big eyes.

"Oh my! Well done!" applauded Myriam. "You're a clever little girl."

As Myriam watched the small child wobble about, balancing herself on her unsteady legs, she contemplated her own feelings. Was she more drawn to the baby than she had been before her miscarriage? She didn't think so. She felt a strange wave of emotion but it wasn't sadness, or longing, or regret. It was more like an appreciation of the precious, little life that was in front of her.

Myriam had talked with Kitty only once about that night back in June. The conversation had been long and she had asked Kitty many questions about childbearing and childbirth. It was a subject that Kitty seemed to know a lot about, both from her own experiences and from those of others, and Myriam had learned much from her. At first Myriam had wondered if her situation was a rarity, if there was something wrong with her, but she had learned that to lose a baby was not actually uncommon. Nor was it uncommon to struggle to conceive. This was something that Myriam had wanted to share with Rose but that would mean telling Rose about what had happened, and she wasn't ready to do that. She still hadn't told Jim so there was no possibility that she could tell Rose.

There was one question that Kitty had not been able to answer though. Myriam had asked her if she would now feel differently. Prior to the miscarriage Myriam had not really felt any need to have a baby, certainly not in the same desperate way that Rose did. She was now worried that the loss of that child would create in her a strong desire to try for another.

She was relieved to find that the interaction she was having with Emeline was not provoking within her any obvious yearning or longing for a baby. She certainly found the small girl delightful and was drawn to her, but she felt no wistful, motherly pangs. Myriam was relieved about this because, in truth, she was scared. She was scared that if she felt those emotions then she may feel the need to purposely try and conceive again. That thought frightened her because she didn't want to lose another baby, not a second time.

Thirty-five

February 1842

Myriam had known that she was carrying a baby for about three weeks before she had her second miscarriage.

She had woken up one morning and gone downstairs to light the kitchen stove. Once the coals were burning, she placed a kettle full of water on top to steadily boil. It was cold outside. The night sky had been clear and full of bright, twinkling stars. Dawn was breaking but it was still dark. Taking a lantern down to the hen-house, Myriam smashed the ice that had formed on the water bowl and collected the eggs. They felt warm against the skin of her cold hand. She returned to the house and lit the fire in the front room. Back in the kitchen, steam was puffing out from the boiling kettle and so Myriam poured it into the teapot and left the tea to stew while she set about preparing some breakfast for Jim.

He had left the house earlier to break the ice around the lock. It was not as cold as it had been during previous weeks but the water on the gates still froze most nights. Jim was always outside early, before it got light, to ensure that everything was ready for when the boats would begin to arrive, shortly after daybreak.

Myriam poured herself a cup of tea and added some milk to it. She took a sip and placed it back on the table, frowning. It tasted strange, as if the milk was off. Thinking that it was odd that the milk was off already, especially with this cold weather, Myriam decided that they would have to drink their tea black. She didn't mind, they had always drunk their tea without milk when she had been a girl anyway.

Cracking four eggs into a pan, Myriam then went to take some bread from the parlour. Coming back into the kitchen, the smell of the warm yokes hit her senses and her stomach lurched violently. Her throat made a retching noise and she ran to throw the back door open. She managed to lean her head outside just in time as the muscles in her stomach and oesophagus contracted, causing her to vomit uncontrollably.

Wiping her mouth with a towel and taking a sip of cold water to wash away the bitter taste of bile, Myriam felt her hand shaking. She had been in this position before; the aversion to tea, the strong reaction to the taste and smell of eggs. It was the same as before, only this time she knew the reason for it. Myriam knew this time that she was expecting a baby.

She told Jim that evening when he finished work. She had gone back to bed after serving him his breakfast and he came in from the lock concerned about her.

"There's something I need to tell you," she said, holding out her hand and beckoning him to sit on the bed with her. "I think, I mean, I'm quite certain that I'm with child."

"With child?" he asked, clearly astonished.

231

"But how?"

Myriam raised her eyebrows at him.

"I mean, I know how. Obviously I do," he explained. "But you said that you're quite certain, how do you *know* that you're with child?" he asked.

Myriam told him about her sickness earlier that morning and about how that was a sign.

"I also know for certain because this happened before," she whispered softly.

He looked at her, confusion all over his face. "Before?"

"Yes. Do you remember last summer when I was poorly for a few weeks? It was the same time as Bill and Josephine's wedding and as..."

"As Mr Thomas' death," he interrupted. "Yes, I remember."

There was a moment while he recalled how she had been back then. He remembered her being very ill and he remembered being worried for her, especially when they had returned home from the wedding. After that it was a bit blurry, he could only remember waiting in the woodshed at the doctor's house and then going back to the lockhouse alone.

"But if that was... Then how?... What happened to...?" He couldn't finish the sentences or ask the questions. He realised what must have happened and he didn't want her to say it.

He reached out and stroked her face gently. "I'm sorry."

"Why are you sorry?" she asked.

"Because I wasn't there."

"Nonsense! Mr Thomas needed you. And besides, you weren't to know what was happening. I didn't even know what was happening until Kitty arrived and told me."

He nodded and leaned forward, giving her a soft kiss. She moved closer to him and they held each other tightly. She was relieved to have finally told him. It had felt like a heavy burden having this secret which she had never meant to keep from him. Now he knew and she felt like she could breathe freely again.

"Will it happen again?" he asked after a few minutes.

Myriam sat back and looked directly into his eyes.

"I honestly don't know," she replied.

He swallowed back a small lump of emotion that had formed in his throat.

"Are you scared?"

"A little bit," she nodded.

"If it does happen, I'll be here this time," he promised and pulled her close to him again.

Thirty-six

April 1843

It seemed to everyone that the day of Mary Price's marriage to Samuel Haynes would never come. Finally, after what had felt to Mary like an eternity, the long-awaited day arrived.

Mary and Eliza's younger brother Jacob had gradually taken over the farm work during the past year. Under the watchful direction of Mr Price, he was now capable of running everything with the help of some hired labourers when they were needed. Samuel and Mary officially began their courtship in December of the previous year but, much the same as it had been with Jim and Myriam, there had already been conversations and there was an understanding between them both. The courtship was therefore a mere formality. On the same day that the courtship was announced the date of the wedding had also been decided upon and now, to Mary's delight, that day was finally here.

It was a cool, spring morning. The night before had been clear and crisp and as the sun rose above the town, wisps of mist hovered above the cold surface of the canal. The white haze of cloud stretched across the low-lying fields to the River Cherwell. Jim and Myriam were both up earlier than usual to make a start on some of the tasks around the house and the lock. Jim had arranged for a young lad who worked in Mr Dickenson's coal shed to look after the lock for the day, but he wanted to deal with the level reports and a few other things himself before the boy arrived. Just before noon Jim and Myriam were both dressed in their best clothes, ready to make their way to Bodicote.

Walking along the tow path, the mist had lifted and there was a feeling that new life was bursting around them. Small lambs were bleating in the fields and blackbirds, thrushes and finches were singing loudly from the hedgerows. To the side of the tow path there was an array of colours. Shoots that had budded at the beginning of the month were now open and fresh leaves of all shades of green were filling the empty spaces between the branches. Yellow primroses and pink campions were shooting up from the verges. Every so often, dotted amongst the hedgerow, they passed wild fruit trees which were now beginning to blossom. Myriam breathed in deeply and could smell the faint floral scent from the creamy white flowers. Passing an apricot tree covered in snowflake-like petals, she reached out, picked a blossom and then took a small nibble from the petal. It tasted sweet and she could just about detect the mild flavour of the apricot fruit that the tree would produce months later. Jim shook his head and smiled at her.

"You're always eating something from the hedgerows," he laughed and took hold of her hand.

"Mother used to take us out for walks regularly and teach us about what we could eat. We'd often return home with baskets full of goodies." She smiled at the memory and squeezed his hand.

She thought how nice this was, just the two of them walking along together. Running the lock was a busy job and Jim rarely allowed himself a break. Once the sun had set each day, they would enjoy time together in and around the lockhouse but to have this moment to themselves during the working day was a precious gift.

After her second miscarriage, just over a year earlier, there had been a few moments when she had felt that a slight distance had developed between them. Myriam had struggled for some time to enjoy intimacy together, afraid of what it may result in. Jim had never complained, he loved her too much to do that, but she knew that they had briefly, for a short time, felt somewhat detached from each other. She had worked hard to reconnect though, both emotionally and physically, and it thankfully hadn't been too long before they had returned to their usual comfortable, content existence.

They crossed the canal, climbed the hill to Bodicote and arrived at St John's chapel in plenty of time for the wedding. The north side of the chapel was surrounded in timber scaffolding. This small church was desperately in need of renovation and plans were under way to begin much needed repairs. The tower had been declared unsafe and so was being pulled down. Work had not yet begun on the inside but there was talk of extending the aisles, renovating the windows and completely renewing the pews in order to create more room for the growing congregation.

Myriam had many memories of this small churchyard as a child; running around after services with Eliza, Mary and other children from the village whilst their parents stopped to talk with one another.

They made their way inside and Myriam could see that it really was in need of repair. She felt that it looked quite neglected. They sat down on a creaky, old pew and it wasn't long before Rose and Tom arrived and joined them. They had driven in from town using one of the coaching inn's small carts. Jim and Myriam were planning to ride back with them that evening.

Myriam greeted Rose warmly. She had consciously pulled away from her sister over the past eighteen months but she was now pleased to see her on this happy occasion. Afraid to tell Rose about the loss of the two babies, Myriam had found that it was easier to avoid spending prolonged time together and any conversations that would inevitably take place as a result. Brushing her seclusion off as a result of being tied up with matters at the lockhouse, she had kept her association with Rose limited to brief, public occasions such as at the marketplace. It pained Myriam to have this withdrawn, parted relationship with her sister and she sensed that Rose felt the same, but Myriam couldn't face the reality of what Rose's reaction would be to her own pitiable struggles.

The inside of the church was full and it wasn't long before Mary and her father arrived. Rays of light from the stained-glass windows poured onto Mary's exuberant face. Myriam glanced over at Samuel as he watched his bride walking towards him. Samuel had always been a quiet boy when they used to all play together. As small children, Mary's vivacious character had sometimes scared him away, even reducing him to tears at times. However, as they had grown up, they had both become drawn to each other.

He found her zest for life excited him and she found him to be the calming influence that she had needed when things on the farm had become fraught. Completely opposite in nature, they complemented each other perfectly.

The small service began and Myriam listened, watching Mary as she stole quick, happy glances at everyone around her. Myriam knew how she was feeling. There had been a time when she too had thought that her own wedding day may never come. Myriam recalled the disbelief she had felt when she had put on her gown, and then entered the church and seen Jim there, waiting for her. It had been the happiest day of her life.

Jim nudged against her shoulder and leaned closer to whisper in her ear.

"Who is the rather sullen looking chap over in the corner?"

Myriam looked around and her eyes rested on George Webb. It was true, he looked very moody and sulky. George had also grown up in the village, although his family were not from a farming background. He had played with them all as children but Myriam had never really liked him. He had been a sly and malicious child, having been overindulged and pampered by his mother. It wasn't a secret that George had always had his heart set on Mary, but Myriam knew that her friend would never have been interested in him. Mary was kind at heart and that was what had drawn her to Samuel with his equally amiable manner. George was still devious in his ways, always pushing himself ahead, often to the detriment of others. No; sadly for him, Mary had never returned the feelings.

"That's George Webb," she replied, keeping her voice low. "He's always wanted to marry Mary. To be honest I can't imagine why he's here, other than to torture himself."

Samuel and Mary were soon saying their vows to each other and Myriam couldn't help but notice the emotional tears that Mr Price was failing to hold back. He owed a lot to Mary and it warmed Myriam's heart to see his love and appreciation for the sacrifices that his daughter had made. Little Emeline, now two years old and wearing a beautiful white dress, was acting as both flower girl and ring-bearer. She shyly handed them their wedding rings, giving each of them a kiss on the cheek as she did so. A gentle murmur of endearment sounded through the room as everyone in the congregation 'cooed' at her.

Once Samuel and Mary had been introduced to everyone as 'Mr and Mrs Haynes', they made their way up the aisle together towards the exit. Mary skipped her way out of the church almost dragging Samuel along with her. The wedding guests gathered for a while outside, taking it in turns to congratulate the newly-weds. Soon though, dark heavy clouds drifted over above their heads, blocking the bright rays of sunlight. As small drops of rain started to fall upon them, Mary lifted up the hem of her skirt, grabbed Samuel by the arm and shouted out to everyone, "Quick! First one to the barn gets extra home-made wine!"

Thirty-seven

Jim and Myriam arrived at the Prices' barn breathless and damp from the rain shower. Stepping inside and straightening out her crumpled skirt Myriam gasped at the transformation that had taken place inside the building, which was usually used to store hay and animal feed.

Bunting and paper streamers were hanging from around the walls. Vases holding simple flower arrangements had been placed in the centres of tables, and small lanterns were dotted around. It looked magical.

"Someone has been hard at work in here," wheezed Rose, trying to catch her breath from the exertion of running.

"Yes," agreed Myriam. "And I'll give you one guess who it was." Looking around she caught sight of Eliza, who had also walked in from the rain but more resembled someone who had taken a leisurely walk on a dry, sunny afternoon. Always immaculate in every way, everything that Eliza touched seemed to turn to gold and the decorations in the barn were a testimony to that.

Tom appeared beside them carrying two glasses of wine.

"It might not be ale, but Mrs Price's home-made wine is the next best thing."

He handed a glass to Rose and chinked his own

against it, giving her a little kiss at the same time.

"Cheers love."

Rose smiled and took a sip.

"Oooh yes, it is delicious! Jim, Myriam are you going to get some?"

Jim didn't usually drink alcohol. He had seen too many drunkards passing by the back streets in town and he didn't like what the effects of fermented liquid did to the human mind and body; but he made exceptions on special occasions and today was one of those occasions.

"I'll go and get us a glass," he said, and made his way over to where the wine was being served.

"I wonder what we'll be eating?" said Rose. Her stomach was making rumbling noises at her.

"I thought I could smell something delicious on the way in," Myriam replied. "I imagine whatever it is, if Eliza has taken care of the preparation, then it will be outstanding."

Jim returned with his and Myriam's wine just as Samuel clapped his hands to get everyone's attention.

"Firstly, thank you all for coming. Mary and I made it at last!" he shouted joyfully and everyone laughed. "You'll be pleased to know that the rain has stopped which is a good thing as the food is outside. There are no formal seating arrangements so sit wherever you want, with whomever you want. Enjoy the dinner and later we'll have a good jig to celebrate!"

There was a cry of three cheers and everyone made their way outside to collect their food. It was a simple meal of warm, crusty rolls, filled with hot slices of pork that had been cooking over a fire since the morning. Myriam was right, everything was outstanding and no one complained about a thing. There was plenty of wine to go around and as the evening continued, all the guests enjoyed a relaxed and happy party.

Once the music began, Jim and Myriam danced and danced until their feet were sore. Myriam's cheeks shone a rosy hue of red as she jumped and spun around. Jim was also enjoying himself. As their fifth dance ended and everyone applauded, he looked over at Myriam and smiled. They hadn't had such a relaxed, memorable evening as this for a long time. Life at the lock had become so busy. He thought back to the days when they had first met and everything in his life had centred around those Friday evenings each month when they could be together. It reminded him very much of those days, dancing with her now.

Panting for breath and in need of water, they stepped outside into the cool night air. A few small fires had been lit within small circles of stone about the farmyard and guests were grouped together around them, keeping warm while they talked to each other. Tom, having drunk quite a lot of the wine, was talking in a loud, animated voice to someone nearby. Jim and Myriam moved away and stood at the edge of the farmyard.

"What's that noise?" asked Jim hearing a distressed bleating from one of the nearby sheds. From the cracks between the doors, they could see the flicker of a lantern inside.

"Let's go and see," said Myriam, walking over

towards the shed.

Slowly easing open the door revealed to them Jacob. He was on kneeling the ground and fussing over a clearly uncomfortable ewe.

"Jacob, is everything all right?" asked Myriam.

Jacob looked up, his face was flushed and he looked worried.

"She's a maiden ewe, and it's not going too well."

"I thought lambing was finished," commented Myriam.

"Mostly it is, we've just got half a dozen left over and this one's decided on tonight," he puffed out his cheeks. "I'm not sure if the lamb will make it, seems to me it's taking too long."

In the shadows of the barn Myriam could indeed see the shapes of other sheep, all fat and heavy with lambs. They were resting on the soft bedding of straw while awaiting their moment to give birth. She turned her attention to the ewe which Jacob was dealing with. The animal was lying on the ground and looked a little distressed.

"Shall I fetch someone to help?"

"No," Jacob replied. "It's Mary's night, I've got to do this myself."

"Then I'll help you," said Myriam dropping to her knees and rolling up the sleeves on her dress. Jacob stared at her. "Jacob, I've helped with lambing on this farm since before you were born."

He nodded and moved aside to let her see. Myriam had a quick look, the lamb's head was already partway out but Myriam couldn't see the front legs.

"We're going to have to get those legs out first. You need to push the head back in and pull them. You know how to do that don't you?" she asked.

"Yes, of course, it's just the ewe won't stay still."

"Not to worry, I'll hold her while you pull the lamb."

Myriam took a firm hold of the sheep who, despite being tired, was fighting against them. Myriam held her tightly and spoke softly while Jacob pushed the head back and then reached his hand in to find the lamb's front legs. Locating them, he grabbed hold of the lamb's hooves and slowly pulled the small, slimy baby out from the back of its mother. Carefully easing the head out he laid it on the ground.

"Check it's breathing," reminded Myriam.

Jacob cleared the lamb's nostrils and placed it in front of the ewe's head. She was tired though and didn't take any notice of her new baby.

"Jacob, do you have any sugar water ready?" asked Myriam.

"Yes, but it's in the house."

"Jim, would you be able to get it?" Myriam looked at Jim. He had been standing, watching with his mouth open wide, amazed. "Jim!"

He snapped into action. "Yes, of course. I'll go now."

Jim fetched the sugary water which they gave to the weary mother. She failed to respond to the lamb though and it seemed to Myriam that something still wasn't right.

"Jacob, I think she may have twins," she said,

watching the movements of the sheep's side.

"Yes, you could be right."

"Can you check?"

Jacob reached inside and nodded. "You're right, but I think it's facing the wrong way."

"Can you turn it?" she asked.

Jacob's eyebrows knitted together anxiously. "I've never done that before."

"Not to worry." Myriam stood up. "Swap places with me, and Jim, can you help us, we need to get her standing up.

Jim helped to get the ewe in a standing position and they grabbed armfuls of straw which they bunched up under the sheep so that her back legs hung down slightly.

"Now, hold her still," instructed Myriam, as she reached her arm inside the ewe.

Moving her hand about, Myriam could feel a tangle of legs. She looked across at Jacob.

"I think she's having more than twins, there's still two in here."

Gently she began to move the lambs around, gradually separating them from one another while being careful to not cause any injury to the mother. After a while, she had the first lamb facing the right way.

"Now we need to get her to lay down again," she instructed Jacob and he pulled the ewe onto her side and held her. Slowly Myriam began to pull the lamb out, easing the head out too. The second lamb slipped out onto the ground and Myriam beckoned Jim to come closer.

"Here, you can do this bit," she said taking his hand. "Wipe the fluid clear of its mouth and nostrils."

Jim broke the sac of viscous liquid and pulled it away from the lamb's face.

"Now, take a piece of straw and just tickle it's nose, like you saw Jacob do earlier."

Jim did as she said and the lamb began to cough and snort as air filled its lungs.

"Incredible," he choked, amazed by what Myriam had been capable of doing.

"It's not over yet," she smiled.

The third lamb was in the correct position. As the feet emerged from within the mother, Myriam again gently aided the head out and the body then followed. Breaking the fluid sac, and wiping the liquid from the lamb's nostrils, Myriam waited a few moments. With no reaction from the tiny creature, she took hold of the back legs and held the lamb upside down. Its lungs soon reacted and the lamb started breathing.

Myriam held the small, floppy creature and cradled it for a moment in her arms. It was slimy and covered in messy liquid but Myriam didn't mind. She felt a small wave of emotion come over her. It gave her a strange sense of fulfilment to have helped this little thing into the world, she felt warm inside because of it. Myriam carefully placed the lamb beside its mother. Revived now by the sugar water she was already beginning to clean the first two lambs. For a moment it seemed that she might ignore this third one but they waited, and soon she gave it the attention it too needed.

"Keep an eye on her," advised Myriam,

standing up. "Make sure she is feeding them all. She will most probably struggle to nurse all three. You may need to raise one yourself, or try to adopt it onto another ewe."

"I'll see how she goes," replied Jacob. "Thank you. I think you saved all their lives tonight."

Myriam smiled weakly. The burst of energy that had come over her when she had leapt into action had now left her feeling tired.

"I'm sure you would have managed it, but I'm glad I could help." She felt her legs shake a little beneath her and turned to Jim. "I think it may be time to go home."

He nodded. She didn't need to explain how she was feeling. He had seen the look in her eyes as she had cradled the small lamb and he knew that it had been a special moment for her.

They stepped outside the shed and went to look for Tom and Rose to see if they were ready to leave. Tom was still outside in the yard, now shouting angrily at another guest. Myriam had no idea what had riled him, but she could see that he was under the influence of the wine. Rose and Andrew were gently coaxing him, trying to calm him down. She sighed and looked at Jim.

"I'll deal with it," he said and patted her gently on the arm.

Jim went to get the pony and cart. He lit a couple of lanterns to take along with them and then pulled up alongside the yard.

"Get in Tom. It's time to go," Jim said firmly.

Tom turned his vexation towards Jim. "What

are you doing driving my cart?"

"No questions Tom. You get in, or you walk."

Myriam wasn't sure if Tom would protest but Jim's voice was both calm and forceful. Everyone around them watched, waiting to see what would happen next. Jim held Tom's defiant stare until Tom was forced to look away first.

"Right then," said Jim, as Tom was helped into the back of the cart by an embarrassed Rose. "Let's get back to Banbury, shall we?"

Thirty-eight

A few days after Samuel and Mary's wedding, Myriam walked up to the coaching inn to see Rose. It had been months since she had paid a visit to her sister but she felt that she needed to now, especially after what had happened with Tom at the wedding. He had fallen asleep in the back of the cart on the way home and so caused no further upset or confrontations, but Myriam wanted to speak with Rose, just to make sure that everything was all right.

She felt nervous. She knew that since the miscarriages she had been avoiding Rose and now it seemed strange to be seeking her out. Myriam felt sad and disappointed with herself for allowing their close relationship to suffer as she had. It had been no fault of Rose's. It was all Myriam's doing and she knew that wasn't fair on Rose. Approaching the inn, she felt ashamed of her cowardly behaviour.

She arrived in the yard and went over to the kitchen door. She had timed her visit to coincide with the end of the breakfast rush. Most of the staff usually had time then to take a short break and she hoped that Rose would be able to do so today.

Josephine was outside, with Bill, sitting on a small bench beside the kitchen door. She saw Myriam and got up to meet her.

"Oh, I feel like I haven't seen you for so long!" she cried. "But look at you! You look so well. Life as a lock keeper's wife must suit you."

Myriam smiled. Josephine was such a sweet girl.

"I can see that married life is treating you well too," she said, glancing at the small bump on Josephine's stomach. "Rose told me when I saw her at the wedding about your news. Congratulations to you both!"

Bill stood up and wrapped his arm around Josephine.

"We're both very excited."

"And so you should be," smiled Myriam.

"Are you looking for Rose?" asked Bill.

"Yes, I was hoping to catch her while she had time for a short break."

"She's taken her break at home today," said Josephine. "I think she needed to sort a few things out for Tom."

"Oh really?" Myriam had no idea what could need sorting out for Tom.

"Yes, he's going to collect young Mr Hamilton from Oxford later today. It's all everyone can talk about here, Mr Hamilton I mean, not Tom."

Myriam laughed. "No, I expect talk about Tom isn't an overly exciting subject, but I'm interested to hear about young Mr Hamilton. I'll go and find Rose. Perhaps she can fill me in on all the gossip I've missed since not working here."

Myriam made her way across the yard to the small lodging that Tom and Rose had at the back of the stables. Tom was hitching two horses up to the large coach that belonged to old Mr Hamilton. She called out 'hello' to him and then went on to knock at

Rose's door. Pushing it open she leaned in and called out. Rose appeared from behind a doorway carrying a basket of food.

"Myriam, duckie. Well, what a nice surprise! Come in. I just need to give this to Tom so he can get going and then I'll be back with you."

Rose ran out with the basket and returned a few moments later having given it to Tom. Myriam heard the sound of hooves and looked out the window to see Tom driving the coach out of the yard.

"What's this I hear about young Mr Hamilton returning?" asked Myriam.

"Yes, everyone is very excited about it. You must remember him?"

"Of course I do. He moved to London about a year after we started working here."

"That's correct," said Rose. "I didn't realise but apparently the Hamiltons have another establishment in London. It's a hotel, I think. It's located somewhere in the centre of town, or did they say it was out by Richmond? Anyway, young Mr Hamilton has been there all this time. He was being trained to run the place by whoever it is that has been running it, some manager or something, I think."

Myriam smiled to herself at Rose's way of relaying information. Half of the facts were always missing but that was what made it so interesting to listen to her.

Rose continued, "Apparently old Mrs Hamilton wants to return to London to be closer to her family and so Mr and Mrs Hamilton are planning to move back sometime over the summer. Miss Jane already married a couple of years ago if you remember and

251

now has a little girl I heard, so I expect that they will enjoy living closer to her too."

Myriam remembered the Hamilton's daughter Jane. They were about the same age. Miss Jane had always been kept very strictly in the private part of the inn, the area that belonged to the Hamiltons, and had never been permitted to mix with the staff. Myriam had sometimes seen her when she used to go out somewhere with her mother. She remembered her looking like a kind, yet quiet girl. As soon as she had come of age Miss Jane was engaged to a banker in London and had moved away. Myriam hadn't heard anything of her since.

"Anyway, to cut a long story short, young Mr Hamilton is moving back here to run the inn in the place of his father," concluded Rose.

"And does he have any family? A wife, or children?" asked Myriam. She was curious. Young Mr Hamilton had left years ago but she remembered him well. He loved being in the yard, chatting with the stable boys. Everyone had liked him very much.

"A wife yes, but no children."

"It all sounds very exciting," agreed Myriam. "But why has Tom gone to collect him, what has happened to old Mr Hamilton's personal coachman?"

"He's unwell this week." Rose stepped forward and clutched Myriam's hand enthusiastically. "This is the most exciting part! If everything goes well today, this could be Tom's chance of a raise. Everyone's commenting about it. Young Mr Hamilton will want to run things his way, he may well have a shuffle about of the staff. The first person he'll see today is Tom. I hope he makes a good impression. Wouldn't it be wonderful if Tom moved up to the position of personal coachman?!"

Myriam nodded and tried to look as excited as she could but Rose knew her better.

"What? Don't you think our Tom is good enough for a raise, or a promotion?" she asked.

"Of course I do," assured Myriam, thinking carefully about her choice of words. "It's just, well...do you think he would be reliable enough? It's quite a responsibility."

"My Tom is very reliable!"

"Yes, I know he is," agreed Myriam. It was true, Tom could be a very dependable person, but he had let them all down on the night of Mary's wedding. "It's just that sometimes, if he's had a drink, he's not quite so reliable."

Rose let go of Myriam's hand and stepped back. "What happened at the wedding was a one off, an accident. Poor Tom is accustomed to drinking ale. That wine was very strong in comparison. Before he had a chance to realise that, it was too late."

Myriam sighed and smiled. What Rose had said was true. Mrs Price's home-made wine had been quite strong. She had also felt its effects immediately that evening.

Rose shrugged. "Tom is very sorry that he caused a bit of fuss. He's been ever so apologetic about it."

Myriam nodded. "I'm sure he has been. Rose, I know Tom is well meaning. It's just that, well to be honest, I do worry about his drinking."

"Only because we had a father that wouldn't

touch the stuff and you have a husband who is very much the same. Most men work hard to provide for their families and then have a little bit of time with their friends, chatting over a drink or two."

Myriam pondered the point that Rose was making. It was true, even Luke frequented the ale establishments at the end of a busy week and Kitty had no issue with it. Maybe Rose was right and she had a very unbalanced view of everything. Jim was quite unusual in his habits when compared to other men and her opinions were based on this experience and that of a father who insisted that alcohol had come from the devil.

"Yes, Tom works very hard," she conceded. "I hope that he does get a raise or a promotion."

There was a moment of silence. It felt awkward, and Myriam wished for a moment that they could go back to being just the two of them, at home in Bodicote with their parents. Back to a time before the coaching inn, or Tom or even Jim had ever been dreamed about. But she knew that could never happen. Time moves on, circumstances change and it is important to keep on enjoying the good things that you have. Myriam stepped forward and gave Rose a kiss on the cheek.

"What was that for?" Rose asked.

"I've missed you," shrugged Myriam.

"I've missed you too, duckie. You should pop by more often."

Myriam nodded. "Yes, I should," she agreed, and made a promise to herself that she would do.

Thirty-nine

March 1844

The winter that spanned eighteen forty-three and eighteen forty-four was long and cold. The autumn months that led up to it had been exceptionally mild and wet. This meant that when the temperatures suddenly dropped overnight, it had caught everyone by surprise. Morning after morning, the ground was covered in thick frost and the air was icy. Even on the brightest days, the sun still failed to melt the ice where it had frozen on the ground.

The freezing temperatures resulted in even more work for Jim. He had spent most of the days over the past few months breaking the ice on the canal. Each morning, he would wake to find the lock completely frozen with the gates stuck solidly together. The thick layers of ice on the canal meant that, until the ice breakers had been through, many of the boats made slow progress. Important deliveries were late in arriving and as a result some necessities had to be rationed. It was hard for many. Things were hard for the canal people, hard for the businessmen and hard for the townsfolk.

Myriam was certain that she had never seen so much snow in one winter. Day after day she cleared the pathway through the garden which led to the chicken run. Even now, almost halfway through the month of March, the snow continued to fall and she woke, once again, to the sight of a white blanket covering the world outside her window. She dressed, put on her winter coat and made her way down the garden to check on the hens and collect their eggs.

Reaching the run, she saw that once again, a hole had been dug out overnight from beneath the fence and the catch on the hen-house door was broken. Her heart sank as she quickly climbed into the run and looked inside the house. Feathers flew out at her, and making a quick count she was dismayed to see that one of the chickens was missing.

"Oh Enid," she sighed.

This was the second time that the fox had managed to get into the run and catch one of her chickens. Myriam couldn't help but cry. She knew it was silly. They were only birds but, in the absence of any children to care for, her hens had become her much loved little girls. She had even named them. A few days ago, it had been poor Ethel's feathers that the fox had left behind. Myriam couldn't help it, she was devastated when something happened to them.

Walking back to the lockhouse, she despondently made breakfast and thought about what needed to be done that day. With two hens having been taken in the last week they were now low on chickens and therefore low on eggs. Having decided to go into the market and see about buying some new hens, she finished up her jobs in the house and, after letting Jim know where she was going, headed off towards the marketplace.

Myriam arrived at the marketplace and immediately went over to where Mary and Eliza had their stalls. She always made sure to pop and say hello to her friends first in case they had anything that she was looking for. Eliza was there with Andrew.

"Did you leave Emeline at home today?" asked Myriam.

"Yes, it's far too cold for her to be standing idly here beside us all day," replied Eliza.

"And what about Mary?" questioned Myriam. "It's not like her to stay at home."

Eliza smiled and stole a glance at Andrew.

"She's not too well." Eliza leaned forward and whispered into Myriam's ear. "I'll tell you because you're her oldest friend. Between you and me, I think that she is expecting."

"Really?" gasped Myriam.

"I can't be sure, but I do know the signs. I'm almost certain that a little cousin for Emeline is on the way."

"Well, if so then I'm happy for her," said Myriam. "Once this cold weather has passed, I'll walk out to see her."

Eliza was about to respond when Josephine appeared beside them carrying her small baby girl. Although Bill was still working at the inn, Bill and Josephine had moved into a small house of their own across the other side of the town and so Myriam hadn't seen Josephine since her baby had been born. Myriam peered at the sleeping girl, wrapped up tightly in a blanket and told Josephine that she was the prettiest little baby she had ever seen. She also thought that Josephine looked very well and it was clear that she was content in her new role as a mother.

"Myriam, is everything well with Rose?" asked

Josephine.

"Yes, I think so," replied Myriam. "Why do you ask? Have you reason to think otherwise?"

"Only that Bill asked me if I minded collecting a few things for the inn. He said that Rose has been off work for almost a week and I thought that was very unlike her."

Myriam frowned. Josephine was right; Rose never got sick and certainly never took time off work. Something must be wrong.

"Do you have the things for the inn already?" Myriam asked.

"Yes, I was about to drop them off on my way home."

"If you like, I can take them," offered Myriam. "That way I can look in on Rose at the same time."

"That's a perfect idea," agreed Josephine and handed her the basket.

Once at the inn, Myriam delivered the basket to the kitchen and then went over and knocked gently on Rose's door. After a few moments Rose answered. She was pale and looked tired, as though she had hardly slept.

"I heard that you've not been well," said Myriam, stepping inside and closing the door behind her. It felt cold inside the small room. The fire had been lit but was dying out so she went over to stoke some life into it.

"I'm sorry," apologised Rose, sitting in an armchair and wrapping a blanket around herself. "I meant to keep that alight but I didn't have the energy."

Myriam looked around the room and noticed the bowl at the side of the chair. It looked as though Rose had been vomiting.

"What is it? Have you eaten something bad?"

"No, I don't think so."

"Have you caught some sort of sickness from someone?"

Rose shook her head.

"What is it then?"

Rose looked up at Myriam and smiled faintly. As their eyes met and Myriam saw the small sparkle in her sister's tired, fragile eyes she knew what was causing her sickness.

"You're with child!"

"I think, I think..." Tears rolled down Rose's face as she tried to speak and Myriam rushed over to her. Rose was nodding, it was clear to Myriam that she was trying to say that yes, she thought that she was finally expecting a baby.

Myriam knelt beside her and held her hands tightly.

"No one deserves this more than you do!"

Rose laughed. "I can hardly believe it. I've dreamed for so long about this. If I didn't feel so sick, I would run and jump for joy. But I don't want to count my chickens before they hatch."

At first Myriam didn't understand what Rose meant. Her thoughts went to poor Enid and Ethel who had been taken by the fox.

Rose read the confused look on her face. "Some women get this far and then lose the baby. I've heard about it."

Myriam stood up and clutched onto a nearby table to steady herself. Was now the time to reveal her secret to Rose? No, she decided, not today. Instead, she steered the conversation in a different direction.

"Well, from what I hear, you're not the only one hatching a chicken just now."

"Really, who else is?" asked Rose.

"I just found out that Mary is at home displaying symptoms very much like your own."

"Oh Myriam, wouldn't that be wonderful for Mary and I to carry children together and then to watch them grow up together?"

"Yes," agreed Myriam with a smile. "That would be wonderful."

<u>Forty</u>

October 1844

Rose and Mary did spend the next few months carrying their unborn babies together. The cold winter ended and the spring months which followed were mild but wet. It felt as though spring never ended and it wasn't until the end of August that the country was hit by an Indian summer. By this time, both Rose and Mary were carrying large bumps in front of them and the hot, sticky heat made everything very uncomfortable.

Up until then Rose had successfully continued working. She was blessed with naturally good stamina and a work ethic to rival any man. As a result, she had been able to keep doing her jobs in the kitchen. Young Mr Hamilton was visibly impressed with her and frequently commended her for her hard work and efforts.

The changeover of management at the inn had gone smoothly. In July, old Mr Hamilton and his wife had made their move back to London, leaving everything under the care of their capable son. Everyone that Myriam spoke to praised him as an employer and said that they had never worked under someone so reasonable and kind. Tom had indeed been promoted, as Rose had hoped he would be, to Mr Hamilton's personal coachman and as a result had received a wage increase. It was good timing with the baby on the way.

The warm, late summer had continued almost until the end of September and Myriam had enjoyed spending as much time outside as she could. She enjoyed being out by the lock, chatting with passers-by and watching Jim while he worked.

He also loved her company. It was busy work, running the lock and keeping the road traffic moving at the same time but it made him content to have her nearby. He would often glance over to her from across the canal and smile as he caught sight of her daydreaming. Her attention would be on some small bird flitting about in search of worms or a butterfly resting its tired wings in the warm sunlight. Jim's days were so occupied, so tied up in the boats and the continual opening and closing of the lock gates that he rarely took time to stop and enjoy what was around him. Myriam though, never let a moment go by without noticing the small things. It was only when Jim observed her watching something that he too then saw it and also paused for a moment to appreciate it. She opened his eyes to so many things.

Late one Friday afternoon, Jim and Myriam were sitting together outside the lockhouse. The canal was calm for a change and Jim was enjoying a brief moment of rest. At the market the previous day, Eliza had excitedly informed Myriam that Mary had given birth to a healthy baby boy. Myriam was delighted and was now happily telling Jim the news. She was debating whether it would be possible to walk out to the Haynes' farm the next day to see her friend and her new little baby. 'David' was the name that Eliza said he had been given. Myriam was eager to meet little David Haynes.

It was Jim who saw the young boy run across the lock gate and approach them. Standing up, he intended to reprimand the boy for rushing across the high, narrow gate in the faded, evening light. The boy spoke first though, not giving Jim a chance to say anything.

"Mrs Bailey, please?" spluttered the boy in anxious, hurried words.

Myriam stood up. "That's me. What is it boy?" She recognised the child, although she wasn't sure where from.

"It's Mrs Watkins. I've been told to send for you. Her baby is coming."

Of course. This boy was the grandchild of the cook at the inn. They must have sent him to fetch Myriam. She clutched at Jim's arm.

"Rose's baby is on the way! What use am I? How am I to know what to do?" she cried to him.

Jim thought for a moment. Myriam seemed slightly panicked and it was very unlike her to get flustered at anything. She must feel anxious about what her role would be in this matter.

"Why don't you see if Kitty will go with you? She's had enough children of her own and I know she has attended many other births in her time," he suggested.

"Of course!" Myriam kissed him. "Kitty is the perfect person to assist."

Myriam ran inside the house to collect her coat and a lantern. It was now almost dark and the temperature had dropped. "I'll go to Kitty right away and see if she will come with me."

Kitty was more than willing to assist Myriam and quickly packed a basket full of towels to take with them. They both arrived at the inn as the last of the daylight had faded on the horizon. Light was flickering across the stable yard from Rose's window and with a quick knock on the door, they let themselves in. Myriam was relieved to see that Ingrid, the head cook was there. It was her grandson that had been sent to the lock to call for Myriam. Ingrid had three children of her own and seven grandchildren.

Rose was upstairs in the bedroom. The small fireplace was roaring with crackling logs and a kettle of water was hanging above the flames. The room felt warm and Rose looked hot. Her hair was already plastered down her neck, wet from the perspiration that was covering Rose's face and body.

Taking off her coat, Kitty opened the small window a little.

"It's a good thing you have the fire and water ready but we need to keep Rose comfortable," Kitty said, thanking Ingrid for her efforts. She was gracious with her words, not wanting to step on the older woman's toes in any way.

Looking around, Myriam could see that there were just the four of them in the room. They had passed no one else on their way through the small house and up the stairs.

"Where's Tom?" she asked.

At that moment a contraction came over Rose and she yelled out at the pain. Kitty pressed a cool towel across her neck and held her hand.

"Have you timed how far apart they are?" she asked, once the contraction had subsided.

"Yes, they are at about ten minutes," said Ingrid.

"Well, that is good news. Hopefully we'll have a new little baby here before the end of the day," smiled Kitty.

Myriam went over to Rose and stroked her face. Rose smiled up at her.

"I don't know where Tom is," she said. "Some of the lads have gone to search for him."

Myriam tried not to frown. It was Friday, she knew exactly where Tom would be and she didn't like it.

"I'm sure he'll be here soon," she assured Rose.

For the next hour not much changed. Rose kept getting contractions and in between they talked happily together about town gossip. Once the contractions were just two minutes apart Rose told them that she was feeling an urge to push. Kitty told her to resist it until they were one minute apart. Before long she informed Rose that it was time to start pushing.

As the next contraction came Rose began to push. She had been pushing for some time when there was a noise from downstairs and a door banged. Rose was crying out at the exertion when a voice called up to them.

"Rose, Rose, is that you?"

"Tom!" she cried gasping for breath.

Myriam went down to him. For a brief moment she felt pity for him. He was standing there, twisting his cap in his hands and clearly distressed by the noise that he had heard coming from upstairs. But then as she stepped forward, she could smell the sweet ale on his breath and her pity for him left.

"The baby is coming," she said, plainly stating the facts.

"And, is everything all right?" he asked.

"Yes, I think so," she replied. Angered to think that he had been sitting in some alehouse all this time, she kept her words short and to the point. "Will you wait down here or outside?"

"Erm, I think it would be best if I wait outside," he hesitated, before heading towards the door. "I'll be in the stables if you need me."

"Tom," called Myriam, as he went to pull the door closed behind him. "Make sure you stay nearby. Rose needs you here."

He nodded and pulled the door to. Myriam made her way back upstairs. Rose looked at her as she came over to the bed and dabbed a cool cloth onto her sister's flushed face.

"Is Tom here?" Her eyes were wide and wild, tired already from the exertion.

"Yes," she smiled. "He'll be waiting right outside."

"Good," sighed Rose. "Let's hope he's not waiting too long."

Kitty was fussing about at the other end of the bed, examining Rose. She looked up at them both and Myriam saw the concerned looked on her face.

"What is it?" asked Myriam, not sure what to expect at this stage.

"It's not the head I can see and what I'm feeling is far too soft. I think the baby is breech."

Forty-one

"I think we may need to send for a doctor. Although, I'm not sure if there is time to wait," said Kitty, standing up and wiping her hands on a towel.

"Surely we don't need a doctor. Can't you manage it?" protested Rose. Her voice was weak and she was tiring from all the effort that she had exerted until now. She was reluctant to have a man attend to her.

Myriam frowned. Why was Kitty so concerned? Lambs were in the breech position all the time and it was just a matter of turning them.

"Can't we turn it? I've turned lambs many times?" she asked innocently.

Kitty shook her head and smiled kindly. "It's a bit different with a human baby."

Myriam nodded and stole a glance at Rose. She seemed exhausted and the energy appeared to be draining from her.

"Is it necessary to send for a doctor?" asked Myriam

"I'm afraid it is," Kitty replied. "I attended a breech birth a few years ago. It's an extremely delicate and skilled thing to deliver the baby safely, with very little room for error. I assisted the doctor at that time and I'm fairly confident that I can remember what was done. With Rose so far along, I'm concerned about whether we have time to wait for the doctor, but I would like to send for him anyway. If we need to, I'll start delivering as best I can."

Kitty looked at them all, from one to the other, each in turn and they nodded in agreement. With the decision having been made to send for the doctor, word was quickly sent outside and someone was sent to fetch him.

"Now Rose," said Kitty. "The main thing is that you don't push at all. Each time you get the urge to push you must resist it or we'll be in trouble here."

Rose, visibly upset and distressed, laid her head back and took deep breaths, trying to relax herself. Myriam thought back to the maiden ewe and her triplet lambs at Mary's wedding. She had been exhausted too.

"Ingrid, could you mix up some hot sugar water for Rose please?" she asked and Ingrid hurried down to the kitchen.

Myriam levelled herself alongside Rose's large, swollen tummy.

"Do you mind if I try something?" she asked Kitty.

"If you think that something may help then try it." encouraged Kitty, carefully monitoring the baby's position.

Myriam began to gently massage and rub Rose's stomach area. Her hope was that some calm would spread to both Rose and the baby. It seemed to be working, at least for Rose. Despite the contractions she was managing to control the urges to push. Rose drank the sickly-sweet sugar water when Ingrid returned and could feel her strength reviving. After some minutes Kitty informed them that she could feel one of the feet and would try to deliver the leg.

"Rose, you're doing so well. I want you to focus on keeping your breaths slow and keep resisting that urge to push," she encouraged.

Rose was listening carefully and nodded.

Gently and slowly Kitty delivered the first leg. After a brief pause to settle her own nerves, she successfully located and delivered the second leg. Beads of perspiration had formed across her forehead and the back of her neck. She felt hot and sticky. Glancing at the door, in the vain hope that the doctor would appear through it, she took a deep breath.

"I'm going to continue with the arms now. Rose, this many cause some strange sensations as I move the baby around," Kitty warned.

Kitty began to turn the baby ninety degrees until she was able to carefully deliver the left arm. Then, turning the baby a full one hundred and eighty degrees the other way, she also delivered the right arm. It was a very delicate process and Kitty was anxious not to cause any damage to either Rose, or the baby.

"This is good Rose, you're doing so well," Kitty encouraged her, as she allowed the baby to hang for a moment. "I'm almost ready to deliver the head. This will be the hardest part for you Rose, but we'll just go really slowly."

Kitty glanced hopefully at the door one final time before taking hold of the baby's feet with one hand. As she eased the baby's body parallel, supported on her other arm, she used her fingers to locate and cover the baby's mouth to avoid any fluids being breathed in.

Kitty now instructed Rose to assist her with small controlled pushes.

Beads of sweat again began forming on Rose's forehead, and were soon running into her eyes. Her face was scrunched up as she made efforts to absorb the pain.

"One more Rose," called Kitty. "He's almost out."

"He? Did you say..." Rose groaned as she was interrupted by a final urge to push. She exhaled all the air out of her lungs, with her eyes pinched tight while Kitty gently pulled the baby boy free and wrapped him in a blanket. She took hold of Myriam's hand and placed the small bundle into her arms. The tiny baby opened his mouth and let out a cry to announce his arrival into the world.

Rose's eyes flashed open and she tried to sit herself up.

"Stay there, stay there," urged Myriam and stepping forwards, she handed the precious little boy to her sister.

Standing back and watching them both, mother and newborn son, Myriam felt an odd wave of emotion accompanied by a longing from deep within come over her. Tears built up behind her eyes. At that moment, Myriam felt it. She was overcome by the same feeling that Rose must have had constantly; the desire for a baby. It hit her from nowhere and she gulped, trying to swallow the emotions that had suddenly been awoken inside her. She looked down at her hands and saw that they were shaking. Glancing over her shoulder, she saw that Kitty was watching her, concerned. Myriam smiled and wiped a tear as it escaped and ran down her cheek. Kitty stood up and gave her arm a gentle squeeze.

Rose looked up at all three of them, Myriam, Kitty and Ingrid.

"He's so perfect," she whispered. "Thank you all so much. I don't know what would have happened if you hadn't all been here."

The tiny baby had now stopped crying and was sleeping peacefully in Rose's arms.

There was a knock at the door and in walked the doctor.

"Late again, am I?" he said, observing Rose and her new baby. He made an examination of them both and then turned to face Kitty. "Very well done, Mrs Freeman. Very well done indeed! It may not have been such a happy ending had you not been here."

Kitty smiled weakly. Her hands were still shaking from all the adrenalin that had rushed around her body during the delivery.

"I only followed the process as I had observed it from you, Sir."

The doctor nodded. "And you no doubt kept a calm head. I commend you for it."

Once the room and Rose had been cleaned up, Myriam went to find Tom. He was pacing out by the stables, swinging his arms around to keep warm. It was now well past midnight and the night was cold. For all his flaws, Myriam could see that he was genuinely concerned. She walked over and he picked up his lantern, holding it high to see who was approaching him.

"Myriam," he said. As he spoke, puffs of cold

air dispersed from his mouth. "What the devil is going on in there? I've been waiting for ages and I saw the doctor was sent for too."

Myriam smiled at him and placed her hands on his shoulders.

"Tom, I'm very happy to tell you that you are now father to the most beautiful baby boy I think I have ever seen."

"A boy?" he exclaimed. "A boy, did you say? Our Rose has had a boy?"

"Yes!" Myriam laughed. "Now get yourself inside and see them both."

Tom grabbed Myriam's faced and kissed her. She squirmed away from him still laughing. "Go on inside will you, you fool! And please, don't ever do that again!"

Tom disappeared into the house and Myriam's laughter turned to a chuckle before she then fell silent, quietly reflecting on her own twisted and confused emotions. It was Kitty who interrupted her thoughts. She had said goodbye to Rose and was ready to leave. Together they walked back through the dark, quiet town.

"Kitty, it was quite outstanding back there, what you did," said Myriam. "Thank you so much, for everything."

"After all that effort, it was rewarding to see Rose looking so delighted with everything," said Kitty.

"Yes, it was," agreed Myriam. "Rose has waited so long and dreamed so hard about having a baby. I'm very happy for her." She tried but Myriam failed to hide the flat tone within her voice.

As they walked, Kitty glanced across at her. It was a clear night with a bright, almost-full moon. The silvery light was shining on them both.

"*Hope deferred maketh the heart sick: but when the desire cometh, it is a tree of life.*" quoted Kitty.

"What's that from?" asked Myriam.

"The Bible," Kitty answered her. "It's from Proverbs."

"What does it mean?"

"It means that when our dreams are delayed or something we are in expectation of is postponed, it can make our heart feel sick."

Myriam thought back to those long months before she had finally married Jim, when she had been so violently in love with him but their hopes and expectations had been put on hold. She thought of Rose and the anguish she had felt at being unable to conceive a child. Myriam smiled faintly at Kitty.

"I've known how that feels."

"And then when the thing hoped for finally comes, you burst into life. It is as if your entire soul is renewed," encouraged Kitty.

"That's a very good way to describe it."

"But it's true, isn't it?" pondered Kitty.

"Yes, I suppose it is," Myriam agreed. She still wasn't entirely sure what point Kitty was trying to make.

Kitty stopped walking and turned to face her.

"Just remember that if ever you have any future dreams delayed, stay hopeful and remain expectant. You never know, you may just burst into life again when what has been postponed finally arrives."

Forty-two

May 1846

"Don't worry Joshua, it won't hurt you. Just stroke his neck gently, like this."

Myriam took hold of the little boy's hand and showed him how to stroke the soft hair on the pony's neck. She had lifted her nephew up off the ground and was holding him against her hip so that he was able to reach the animal more easily.

"You're getting too big to carry," she said, setting him back onto his own two feet beside her.

Joshua looked up and smiled at her and she felt a warm glow inside. It melted Myriam's heart when her nephew smiled at her like this. He was a funny little boy. He was so quiet and reserved when compared to Mary's son, David. Joshua always wore a serious expression on his little, round face. She thought that he appeared already older than his years and his contemplative mood was an indication that he was in fact going to be a very intelligent young child. Little Joshua Watkins didn't give away his smiles easily and so on the few occasions when he did allow his mouth to open into an upwards grin, with his eyes all twinkly just like his mother's, it was something special to see.

The boatman who had stopped to open one of the swing bridges now continued on his way, and

Joshua watched as the pony disappeared along the tow path and out of sight. Myriam wondered if she should close the bridge again as the boatman had left it open, but she decided against it. The bridges outside of town were normally left open as the canal was much busier than any of the small village roads. Any moment now, another boat would come along, so it was best to leave the bridge up.

"Come on then young man," she said, taking hold of Joshua's hand and leading him towards the town. "Let's get you back home, shall we?"

Joshua began to walk alongside her, sucking on the thumb of his free hand.

"And you can take that thumb out of your mouth too," she chided and gently pulled his hand down. "If you fall over, you'll only hurt yourself."

He stared at her for a moment with his usual solemn expression and Myriam chuckled to herself. It made her laugh sometimes when she looked at little Joshua. Both of his parents were two of the most open-mouthed people you could meet. Rose always had a smile on her face and a twinkle in her eye and Tom was a cheeky, mischievous sort, constantly joking about something. The two of them had somehow managed to create this quiet, pensive little boy. Joshua's reserved manner wasn't a negative thing though. Myriam thought that it actually endeared people to him. He didn't tend to stamp and scream like some children did and he played well with others, never snatching at objects or toys. He was happy and content to watch those round him, joining in if he felt like it.

They were returning from spending the

morning with Mary and David out at the farm. The two boys, both now about eighteen months old, had played together happily. David was already a lot more stable on his feet than Joshua. He was able to run easily and clamber about, thus avoiding the various obstacles which lay all around the farmyard. Joshua had followed him about as much as he could, but he had started walking later than David and so his legs were less steady and he was not yet confident enough to pick up speed and try running.

It had been lovely to sit in the sun with Mary and watch the two of them together. Myriam had thought that Mary looked well. It seemed that being a mother had calmed her slightly. She appeared less wild and less brash than she had used to be. Possibly it was the effect of being married to Samuel too. He was such a calm man who never seemed to get flustered or ruffled. Myriam thought that he and Jim were very similar. It was a shame that they were both so busy with their respective work, as she felt that they could be good friends.

David was a sweet boy. He was always smiling, and was often caught laughing to himself, amused by something that he had found funny. He already had a mass of blonde, wavy hair, just like his mother's. Myriam and Mary had laughed at how different the two boys were to look at. Joshua, with his hazelnut hair and big, brown eyes, wearing his usual serious expression, had spent the morning toddling around after the energetic, laughing, blue-eyed David with bits of straw and leaves sticking out from his fair hair.

"Up, Iriam, up," said Joshua, standing still and holding his arms out at her. He still hadn't mastered the pronunciation of her name fully. Myriam smiled.

He had walked a lot today and it was no wonder that he was now tired. She picked him up and carried him, adjusting his weight every few steps. He really was beginning to get heavy.

Myriam loved the days when she could take care of Joshua. Young Mr Hamilton had spoken with Rose not long after the birth. It seemed that Ingrid was hoping to soon retire as head cook and Mr Hamilton told Rose that she was his first choice as a replacement. He told her that nothing was required urgently, especially as she had a new baby to care for, but asked her to consider if she thought it was something she could do. Rose was delighted, she had worked hard for years and had always dreamed of working her way up through the kitchen to head cook. Between Tom's family and Myriam, they had come up with a plan that would enable Rose to achieve this dream. Ingrid had agreed to stay on for four days a week for the first year and then to cut it down gradually after that. As Joshua would get older, Rose's plan was to be able to take up the position completely. The arrangement meant that at least one day each week Myriam looked after Joshua and she loved it. It was her time alone with the little boy.

When he had been born, she had been surprised by the strong attachment that she had instantly felt towards him. Jim was fond of him too and enjoyed playing with him, but it wasn't the same. It felt as though Joshua was a part of Myriam. She felt that he was a special link between her, Rose and their parents. She loved looking after him.

Myriam had hoped that the emotions which had been stirred within her on the night of Joshua's birth would not last for long. She had hoped that they would be just a few fleeting sentimental thoughts, brought on by the intense situation of successfully helping to bring a new human life into the world. However, as the months had gone by, she found that the desire she had felt that night to be a mother had remained with her. Kitty had spoken about a persons' dreams and expectations in life being delayed and Myriam now felt that her hopes were tied up in something that wasn't going to ever happen. After her miscarriages she had been frightened of ever carrying an unborn child again; but now that it was something she wanted, it seemed to be eluding her.

Jim though felt differently. He felt deeply anxious for her. He didn't want the same thing to happen again as it had before. Usually, they were of the same mind in everything, united in agreement about what they both wanted in life, but this subject had caught them both off guard. Jim admitted that he would love to be a father but would rather not experience any more pain in order to achieve it. While they were still happy together and loved each other very much, Myriam felt that a small crack had now developed between them and she wished that it could be smoothed over. For a while, she was convinced that the only thing which could fill this gap would be a baby, a child of their own. However, she had done much thinking about it over the recent weeks and had decided to try to put her maternal feelings aside, hoping that they might disappear and then she and Jim would somehow be completely connected again.

Myriam reached the inn and Rose had the door to her place open, waiting for their arrival.

Once Myriam had placed Joshua on the ground, he made his way over to the door calling 'mummy' as he went. Rose appeared in the doorway.

"There you are my gorgeous boy," she cried and picked him up, smothering him in kisses. "Did you have a nice day with Aunty Myriam?"

Joshua didn't reply, but wriggled his way back down to the ground and then wandered inside the house.

"Have you time for a cuppa, duckie?" asked Rose.

"That would be nice," replied Myriam. "We've just come directly from Mary's place."

"Oh, how lovely! How is she? And how is David?"

"They're both very well." Myriam sat down on a small chair and rested her feet. "David is a delightful little thing, so full of smiles and laughter."

"He gets that from his mother I expect," said Rose, as she handed Myriam a cup of hot tea and a slice of freshly baked sponge.

"Thank you. Yes, he must do, although I don't think he's going to be wild like she is. He seems to have Samuel's calmness."

Rose sipped from her teacup. "Isn't it fascinating how their little characters develop. I wonder what sort of child you and Jim would have?"

Myriam flushed red and she quickly took a bite from the soft, sweet cake. There was a pause and Myriam could feel Rose watching her.

"Duckie, I've wanted to ask for a while and not really known if I should do, but I feel I need too." Myriam knew that this moment was well overdue. She looked up at Rose, knowing what her next words would be.

"Are you having the same problem that I had for all those years?"

Myriam swallowed the food that was in her mouth. How could she answer that?

"In a way, yes. And yet, at the same time, no."

Rose shook her head. She didn't understand what that answer was supposed to mean. Myriam took in a deep breath and explained.

"I have fallen with child two times, but I lost both of them."

Rose frowned and then reached out to hold her sister's hand.

"I'm fine," Myriam assured her. "It was a long time ago now, when Jim and I were first married. After that I didn't want it to happen again and besides, I'd never felt that maternal longing that I know you did for so long." Myriam paused for a moment. Now she had said that part out loud, she might as well admit the rest to Rose. She continued, "To be completely honest though, since Joshua was born, I've begun to feel differently. I would now like to be a mother and to have a child of my own. However, it's something that doesn't seem to be happening for me. It seems to me that it may now be too late."

"Nonsense!" replied Rose. "Look at me and look how long I waited. You're still very young, duckie. I don't believe it's too late. I believe that miracles can happen at any time."

Myriam smiled weakly. She wished she could have Rose's confidence.

Forty-three

January 1847

"Can you find the red hat?" asked Myriam, and then applauded as Joshua picked out a bright, scarlet hat. "What about the blue hat?"

Joshua stared into the small basket and thought about it. He reached in and handed a brown, woollen hat to Myriam.

"Almost darling, but not quite. This one is brown. *Brown*," she repeated and popped the hat onto his head, pulling it over his eyes.

Joshua took the hat off, put it back into the basket and then began to wander off away from her. He was bored of that game.

"Hey, where do you think you're going?" called Myriam. She closed the lid of the basket, placed it inside the front door, grabbed both of their coats from where they were hanging and then chased after him along the tow path. Neither of them were suitably dressed to be going off for a walk in the cold weather.

After Joshua had been born, Myriam had started to lovingly knit him little things to wear, constantly working on something new to keep up with his continual growth. With leftover wool she had made an assortment of hats, scarfs and gloves and during the winter months, was selling many of them to people along the canal. A boatman and his wife had just stopped to buy a couple of pairs of gloves and so Myriam had stepped out from within the warm cottage to see to them. She and Joshua had been inside all morning, keeping warm by the fire but it seemed that now he wanted to be outside for a while.

"Here, put this on or you'll get cold," she insisted, as she caught up with him and forced him to put the coat on. He tried to wriggle away from her, impatient to keep moving, but gave in after she firmly held his hand and pushed it inside the arm of his coat.

"It's for your own good," she said, finally releasing him once the buttons on his coat were all done up. He was quite a headstrong little thing. It reminded her so much of herself sometimes. She could remember her own parents firmly insisting that she wear a bonnet to protect her from the sun and her own feelings of defiance as she would try to undo the laces and take it off.

"Where are we going Joshua?" she asked, following him as he continued along the tow path.

"Horsey," he replied and kept walking.

Tom often took Joshua out into the stables with him while he was working and as a result, Joshua loved the giant creatures. There were a couple of farm cobs that grazed in a field just along from the lockhouse and Joshua knew exactly how to get to them. Reaching the field where they were, he climbed onto the fence and tapped his tongue against the roof of his mouth in the way that his father had taught him to do. The two horses heard the clicking noise and looked up. They both then began to walk over towards the two humans.

"They'll be disappointed to find out that you

forgot to bring the carrots," said Myriam, standing beside him with a hand against his back in case he should lose his balance and fall.

Joshua looked at her and registered what she had said. Tears started to fill his eyes. They usually brought some sliced carrot with them when they would visit the horses. Joshua loved feeding it to them, holding his hand as still as he could so that they didn't jump or flinch.

"Oh, don't worry. It's all right," she soothed. "I have something else they might like."

Myriam reached into her pocket and brought out a small paper bag. Inside were a dozen or so mint-flavoured sweets. She had bought them to give to Joshua as a treat.

"Here you go," she said, handing him the bag. "Only one though because they are very sweet," she insisted, as Joshua held his hand out flat with the small, white mint in the middle of his palm and offered it to the first horse. It was a black horse with long, dark eyelashes and a thick black mane. He stretched his nose out towards Joshua's open hand, snorting puffs of warm breath into the cold air and then gently took the mint. Joshua laughed as the horse's wet tongue licked across his fingers. He pulled his hand away and wiped it on his trouser leg.

Myriam shooed the first horse away to let the second come near. This one was covered in brown and white patches with hairs around his nose that made him look as though he had a moustache. He could smell the mint flavour and was already stretching his nose out and rubbing it against Joshua's arm. Joshua squealed in delight and held the mint out for him to take. The horse snatched at it quickly, worried that his field companion might try to get in again before him.

Both the horses stood for a while beside the fence hoping for more offerings from the little boy, but Myriam had taken the bag of sweets back and returned it to her pocket. In time, the two animals realised that there were no more treats being offered that day and they wandered back across the field, nibbling at mouthfuls of grass as they went.

Joshua shivered and Myriam decided that it was time to head back inside.

"Come on you, I need some help to get lunch ready for your uncle Jim," she said, taking his cold hand and leading him back along the tow path.

Back at the lockhouse, Myriam settled Joshua in the front room, giving him a few small toys to play with while she stoked the stove into life and began to prepare some lunch for the three of them.

She brought a pan of water to the boil and placed three eggs into the bubbling water. After a few minutes, using a ladle, she lifted them out of the pan and rinsed them with cold water in the sink. Leaving them there to cool, she cut some slices of bread which she had bought fresh from the bakery that morning. Once the bread was sliced, she laid it out on the side, ready to be filled with some butter, the eggs and a shaking of salt. As soon as the eggshells were cool enough to handle, she took a spoon and tapped each one, firmly enough to crack it but not so hard that it was completely crushed.

Myriam was halfway through removing the second shell when the smell of the warm, cooked egg hit her nostrils. Her reaction was as instant as it had been on previous occasions. Hastily grabbing a bucket from underneath the sink, Myriam managed to catch everything just in time.

After washing her face, Myriam went into the front room to check on Joshua and to check that the fireplace was still warm. She added another log to the fire and then sat on the couch. Laying her head back for a few moments, she closed her eyes.

For over two years now, she had thought about this moment; the discovery that she would once again be expecting a child. She had tried to imagine how she would feel but nothing had prepared her for the tumultuous emotions that were now storming around inside of her being. She felt relieved, elated, petrified and anxious all at the same time. What if she lost this one too? She pushed that idea away, refusing to allow it to dominate her thoughts. If she worried about it, it would do neither her, nor the small life that was now inside her any good. She must try to be positive and hopeful, although also realistic about the possibilities.

She was so deeply involved in her own thoughts that she hardly noticed as Jim walked in, looking for his lunch.

"Is everything all right?" he asked.

Myriam leaned forward in the chair. "I was just sick." She looked at him and he frowned. "I was preparing the eggs when it happened," she explained.

Now he understood what she was saying. Jim took his cap off and sat next to her. Joshua continued playing with a small ball on the floor in front of them.

"I know we haven't felt sure about this," she said. "And I know you are happy if we stay as we are, just the two of us, but..." She hesitated and took hold of his hands. "But I feel I need this now."

He squeezed her hand gently and gave her a soft kiss on her forehead.

"I know you do. I just hope this doesn't go as it has before."

"I know that's a possibility," she admitted. "But it doesn't stop me feeling so excited that I've... no, I mean, that *we've* been given a chance again. I'd started to think that all my chances of being a mother were over. If the worst were to happen and we were to lose the baby as we did before, then that may well be so, but I'm grateful for this opportunity. I'm grateful for *our* opportunity."

Her expression was earnest. She was more expectant than he'd ever seen her before. As he thought of what may happen if she was to lose a third baby his heart fluttered for her, for *them*, but he couldn't deny how much this meant to her and if he was honest, to him too. He hadn't wanted to admit it before, but the prospect of being a father was something that excited him greatly. He could think of nothing better than having something that was part of both him and Myriam. Something that only they would share.

She was still staring deeply into his eyes, waiting for him to say something, anything that would let her know that he also shared her trepid enthusiasm.

"I'm grateful for this opportunity too," he said, holding her tightly to him. As he held her, they both heard a rumble. His stomach growled loudly, reminding them all that it was well past the time for lunch.

"Shall we leave the eggs for today and eat something else?" Jim asked jokingly.

"Oh please," she laughed. "I can't even bear to look at them!"

Forty-four

May 1847

Myriam heard the waters lapping against the bank of the canal and turned to look up towards the lock.

She had been watching a small sparrow coming and going from the hedgerow behind where she was sitting, on her usual bench. Each time the bird returned and then disappeared into the flourishing canopy of green leaves, Myriam could hear high-pitched chirping coming from a nest that had been built within the bushes. She observed that the adult bird was working hard, returning each time within just a few minutes to deliver a fresh load of food to the numerous hungry mouths that were awaiting.

Her attention was now pulled away from the family of birds, who were hidden somewhere out of her sight, and she saw that one of the regular boatmen was driving his boat down the canal. He was a young man with a cheery face and a pleasant disposition. As he walked by where she was sitting, leading his horse steadily beside him, he tilted his cap and greeted her.

"You're looking exceptionally well Ma'am," he said and flashed her a cheeky smile.

"Thank you Arnold, I feel exceptionally well," she replied.

"So I hear! I've just being chatting to Jim," he

said. "I'll be seeing you both on my way back up in a few weeks then." He glanced down at her hands, which were folded across her stomach and nodded, continuing on his way.

Once he was gone, and the waters had once again settled and calmed down, Myriam closed her eyes and listened to the sounds around her. Voices could be heard, far away in the distance. The voices were of men, working in the coal yards and timber sheds that lined the canal. Louder though and closer to her, were sounds of the countryside. Lambs were bleating in the fields, birds were singing in the trees and bees were buzzing amongst the flowers.

Hearing a swish from the reeds and the faint sound of water rippling nearby, she opened her eyes and saw the two adult moorhens with this year's young swimming about beside them. Each year she had watched these fascinating families grow and mature from her seat on the bench.

How her moods had changed over the years as she had sat on this bench and watched the countryside grow around her. Some days she had sung, quite literally, out loud to the world. Overjoyed at her life and promises that had lain ahead of her. Other times she had quietly wept, allowing the waters to listen to her sorrows and to soak in her tears. This canal had become the centre of her life. It was the place where she had first seen Jim, when he had been nothing more than a stranger to her with dark, mysterious eyes. Since then, they had walked alongside, worked on, and lived next to this ever moving, yet never changing waterway. Her whole life was now caught up within these waters.

As Myriam now sat, watching the small black birds moving around, she reflected, as she did at this time every year, on how much she loved the springtime season. It was a time of growth and regeneration. A time of new beginnings and new life. *New life.* Myriam's hands instinctively rubbed her stomach and the small bump that was now visible.

Mary had walked along the tow path to visit her earlier that morning. With David bouncing along beside her, she had looked tired as she had struggled to carry her own slightly larger, slightly heavier bump. Mary's second child would be arriving in a month or two and Myriam couldn't help but wonder whether her child and Mary's would become close friends, just as they were.

She found herself allowing her thoughts to drift more and more into these future daydreams as the time went by. Her bouts of morning sickness and violent aversions to the smell of eggs and the taste of tea had subsided. She now found that she was craving cheese in large quantities and her energy, which she had initially lost, had returned to her. Now that she could see a change in her body and the way that it was moulding itself around the life that was developing inside, she finally felt sure that the baby was growing as it should be. Until then, she had been nervous, unsure as to whether it was really there. She had felt uneasy and scared to believe that it had really existed. However, that was before she had felt those first few movements. They had started as just a strange flutter, an odd sensation that she had never felt previously, not even on the days when she had been at her hungriest.

To Jim's dismay these movements could only

be felt by Myriam. She had taken hold of his hand on many occasions and placed it on her stomach insisting that he must be able to the feel the same things that she was, but he hadn't. It had frustrated him at first but he was learning to be patient. In time he would feel their baby kick. Until then, he was simply feeling relieved. He was satisfied that this time, everything was progressing as it should; this time, it was all so different for them both.

It was now late in the afternoon. The canal was quiet and so Jim walked down to join Myriam on the bench. They sat companionably, as they often did, watching the water.

"How was Mary today?" he asked.

"She's well," Myriam replied. "Did you see how big she is now? I don't think she will be walking into town again before the baby arrives."

"She looked tired," he agreed and brushed a strand of hair from her eyes.

"I do hope that our two babies will be good friends." Myriam's eyes were wistful, she was once again daydreaming about the future and what life for their child would be like.

Jim smiled. "I'm sure they will be."

A noise was heard from up by the cottage and Jim looked up to see a late arrival at the lock. He stretched his hands out and prepared to stand, ready to go and open the gates.

Before he could get up to go, Myriam suddenly reached out and placed her hand on his arm.

"Wait," she said, taking hold of his hand and placing it onto her stomach.

"Myriam, I can't feel anything," he protested. "Besides, there's a boat at the lock."

"Shush," she said and gently pushed his hand against her bump more firmly.

They both sat, silently waiting.

"There!" she said, as he let out a gasp.

He looked at her.

"Did you feel it?" she asked.

He nodded. He was holding his breath. He felt another small movement, a tiny push against his hand.

"Was that it again?" he asked.

"Yes."

Jim felt his eyes filling with tears as emotion overcame him. Myriam raised her other hand and lovingly stroked his face.

"Woah, that one was strong," said Jim, as he felt a third nudge from her stomach.

"He's got a good little kick," she smiled.

"*He*? What do mean he? It might be a girl," Jim laughed.

As the possibility crossed Myriam's thoughts that this small life which she was carrying inside of her might indeed be that of a little girl, she looked at Jim and nodded happily.

"That would be lovely!"

THE END

NOTE FROM THE AUTHOR

When I wrote my first novel, 'One Fine Lady', I was writing from an inspiration based on my own feelings of nostalgia. The story was very much about places and activities.

Many of my readers enjoyed reading Becky's story and so asked me for a sequel. However, I wasn't ready to write a sequel. There was a different story that I wanted to tell.

My readers had fallen in love with Becky. Now I wanted them to fall in love with her parents, as they fell in love with each other. I wanted to tell people Myriam's story. So, I set out to write this prequel.

With only a few, very brief mentions of Myriam in my first book, the plot was essentially an open canvas. I enjoyed using some of the previous characters and revealing to you their back stories, thus helping you to appreciate them more. It was also fun to create and introduce to you some new characters too.

There was though one area of the story which I found myself agonising long and hard over; the instances of Myriam's miscarriages. At one point I had almost decided not to put them into the book at all. The subject of losing a baby is very difficult. I have family and friends who have experienced this loss and the last thing I wanted to do was cause distress to my readers. I found that I had been trapped by my own writing though. The small snippet of information I had given about Myriam in my first book was, that prior to Becky's birth, she had sadly suffered miscarriages and so I couldn't ignore it or delete it from this book. As I said, I felt trapped. I therefore spent hours and hours trying to tell this part of the story in the kindest way possible. I hope that I succeeded in this and, without causing anyone distress, helped you to connect with

Myriam even more as a result.

I felt that with this book I grew and developed as a writer. With the deeper emotions and more intense realities that are challenged by the characters, I found I had to 'dig deep' within myself at times in order to convey the thoughts and images that I wanted to. I enjoyed getting to know my own characters and travelling with them though life's laughter and sadness. As I wrote, I fell in love with them all. I hope that you did too.

Both 'One Fine Lady' and this book, 'Delayed Expectations,' are set in the market town of Banbury, Oxfordshire, and I thought it would be helpful for the readers to use the map on the front pages for reference. The map features establishments which date back to when Delayed Expectations was set and are still standing today. As with all fiction, a lot of what I write about is from my own imagination but I do think it's nice if people are able to actually visualise the places about which I write.

The lock is the area where I have used my artistic licence the most. Lock 29, on the Oxford Canal in Banbury, would have been a busy place during the nineteenth century. However, the truth is that Banbury has never had a lockhouse beside its lock. The lock keeper for the town would have lived in a house somewhere away from the canal. I have chosen though, to depict the town with a lockhouse in my books and I hope that as you read my stories, you can visualise the imaginary cottage as clearly as I do.

As a self-published author, the whole process of writing, editing, and preparing a book for publishing is a very daunting task. I couldn't have done it without the support of so many:

Sophi, Lianne, Louise, Beth and Gillian have all been

invaluable to me with their help of proof reading and feedback.

My mum did a fantastic job on the editing and I absolutely love her incredible artwork for the cover.

My dad, ever ready to assist me, provided vital technical support I needed for formatting etc.

I would like to mention Margaret Little from the Banbury Historical Society, who patiently replied to my numerous emails regarding the history of the town.

Of course I can't forget my husband, Jordan. His enduring patience with me whilst I was engrossed in my writing allowed me to get it all completed.

Finally, to you dear reader; thank you for purchasing and reading my book. Your support means so much to me. Without an agent or publisher, it's up to me to do all my own publicity. Therefore, reviews make a big difference. It doesn't matter if you don't think it deserves 5 stars, I won't be offended, I'm realistic about that sort of thing. However, reviews do help others to find my book. With that in mind, if you could leave a review, either on Amazon or Goodreads, I'd be so grateful.

Thank you

Abigail

ALSO BY ABIGAIL SHIRLEY

Twelve year old Becky has stopped hoping for any love and affection from her father. Her life alongside the busy canal in Banbury continues as normal until she travels to London, forcing her father to face reminders of what he once had but is now too afraid to embrace.

As Becky makes her journey from childhood into adolescence, she notices that something has changed. Should she open her heart and dare to hope again?

Like the horse drawn canal boats, amongst which this story is set, let yourself be pulled along by this family's story of love and loss.

I thoroughly enjoyed joining Becky on this heartfelt emotional journey. One Fine Lady is an insightful, pleasant, and well-researched window into the life of a small nineteenth-century English town. The diverse characters engender a spectrum of emotions ranging from joy, discovery, anger, sorrow, fear, and hope. Beware, your heartstrings will be pulled.
-DEREK J PACK

ABOUT THE AUTHOR

Raised in Oxfordshire and currently residing in Cornwall, Abigail Shirley loves the simpler things in life. After marrying her wonderful Cornish husband, her heart fell in love with his home county and in particular Bodmin Moor.

She enjoys walking, swimming, cycling and horse riding. The perfect end to a perfect day for Abigail would be sitting by a fire with a glass of red wine and some melted marshmallows, accompanied by a few close friends.

A vivid daydreamer, her mind often drifts away and she enjoys writing short stories and quirky poems as small gifts for her family and friends.

Delayed Expectations is Abigail's second novel.

Follow Abigail on Instagram @abigailshirleyauthor

Printed in Great Britain
by Amazon